喚醒你的英文語感！

Get a Feel for English !

喚醒你的英文語感 ！

Get a Feel for English !

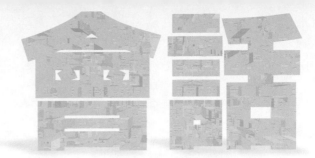

# 會話

## 旅遊篇

### 超盡興！用英文玩遍超 HOT 景點不吃力！

CONVERSATION BOOSTERS－TRAVEL

- ☑ 3 組人馬遊歷不同國家的狀況寫實
- ☑ 14 個自助旅行必經關卡全記錄
- ☑ 42 種海外旅遊狀況教戰
- ☑ 858 個SOS必備詞彙

## 震撼教育

附 **2** 片
歷險CD

貝塔語言出版
Beta Multimedia Publishing

總編審◎王復國　　作者◎Jeffrey Gordon

我們常聽人說：『等我英文學好以後再去環遊世界。』

然而，語言是永遠學習不完的，

學到哪裡，就用到哪裡，

往往會讓學習語言更有成就感。

記得第一次在異國的餐廳點菜，

順利得到侍應生回答時的滿足感嗎？

對了，就抓緊那種感覺，在旅途上學習語言吧！

# 總編審序

　　台灣之外的世界是如何之大！隨著觀光事業的發達，只要是經濟許可又有意願即可隨時擁抱這五花八門的世界，而接觸這一片包羅萬象文化的最佳捷徑即是英文。正因體認到這樣的需求與必要性，「會話震撼教育系列」在時事篇、運動篇、飯店篇、時尚篇以及戀愛篇之後，特地推出了旅遊篇，為的就是能幫助讀者在吸收異國文化的同時，可以減少因溝通不良而產生的誤會，降低出狀況時的機會，甚至幫助讀者除卻在碰上前所未見情況之時的驚慌失措。畢竟，出門在外，誰都會希望煩惱的時候少，而愉快充實的時候多。

　　本書特地設計了三組平行的旅遊路線及角色：他們雖然經歷的關卡相似，卻又各自遇上不同的狀況或是需求。全書統整出十四個必經關卡，包括搭機、抵達當地機場、住進旅館、打聽消息、交通工具、認識當地人、購物、在外用餐、突發狀況、與家人保持聯絡、事務辦理、市區遊玩、回程、和親友分享等主題。承襲「會話震撼教育系列」的學習設計，旅遊篇同樣是以完整故事的呈現方式，搭配自然不做作的對話，建構出一個真實的對話環境。讀者從書中可以真正學習到語言如何使用，而不只是做孤立的單字、片語的背誦。

　　每組人馬所發展出的故事都包含以下五個分別以功能性來做區分的單元：先是主要的「對話」，為故事與對話的主體；接下來是與主題關卡相關的「我要怎麼做」，提供當別人對你做出要求時得體的回應；「解決你的需求」則收錄了可能碰上的問題以及該如何提問的建議；「好用資訊」則特別收錄一些表現國外風情的小物件、旅程中會遇上的

表格文宣或是一些單字的圖解;「旅遊秘訣」傳授旅遊時省時省力的小撇步,幫助您快速成爲旅遊的高手。本書最後整理了一個貼心的字詞檢索附錄,方便讀者在看到字詞的時候搜尋它所在的章節,加深印象。

　　語言的學習也需要「身體力行」。在看旅遊英文的同時也要親身出國去走走、體驗體驗,希望這本書會是您出國時的必備良伴。就算暫時沒有機會出國,希望在我們精心打造的故事環境中,爲您提前展開旅程!

## 大衛 (*David*)

　　才剛拿到加州大學的英文學位的美國人，友善且討人喜愛，去泰國是為了要給自己一份畢業禮物。他對於泰國的佛教傳統挺有興趣的，不過去泰國最主要的目的是要轉換一下心情並且大快朵頤一些美味的辛辣泰國料理。大衛曾聽說過有關泰國女人過分「友善」的傳聞，不過因為他已有一位女友，所以對這一點興趣也沒有。

## 瑪莉 (*Marie*)＆賽麗絲特 (*Celeste*)

　　他們是在同一個台北辦公室裡工作的同事。瑪莉是人來瘋型的派對女郎，賽麗絲特則較為保守。她們瘋狂喜愛著任何和法國有關的事物，兩年前當他們開始策劃這次旅行時，他們還把原本的英文名字「茉蒂」和「琳達」改為法文的「瑪莉」和「賽麗絲特」。再一個禮拜她們就要啟程了，在辦公室根本無心上班。光是想像走出飛機踏上巴黎的土地就讓她們興奮得不能自己。

## 凱文(*Kevin*)＆莎拉(*Sarah*)

　　年輕的英國夫妻正在度蜜月，他們是第一次去美國，目的地是佛羅里達。他們對於那灰暗且令人窒息的英國天氣已感到厭煩，對於在充滿陽光的佛州享受日光浴滿懷了期待。在還未踏上佛州之前，凱文就已愛上它了。這地方好大啊！他已迫不及待要去看鱷魚了。莎拉是比較有所保留的那一個，凱文那橫衝直撞的熱情有時讓她好愛他，但有時也令她好抓狂。

# CONTENTS

序與介紹

冒險開始

**PartIII** 附錄

# CHAPTER 1

# ON THE FLIGHT

## 搭機

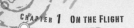

# David

## 大衛

 Dialogue 對話

CD 1-02

**David, a Taiwanese [1]backpacker who just graduated from an American college, is flying to Thailand.**

David : I'm sorry, but I'm pretty sure that you're sitting in my [2]seat.

Man : Are you sure? I did specifically [3]request a [4]window seat.

David : Yes, I think so. Look at my [5]boarding pass. It says 43A. That's definitely the window seat. You must be in the [6]aisle.

Man : All right, let me move my bag.

David : I think you probably need to put that in the [7]overhead bin. Do you want me to give you a hand?

Man : ([8]*Rudely*) No. I want to leave it on the floor.

[9]*Flight Attendant* : I'm sorry sir. It's too big to go under the seat. You'll have to [10]store it overhead.

Man : Yes, hold on. Just wait. I'm sure it'll [11]fit.

David : (*To the flight attendant*) How long before we [12]take off?

Flight Attendant : Another few minutes. I suggest that you [13]fasten your seat belt and put your seat [14]upright.

大衛，一位自助旅行的台灣人，剛從美國大學畢業，現正飛往泰國。

大衛　：抱歉，我很確定你坐的是我的位置。

男子　：你確定嗎？我可是特地要求一個靠窗的位置。

大衛　：是的，我想應該沒錯。你看我的登機證，上面寫了 43A ，確定是靠窗位。
　　　　你一定是靠走道。

男子　：好吧，讓我移一下袋子。

大衛　：我想你大概得把它擺在上方置物箱裡。要我幫忙嗎？

男子　：（無禮地）不必。我要把它放在地上。

空服員：先生，抱歉。它太大了，不能放在座位底下。你必須把它擺到上面去。

男子　：是，妳等一下，我確定放得進的。

大衛　：（對空服員說）我們還要多久起飛？

空服員：再幾分鐘。請你們繫緊安全帶，並把座椅打直。

## Words & Phrases

1. backpacker [`bæk͵pækɚ] *n.* 自助旅行者

2. seat [sit] *n.* 座位

3. request [rɪ`kwɛst] *v.* 懇請；請求

4. window [`wɪndo] *n.* 窗

5. boarding pass [`bordɪŋ͵pæs] 登機證

6. aisle [aɪl] *n.* 走道

7. overhead bin [ovɚ`hɛd`bɪn] 上方置物箱

8. rudely [`rudlɪ] *adv.* 無禮地

9. flight attendant [`flaɪtə͵tɛndənt] （客機上）空服人員（總稱為 cabin crew ，另外，駕駛艙人員則為 cockpit crew）

10. store [stor] *v.* 存放

11. fit [fɪt] *v.* 正好吻合；放得下

12. take off　起飛

13. fasten [`fæsṇ] *v.* 繫緊；扣緊

14. upright [`ʌp͵raɪt] *adj.* 垂直的；打直的

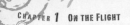

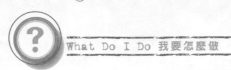

What Do I Do 我要怎麼做

CD 1-03

# Responding to the Flight Attendant's Questions
# 回答空服員的問題

**(1)** Flight Attendant : Can I see your boarding pass, sir?

You : Yes, here it is. My seat is 53J.

空服員 ：先生，我能看一下您的登機證嗎？

你 ：好的，在這裡。我的座位是 53 J。

---

**(2)** Flight Attendant : Do you want to put that in the overhead bin?

You : I'd prefer to keep it under the seat, if that's OK.

空服員 ：您要把東西放在上方置物箱嗎？

你 ：如果可以的話，我想放在座位底下。

---

**(3)** Flight Attendant : Sir, can I get you something to drink?

You : Not now thanks, maybe later.

空服員 ：先生，您需要喝點東西嗎？

你 ：現在不用，謝謝，待會再說。

CD 1-04

Getting What You Want 解決你的需求

# Asking the Flight Attendant for [1]Assistance
## 請空服員幫忙

**(1) You** : Would you please open the overhead bin for me?

**Flight Attendant :** No problem. [2]Hand me your bag and I'll take care of it.

你 ：可以麻煩妳幫我開一下上方的置物箱嗎？

空服員 ：沒問題。把您的袋子給我，我來幫您放進去。

---

**(2) You** : Could you bring me an [3]air sickness bag, please?

**Flight Attendant :** Of course, I'll bring it [4]right away.

你 ：可以麻煩妳給我一個嘔吐袋嗎？

空服員 ：當然可以，我馬上拿過來。

---

**(3) You** : Miss, is it possible for me to change seats?

**Flight Attendant :** Wait until we take off and I'll see if there are any empty ones.

你 ：小姐，我可不可以換位置呢？

空服員 ：等我們起飛後，我會看看還有沒有空位。

## Words & Phrases

1. assistance [ə`sɪstəns] *n.* 幫忙；援助

2. hand [hænd] *v.* 交、遞

3. air sickness bag [`ɛr͵sɪknɪs͵bæg] 嘔吐袋（還有其他的說法： discomfort bag 或是較口語的 barf bag）

4. right away 馬上；即刻

5

 FYI 好用資訊

**flight attendant**
空服員

**fasten seatbelt sign**
繫緊安全帶號誌燈

**air sickness bag**
嘔吐袋

**window shade**
遮陽板

 Travel Tips 旅遊撇步一起走

　　褪黑激素（Melatonin）被很多人認為是純天然的時差特效藥。當眼睛察覺夜晚來臨時，位於大腦中央如豌豆般大小的松果腺通常就會分泌褪黑激素。褪黑激素在晚上被製造出來，以幫助身體調整睡眠或覺醒的週期。理論上來說，搭機時服用褪黑激素補充品可以讓人容易入睡。

# Notes

# Marie & Celeste

瑪莉&賽麗絲特

Dialogue 對話

CD 1-05

**Marie and Celeste are** [1]colleagues **in an office in Taipei. They are flying to France.**

| | |
|---|---|
| *Marie* | : I'm [2]starving. I always seem to [3]get served last whenever I [4]take a flight! |
| *Celeste* | : I'm pretty hungry too. I hope the [5]cabin crew remembered my [6]vegetarian meal. |
| *Marie* | : Here comes the [7]trolley. |
| *Flight Attendant* | : Would you like the chicken with vegetables or the beef with rice? |
| *Marie* | : Beef for me, please. And a glass of [8]red wine. |
| *Celeste* | : I ordered a vegetarian meal when I [9]booked my ticket. Do you have a record of that? |
| *Flight Attendant* | : Yes, it's here on the [10]list. You are Celeste Zhuang? |
| *Celeste* | : Yes, that's right. |
| *Flight Attendant* | : One vegetarian [11]lasagña for you. Anything to drink? |
| *Celeste* | : A [12]can of Coke will be fine. |
| *Marie* | : Come on, Celeste. [13]You won't get very far in France only drinking Coke. |
| *Celeste* | : OK. Half a glass of [14]white wine then, please. And could I have a couple of [15]rolls? |
| *Flight Attendant* | : Of course. I'll be back with the coffee in a few minutes. Enjoy your meal. |
| *Marie* | : Cheers! |
| *Celeste* | : Salut! As they say in France. |

瑪莉與賽麗絲特在台北是同一辦公室的同事，她們正飛往法國。

瑪莉　　：我快餓死了。我每次坐飛機似乎總是最後一個拿到餐點的！

賽麗絲特：我也好餓。希望空服員記得我的素食餐。

瑪莉　　：餐車來了。

空服員　：您要蔬菜雞肉還是牛肉飯？

瑪莉　　：麻煩給我牛肉，外加一杯紅酒。

賽麗絲特：我在訂票時點了素食餐，你們有紀錄嗎？

空服員　：有，我的名單上面有寫。您是賽麗絲特·莊嗎？

賽麗絲特：是，沒錯。

空服員　：您的是一份素千層麵。要什麼飲料呢？

賽蕾絲特：一罐可樂就好了。

瑪莉　　：拜託，賽麗絲特。光喝可樂在法國可行不通。

賽麗絲特：好吧，那麻煩給我半杯白酒。可以再給我幾個麵包捲嗎？

空服員　：當然。幾分鐘後我會把咖啡拿來。請慢用。

瑪莉　　：乾杯！

賽麗絲特：　Salut！在法國他們都這麼說。

## 🚌 Words & Phrases

1. colleague ['kɑlig] *n.* 同事

2. starving ['stɑrvɪŋ] *adj.* 餓死了；餓壞了

3. get served　得到服務

4. take a flight　飛行；搭機

5. cabin crew　機組人員

6. vegetarian [ˌvɛdʒə'tɛrɪən] *adj.* 素食的

7. trolley ['trɑlɪ] *n.* 手推車（除了餐車，也用以指機上賣免稅商品的推車或機場中放行李的推車）

8. red wine　紅（葡萄）酒

9. book [bʊk] *v.* 訂（票）

10. list [lɪst] *n.* 名單

11. lasagña [lə'zɑnjə] *n.*【義大利菜】千層麵

12. can [kæn] *n.*（可樂等的）罐

13. You won't get very far.　行不通。

14. white wine　白（葡萄）酒

15. roll [rɔl] *n.* 麵包捲

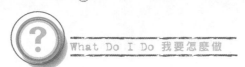

What Do I Do 我要怎麼做

CD 1-06

# ¹Mealtime on the Plane
## 機上用餐時間

**1** Flight Attendant : Did you order any kind of ²special meal?

You : Yes, I ordered a ³children's meal for my son.

空服員 ：您有沒有點任何一種特別餐？

你 ：有，我幫我兒子點了兒童餐。

---

**2** Flight Attendant : Can I ⁴refill your coffee cup, honey?

You : No, thanks. Any more and I won't be able to sleep.

空服員 ：親愛的，要不要再來一杯咖啡？

你 ：不用了，謝謝。再喝我就睡不著了。

---

**3** Flight Attendant : Can you pull down the ⁵window shade, please?

You : ⁶Sure.

空服員 ：可以麻煩您拉下遮陽板嗎？

你 ：當然可以。

## Words & Phrases

1. mealtime [`mil‚taim] *n.* 用餐時間

2. special meal 特別餐

3. children's meal 兒童餐

4. refill [`rifil] *v.* 續杯；再注入

5. window shade 遮陽板

6. Sure. 沒問題。

Getting What You Want 解決你的需求

CD 1-07

# Mealtime on the Plane
# 機上用餐時間

**(1)** You          : Could I have some clean [1]utensils, please?

Flight Attendant : [2]Certainly miss, I'll bring you some in a moment.

你          : 可以麻煩給我乾淨的餐具嗎？

空服員      : 沒問題，先生，等下我就幫您拿來。

---

**(2)** You          : Do you have any red wine left?

Flight Attendant : No, I think there's only white.

你          : 你們還有多的紅酒嗎？

空服員      : 沒有了，我想只剩白酒了。

---

**(3)** You          : Excuse me, I ordered fish and this seems to be chicken!

Flight Attendant : Oh, I'm terribly sorry. I'll change it for you right away.

你          : 對不起，我點了魚，而這似乎是雞肉！

空服員      : 噢，非常抱歉，我馬上幫您換。

---

## Words & Phrases

1. utensil [ju`tɛns]] *n.* 餐具

2. Certainly. 當然可以。

FYI 好用資訊

**boarding pass stub**
登機證票根

Travel Tips 旅遊撇步一起走

　　一份商務艙的餐點加上酒大概要花掉航空公司五十美元的材料費。不過，在食物和飲料上每花一美元，相對就要花三美元在機員服務、準備、裝載以及服侍乘客上，所以一份商務艙餐點的總成本要將近兩百美元。

## Notes

# Kevin & Sarah

## 凱文 & 莎拉

 Dialogue 對話

CD 1-08

**Kevin and Sarah are a young British couple flying to the United States.**

| | |
|---|---|
| *Kevin* | : [1]Check out some of the [2]stuff in the [3]duty-free [4]brochure. It's incredibly cheap. |
| *Sarah* | : Yes it is, if you want a clock [5]shaped like an airplane! |
| *Kevin* | : No, not that. I was thinking about the [6]perfume. Look, Chanel, CK, Revlon.... |
| *Sarah* | : Hmm. That is [7]a bit of a [8]bargain. For a bottle of [9]scent like that, I'd have to pay at least 50% more at home. |
| *Kevin* | : So, would you like one? |
| *Sarah* | : OK. |
| *Kevin* | : I was actually thinking about [10]picking up one of these [11]dual [12]time zone watches. |
| *Sarah* | : Ah, now I see your plan! Ask me if I want some [13]toiletries so that I'll feel bad not letting you buy a watch. |
| *Kevin* | : Uh, I...no...I didn't mean it like that. |
| *Sarah* | : Kevin, I'm kidding. Buy what you want. We're [14]on vacation. Florida here we come! |
| *Flight Attendant* | : [15](*Announcement*) Ladies and gentlemen, the cabin crew will shortly be bringing the duty-free trolley around. If you want anything, please let them know. |
| *Sarah* | : Kevin, now's your chance. |

凱文與莎拉是對年輕的英國夫妻，現正飛往美國。

凱文　：你看看這些免稅目錄裡的玩意兒，還真是便宜。

莎拉　：是很便宜，假如你想要飛機形狀的時鐘的話！

凱文　：不，我不是說那個。我在想的是香水。你看，香奈兒、凱文克萊、露華濃
　　　　……。

莎拉　：嗯，是有點便宜。像那樣的一瓶香水，在國內的店買的話，我起碼得多花
　　　　一半的錢。

凱文　：那，妳想要一瓶嗎？

莎拉　：好。

凱文　：其實我在考慮買一隻雙時區的錶。

莎拉　：啊，現在我知道你的企圖了。問我要不要一些化妝品，是為了讓我覺得不
　　　　讓你買錶會有罪惡感。

凱文　：呃，我……不是……我沒有那個意思。

莎拉　：凱文，我是開玩笑的，要什麼你就買吧。我們是在渡假。佛羅里達，我們
　　　　來囉！

空服員：（廣播）各位旅客，機組人員等一下會把免稅車推出去。如果您需要任何
　　　　東西，請告訴他們。

莎拉　：凱文，你的機會來了。

## Words & Phrases

1. check out　看一看

2. stuff [stʌf] n.（泛指）東西、物品、事物

3. duty-free adj. 免稅的

4. brochure [bro`ʃjʊr] n.【較英式的說法】宣傳品；小冊子

5. shape [ʃep] v. 做成……的形狀

6. perfume [`pɝfjum; ˌpɝfʼjum] n.（女用）香水

7. a bit of ... adj. 多少有點……

8. bargain [`bɑrgɪn] n. 條件優惠的買賣

9. scent [sɛnt] n.【英】香水

10. pick up v. 買，帶，弄到手

11. dual [dʊəl] adj. 雙重的；二元的

12. time zone n. 時區

13. toiletries [`tɔɪlɪtrɪs] n. 梳妝用品（包括洗髮精、香水、牙刷、牙膏等）

14. on vacation　度假的

15. announcement [ə`naʊnsmənt] n. 廣播通知

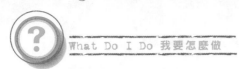

What Do I Do 我要怎麼做

CD 1-09

# Buying Duty-Free Stuff on the Plane
## 在飛機上買免稅商品

**1** Flight Attendant : Which ¹<u>currency</u> would you like to pay with, madam?

You : I think I'll just use my ²<u>plastic</u>.

空服員 ：太太／小姐，您要用哪種貨幣付款？

你 ：我想就用我的信用卡好了。

---

**2** Flight Attendant : Can I ask you to ³<u>sign</u> the ⁴<u>receipt</u>?

you : Sure. Can I borrow your pen for a minute?

空服員 ：可以麻煩您在收據上簽名嗎？

你 ：好的。可不可以跟你借一下筆？

---

**3** Flight Attendant : Would you like us to ⁵<u>ship</u> the items to your house?

You : Sure. I'll write my ⁶<u>address</u> down for you.

空服員 ：您要我們把東西送到府上去嗎？

你 ：好的。我把地址寫給妳。

## Words & Phrases

1. currency [`kɝənsɪ] *n.* 貨幣

2. plastic [`pæstɪk] *n.* 信用卡（credit card 的口語講法）

3. sign [saɪn] *v.* 簽字

4. receipt [rɪ`sit] *n.* 收據

5. ship [ʃɪp] *v.* 寄送

6. address [ə`drɛs; `ædrɛs] *n.* 地址；住址

Getting What You Want 解決你的需求

CD 1-10

# Questions about Duty-Free [1]Goods
## 關於免稅商品的問題

**1** You ：What are the duty-free [2]allowances for the UK?

Flight Attendant：A [3]liter of [4]spirits and two hundred cigarettes [5]per person.

你 ：英國的免稅額度是多少？

空服員 ：每個人一公升酒和兩百支菸。

---

**2** You ：Could you bring me a [6]copy of the duty-free [7]catalog, please?

Flight Attendant：It should be in the [8]seat pocket in front of you, madam.

你 ：可不可以麻煩妳給我一本免稅目錄？

空服員 ：先生，您前座的置物袋裡應該有。

---

**3** You ：How much money do we save by buying duty-free?

Flight Attendant：Items are usually about 40% less than [9]street prices.

你 ：我們買免稅商品可以省多少錢？

空服員 ：通常比市價要便宜四成。

## Words & Phrases

1. goods [gʊdz] *n.* 商品；貨物

2. allowance [əˋlaʊəns] *n.* 所允許的限度

3. liter [ˋlitɚ] *n.* 公升

4. spirit [ˋspɪrɪt] *n.*【英】烈酒（美國通常用 liquor 或 booze 這兩個字）

5. per person 每一人

6. copy [ˋkɑpɪ] *n.*（書、雜誌等出版品的）一份；一冊

7. catalog [ˋkætḷˏlɔg] *n.* 目錄

8. seat pocket 椅背上的置物袋

9. street price 市面價格

FYI 好用資訊

**seat pocket**
椅背置物袋

**towel**
小毛巾

**eye mask**
眼罩

**trolley**
餐車

 Travel Tips 旅遊擻步一起走

各國免稅商品額度比一比：

| 台灣 |
|---|
| 200 支香菸（或 25 支雪茄；或 1 磅菸葉）。<br>1 瓶不超過 1,000 毫升的餐酒（wine）或烈酒（spirit）。<br>價值不超過 20,000 新台幣的物品。 |
| **泰國** |
| 200 支香菸（或 250 公克雪茄；或 250 公克菸葉）。<br>1 公升餐酒或烈酒。<br>價值一千泰銖之個人物品。 |
| **法國** |
| 200 支香菸（或 100 支小雪茄；或 50 支雪茄；或 250 公克菸葉）。<br>1 公升烈酒（或 2 公升餐酒）。<br>50 公克香精和 250 毫升香水。 |
| **美國** |
| 200 支菸（或 50 支雪茄；或 2 公斤菸絲）。<br>1 公升餐酒（二十一歲以上旅客）。<br>非美國居民可免稅攜帶不超過 100 美元的物品。<br>美國居民可免稅攜帶相等於 800 美元的物品。 |

# CHAPTER 2

# ARRIVING AT THE AIRPORT

## 抵達機場

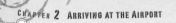

# David
## 大衛

 Dialogue 對話

CD 1-11

David ¹<u>arrives</u> at Bangkok airport after his ²<u>flight</u>. It's hot and ³<u>steamy</u> and he's tired. He goes to ⁴<u>immigration</u>.

*Immigration Officer* : Good morning, sir. May I see your ⁵<u>passport</u>?

*David* : Sure, here it is. The ⁶<u>visa</u> is on page 12.

*Immigration Officer* : Can you also give me your ⁷<u>disembarkation</u> card?

*David* : Oh yes, sorry. I ⁸<u>filled it out</u> on the plane. It's in my pocket.

*Immigration Officer* : What is the ⁹<u>planned duration</u> of your ¹⁰<u>stay</u> in Thailand?

*David* : I think probably only a couple of weeks.

*Immigration Officer* : And are you here ¹¹<u>for business or pleasure</u>?

*David* : Just a vacation. I have to go back to school in the fall.

*Immigration Officer* : (*Stamping passport*) Welcome to Thailand. Enjoy your stay.

*David* : Thanks, I will. Oh, just one thing, which way is ¹²<u>customs</u>?

*Immigration Officer* : Go down the stairs, turn left and follow the ¹³<u>signs</u>.

*David* : Thanks.

經過飛行後，大衛抵達了曼谷機場。天氣又熱又潮濕，而他也累了。他走向入境處。

入境官員：先生，早安。可以讓我看一下您的護照嗎？

大衛 ：好，在這裡。簽證在第十二頁。

入境官員：您可以把入境（記錄卡）也給我嗎？

大衛 ：噢，好的，抱歉。我在飛機上填好了，放在我的口袋裡。

入境官員：您打算在泰國停留多少時間？

大衛 ：我想大概只待幾個星期左右。

入境官員：您到這裡來是為了談生意還是觀光？

大衛 ：只是度假而已。我秋季的時候得回到學校。

入境官員：（在護照上蓋章）歡迎來泰國，祝您玩得愉快。

大衛 ：謝謝，我會的。噢，對了，海關要怎麼走？

入境官員：下樓後左轉，再跟著標示走就行了。

大衛 ：謝謝。

## Words and Phrases

1. arrive [əˋraɪv] v. 抵達

2. flight [flaɪt] n. 飛行

3. steamy [ˋstimɪ] adj. 熱而潮濕的

4. immigration [͵ɪməˋgreʃən] n. 入境處

5. passport [ˋpæs͵port] n. 護照

6. visa [ˋvizə] n. 簽證

7. disembarkation [͵dɪsɪmbɑrˋkeʃən] n. 入境（disembarkation card為入境卡）

8. fill out 填寫（書、報表等）

9. planned duration 準備停留的時間

10. stay [ste] n. 逗留；停留

11. For business or pleasure? 為了談生意還是觀光呢？

12. customs [ˋkʌstəmz] n. 海關

13. sign [saɪn] n. 標示

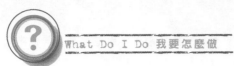

What Do I Do 我要怎麼做

CD 1-12

# Getting through Customs 通關

**1** Official : Good morning, ¹<u>madam</u>. Can I please see your ²<u>landing card</u>?

You : Yes, it's here in my backpack. Wait a second.

官員 ：小姐，早安。可以讓我看一下您的入境卡嗎？

你 ：好的，在我的背包裡。稍等一下。

**2** Official : Do you have anything to ³<u>declare</u>?

You : No, I only have a liter of spirits and some ⁴<u>cigars</u>.

官員 ：您有任何要申報的東西嗎？

你 ：沒有，我只有一公升烈酒和一些雪茄。

**3** Official : Do you mind if I open your bag and take a quick look inside?

You : No, go ahead.

官員 ：您介意我打開您的袋子，很快地看一下裡面嗎？

你 ：不介意，請便。

## Words and Phrases

1. madam [`mædəm] *n.* 【尊稱】小姐；女士

2. landing card 入境卡（=disembarkation card；不同國家所要求的證件會有一點點的出入，有的地方稱 disembarkation card，有的地方稱 landing card，基本上都是入境時須填寫並交給海關的表格）

3. declare [dɪ`klɛr] *v.* （向海關）申報（納稅品等）【註：超過免稅限額的才需申報】

4. cigar [sɪ`gɑr] *n.* 雪茄

Getting What You Want 解決你的需求

CD 1-13

# Paperwork at the Airport 通關文件

**1** You : Could you bring me a disembarkation card, please?

Official: Sure, I think we should still have some.

你 ：可以麻煩你給我一張入境卡嗎？

官員 ：當然可以，我想我們應該還有一些。

---

**2** You : What are the duty-free ²limits for Taiwan?

Official: A liter of spirits, 200 cigarettes and 500ml of perfume.

你 ：台灣的免稅限額是多少？

官員 ：一公升烈酒、兩百根菸以及五百毫升的香水。

---

**3** You : Can you give me a ³multiple-entry visa?

Official: Certainly, but it will be 20 dollars more.

你 ：可以給我多次入境簽證嗎？

官員 ：當然可以，可是要多付二十元。

## Words and Phrases

1. paperwork [ˋpepɚˌwɝk] *n.* 文書工作

2. limit [ˋlɪmɪt] *n.* 額度；限額

3. multiple-entry visa [ˋmʌltɪpļˌɛntrɪ ˋvizə] 多次入境簽證

FYI 好用資訊

## 泰國的入境卡

| | | | |
|---|---|---|---|
| 1 ธันวาคม 2539 | รายการของบุคคลซึ่งเดินทางเข้ามาในหรือออกไปนอกราชอาณาจักร<br>DETAILS OF PERSON ENTERING OR LEAVING THE KINGDOM | | ตม. 6<br>TM. 6 |

**ลำดับที่**
**No.** **TM. MJ 52648**

บัตรขาเข้า
ARRIVAL CARD

| ชื่อสกุล Family name | ชื่อตัว First name | ชื่อรอง Middle name | ☐ ชาย Male |
|---|---|---|---|
| WANG | LING | HUI | ☑ หญิง Female |

| วัน เดือน ปีเกิด Date of birth | สถานที่เกิด Place of birth |
|---|---|
| 6 , 21 , 1997 | TAIWAN R.O.C |

| สัญชาติ Nationality | อาชีพ Occupation |
|---|---|
| TAIWAN R.O.C. | CABIN ATTENDANT |

| หนังสือเดินทางเลขที่ Passport No. | ออกให้ที่ Place of issue | เมื่อวันที่ Date of issue |
|---|---|---|
| X1234567 | TAIWAN | 6/30/99 |

| ตรวจลงตราเลขที่ Visa No. | ออกให้ที่ Place of issue | เมื่อวันที่ Date of issue |
|---|---|---|
| Y1234567 | TAIWAN | 6/30/99 |

| เดินทางมาจาก From | ☐ โดยทางรถไฟ By rail | ☑ โดยทางอากาศ By air |
|---|---|---|
| TAIWAN | ☐ โดยทางรถยนต์ By road<br>☐ โดยทางเรือ By ship | เที่ยวบินที่<br>Flight No. BR123 |

| เดินทางมาประเทศไทยครั้งแรก<br>First trip to Thailand<br>☑ ใช่ Yes ☐ ไม่ใช่ No. | เดินทางมาเป็นคณะท่องเที่ยว<br>Traveling on group tour<br>☑ ใช่ Yes ☐ ไม่ใช่ No. | ระยะเวลาพำนัก<br>Length of stay<br>2 วัน Day (s) |
|---|---|---|

ความประสงค์ในการมา Purpose of visit

☐ ท่องเที่ยว Tourist      ☐ การประชุม Convention      ☑ ธุรกิจ Business

☐ ราชการ Official       ☐ จุดประสงค์อื่น ๆ Others      (โปรดระบุ) (Please specify)

ผ่านไปยัง Transit to

| ที่อยู่ปัจจุบัน Country of residence | ที่อยู่ในประเทศไทย Address in Thailand. |
|---|---|
| | XX HOTEL |
| City/State        Country | |

ลายมือชื่อ Signature _____ บุคคลซึ่งเดินทางเข้ามาในราชอาณาจักร
Person entering the Kingdom

**สำหรับเจ้าหน้าที่**
FOR OFFICIAL USE

อนุญาตให้อยู่ตามสิทธิเดิม

Travel Tips 旅遊撇步一起走

　　假如你想要順利通關，打扮整齊、穿著得體會有所幫助。假如你喜歡把外表弄得髒兮兮，像個長髮嬉皮一樣的話，就比較容易被海關人員盯上，不客氣地對你做徹底的搜身。

Notes

# Marie & Celeste

瑪莉＆賽麗絲特

Dialogue 對話

CD 1-14

**The two girls arrive at Charles de Gaulle airport. They get off the plane, go through customs and decide to ¹change money.**

*Marie* : I think we should go ²<u>downtown</u> first. We'll get a better ³<u>exchange rate</u> there.

*Celeste* : I don't think so. Are you kidding? They'll ⁴<u>rip you off</u>. ⁵<u>According to</u> the *Lonely Planet* ⁶<u>guidebook</u>, the airport is the best.

*Marie* : OK. Let's change it here, then.

⁷<u>*Clerk*</u> : Good afternoon. How can I help you?

*Celeste* : Can we change US$500 into ⁸<u>francs</u>?

*Clerk* : You mean ⁹<u>euros</u>? The franc has been ¹⁰<u>phased out</u>.

*Marie* : Sorry. Yes, euros.

*Clerk* : Can I see your passport please, or some other form of ¹¹<u>photo ID</u>?

*Celeste* : OK. How about my ¹²<u>international driver's license</u>?

*Clerk* : That would be fine. US$500 is around 420 euros ¹³<u>minus</u> our 2% ¹⁴<u>commission</u>. Now, ¹⁵<u>how do you want the money</u>?

*Celeste* : What ¹⁶<u>denominations</u> do you have?

*Clerk* : Tens, twenties, fifties and hundreds.

*Celeste* : Just give me eight fifties and the rest in ¹⁷<u>change</u>, please.

*Marie* : Sorry, how much do you think a taxi to downtown will cost?

*Clerk* : I would guess around fifteen euros. If you walk down to the end of this ¹⁸<u>hall</u> and turn right, you would see a line of taxis.

*Celeste* : Thanks for your help.

這兩個女孩抵達了戴高樂機場。她們下了飛機、通了關，並決定要去換錢。

瑪莉 ：我想我們應該先去市區，在那裡我們會獲得較划算的匯率。

賽麗絲特：我不這麼認為。妳在開玩笑嗎？他們會把妳狠刮一頓的。根據《寂寞星球》旅遊手冊，在機場換是最好的。

瑪莉 ：好吧，那我們就在這裡換好了。

櫃台人員：午安。我能夠為兩位效勞嗎？

賽麗絲特：我們可以把五百美元換成法郎嗎？

櫃台人員：您是說歐元吧？法郎已經停用了。

瑪莉 ：抱歉。沒錯，是歐元。

櫃台人員：那我可以看一下妳的護照，或是任何其他形式的有照證件嗎？

賽麗絲特：好。我的國際駕照可以嗎？

櫃台人員：可以的。五百美元大約是四百二十歐元再扣掉二％的手續費。那，妳要哪些面額的呢？

賽麗絲特：你們有哪些面額？

櫃台人員：十元、二十元、五十元和一百元。

賽麗絲特：那就請給我八張五十元，其餘的就給零錢。

瑪莉 ：不好意思，你認為坐計程車到市區要花多少錢？

櫃台人員：我想大概是十五歐元左右。你們這個走廊往前走到底，然後右轉，就會看到一整排的計程車。

賽麗絲特：謝謝你的幫忙。

## Words and Phrases

1. change [tʃendʒ] v. 換（錢）

2. downtown [`daʊn`taʊn] adv. 往、在市中心（鬧區）

3. exchange rate [ɪks`tʃendʒ͵ret] n. 外匯兌換率

4. rip sb. off 敲竹槓

5. according to... 根據……（的說法）

6. guidebook [`gaɪd͵bʊk] n. 旅行指南

7. clerk [klɝk] n.（旅館）接待員；售貨員；職員；辦事人員

8. franc [fræŋk] n. 法郎

9. euro [`jʊrə] n. 歐元（符號為€）

10. phase out 分階段逐步停止使用（或生產、實行）；逐步結束、被淘汰

11. photo ID 有照證件（＝picture ID）

12. international driver's license 國際駕照

13. minus [`maɪnəs] prep. 去除

14. commission [kə`mɪʃən] n. 手續費；佣金；回扣

15. How do you want the money? 你的款項要以哪些面額呈現？

16. denomination [dɪ͵nɑmə`neʃən] n.（貨幣）面額

17. change [tʃendʒ] n.（找回的）零錢

18. hall [hɔl] n. 走廊

27

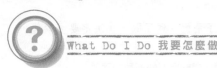

What Do I Do 我要怎麼做          CD 1-15

## ¹**Exchanging Money 換錢**

**① Clerk**    : Can you sign these traveler's checks on the ²<u>reverse</u> side, please?

**You**    : Of course. Do you mind if I borrow your pen?

櫃台人員：可不可以請您在這些旅行支票的背後簽名？

你        ：當然可以。你介意我借一下你的筆嗎？

---

**② Clerk**    : In what currency would you like your money?

**You**    : U.S. dollars, please.

櫃台人員：您的錢要換成哪種貨幣？

你        ：美元，麻煩你。

---

**③ Clerk**    : Please take this ³<u>form</u> to the ⁴<u>cashier</u>.

**You**    : Which ⁵<u>counter</u> is that?

櫃台人員：請把這張表格拿到出納處。

你        ：那是哪一個櫃台？

---

📺*Words and Phrases*

1. exchange [ɪks`tʃendʒ] *v.* 兌換（貨幣）

2. reverse [rɪ`vɝs] *adj.* 背面的；翻過來 另一面的

3. form [fɔrm] *n.* 表格

4. cashier [kæ`ʃɪr] *n.* 出納；出納員

5. counter [`kaʊntɚ] *n.* 櫃台

Getting What You Want 解決你的需求

CD 1-16

# Exchanging Money 換錢

**(1)** You : Can you ¹break this 100 euro ²note, please?

Clerk : Sure. Is a fifty and five tens OK?

你 ：可不可以麻煩你把這張一百歐元的鈔票換開？

櫃台人員：當然可以。一張五十和五張十元行嗎？

---

**(2)** You : What is your commission rate?

Clerk : 2% if you exchange less than US$1000. 1.5% if you exchange US$1000 or more.

你 ：你們的手續費率是多少？

櫃台人員：假如換不到一千美元的話是二％；換一千美元以上則是一‧五％。

---

**(3)** You : Do you ³accept ⁴coins ⁵as well as notes?

Clerk : No, sorry, we can only exchange notes.

你 ：你們紙鈔和硬幣都接受嗎？

櫃台人員：不，抱歉，我們只能換紙鈔。

## Words and Phrases

1. **break** [brek] *v.* 換開

2. **note** [not] *n.* 【英】鈔票；紙幣

3. **accept** [ɪk`sɛpt] *v.* 接受（承兌）；認付

4. **coin** [kɔɪn] *n.* 硬幣

5. **as well as...** 亦、也

泰國、法國、佛羅里達州三地對於我國國際駕照以及普通駕照的承認度參考：

| 泰國 |
| --- |
| 一、承認我國國際駕駛執照。 |
| 二、當事人需持該駕照、護照（具有效觀光旅遊簽證）至泰國監理處繳交二十五元泰幣，經監理處驗證後使用。 |
| 三、攜帶所需文件辦理，可免考換發一年有效期之泰國駕照。 |

| 法國 |
| --- |
| 一、可在當地使用我國之國際駕駛執照，但不可免考換發當地之駕駛執照。 |
| 二、持我國駕照可憑居留證免考換發當地之駕駛執照。 |

| 佛羅里達州 |
| --- |
| 一、不承認我國國際駕駛執照。 |
| 二、承認我國駕照。附該駕照之中文翻譯之文件，經有關當局驗證後，可免路考並經交通筆試之後換發當地駕駛執照。 |

資料來源：http://www.thb.gov.tw

Travel Tips 旅遊撇步一起走

　　內行的旅客在購買當地貨幣的時候，都知道要去哪裡找最划算的匯率。機場過去提供的匯率都非常不划算，但最近的價格都已跟當地的銀行一模一樣。在大城市裡，自動櫃員機非常方便，而且通常都提供公道的價格。在下榻的旅館換錢可能是最方便的選擇，但不會有好價錢。在某些國家，「黑市」的路邊交易者給的價錢最好；但你若是要在街上交易，就得小心不要上當受騙。

Notes

# Kevin & Sarah
## 凱文&莎拉

Dialogue 對話

CD 1-17

Kevin and Sarah arrive at Miami International airport. Their first [1]task is to [2]collect their [3]luggage and find a bus to their hotel.

*Kevin* : I don't know why our luggage always [4]comes off the plane last.

*Sarah* : Probably because we always arrive several hours before [5]check-in, so our stuff gets put on the plane first.

*Kevin* : Hmmm...yeah, [6]that would explain it. I wonder if this is the right [7]carousel?

*Sarah* : Well, our [8]flight number was ER602 and the [9]monitor does say carousel 6.

*Kevin* : Yes, here they come. There's yours and there's mine. Quick, [10]grab a baggage trolley. It might be a long walk down to Customs.

(*Five minutes later*)

*Sarah* : God, it's humid out here. I need a drink.

*Kevin* : Let's wait until we get to the hotel.

*Sarah* : We're staying at the Four Seasons Hotel. According to the brochure they offer a free [11]shuttle bus from outside the [12]terminal.

*Kevin* : That sign says "For all buses go to the north [13]exit." Come on, this way! Follow me!

*Sarah* : Hang on a second! Come back! That bus in front of us says, "Four Seasons Hotel Shuttle Bus."

*Kevin* : Oh. Right. That's probably it then.

凱文與莎拉抵達邁阿密國際機場。他們的首要之務是取回他們的行李，然後找公車到他們下榻的旅館。

凱文：我不知道為什麼我們的行李老是在最後才下飛機。

莎拉：大概是因為我們老是在辦登機手續的幾個小時前就到了，所以我們的東西會先被放上飛機。

凱文：嗯……對，這就難怪了。我懷疑這是不是正確的行李轉盤？

莎拉：嗯，我們的班機號碼是ER602，螢幕上的確寫的是六號轉盤。

凱文：沒錯，來了。你的在那兒，我的在那兒。快，抓一台行李推車來，走到海關可能還要一段距離。

（五分鐘之後）

莎拉：天哪，這裡可真是潮濕。我需要喝點東西。

凱文：我們到旅館再說吧。

莎拉：我們下榻的是四季飯店。簡介上面說，他們在航空站外面有提供免費的接駁公車。

凱文：那塊標示上說「搭乘所有公車請至北出口」。來吧，往這邊走！跟我來！

莎拉：等一下！回來！我們前面的那台公車上寫著「四季飯店接駁公車」。

凱文：喔，對，那大概就是它了。

## 🚌 Words and Phrases

1. task [tæsk] *n.* 任務

2. collect [kə`lɛkt] *v.* 領取

3. luggage [`lʌgɪdʒ] *n.* 行李

4. come off 卸下

5. check-in [`tʃɛk`ɪn] *n.* 辦理登機手續

6. That would explain it. 難怪。

7. carousel [ˌkærə`zɛl] *n.* （行李）旋轉

式傳送帶；行李轉盤

8. flight number 班機號碼

9. monitor [`mɑnətɚ] *n.* （電腦）螢幕

10. grab [græb] *v.* 快快抓住；搶奪

11. shuttle bus [`ʃʌtlˌbʌs] 接駁公車

12. terminal [`tɚmən] *n.* 航空站

13. exit [`ɛgzɪt] *n.* 出口

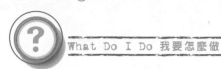

What Do I Do 我要怎麼做

CD 1-18

# Luggage 托運行李

**(1) Clerk** : Do you remember your flight number?

**You** : It was Q504 from Sydney.

櫃台人員：您記得您的班機號碼嗎？

你　　　：是從雪梨起飛的Q504號班機。

---

**(2) Clerk** : Can you ¹describe your luggage, please?

**You** : One large green ²suitcase and a blue ³duffel bag.

櫃台人員：可不可以請您形容一下您的行李？

你　　　：一個綠色的皮箱和一個藍色的簡便行李袋。

---

**(3) Clerk** : Do you need help with your luggage?

**You** : Thank you. But I think we can ⁴handle it.

櫃台人員：您需要幫忙提行李嗎？

你　　　：謝謝你，我想我們應付得來。

## Words and Phrases

1. describe [dɪs`kraɪb] *v.* 描述

2. suitcase [`sut͵kes] *n.* 手提箱；皮箱

3. duffel bag [`dʌfl͵bæg] 簡易行李袋（設計很簡單，手提和肩背皆可）

4. handle [`hændl] *v.* 應付；處理

Getting What You Want 解決你的需求

CD 1-19

# [1]Transportation Away from the Airport
## 離開機場的交通工具

**1** You : Excuse me, where are the [2]rental car companies?

　　Clerk : Down at the other [3]end of the terminal.

　　你 ：對不起，請問租車公司在哪兒？

　　櫃台人員：在航空站的另一頭。

---

**2** You : Can you tell me where the bus station is [4]located, please?

　　Clerk : Go out of the [5]arrivals building and turn left.

　　你 ：可以請你告訴我公車站的位置在哪裡嗎？

　　櫃台人員：走出入境大樓再左轉就到了。

---

**3** You : Does this bus stop at the Ramada Inn?

　　Clerk : Yes, it's the fifth [6]stop.

　　你 ：這班公車華美達飯店停不停？

　　櫃台人員：停，是第五站。

🚌 *Words and Phrases*

1. transportation [ˌtrænspɚˋteʃən] *n.* 交通工具

2. rental car [ˋrɛntḷ͵kɑr] 租車

3. end [ɛnd] *n.* 終端；盡頭

4. located [ˋlo͵ketɪd] *adj.* 位於；座落於（注意使用被動式）

5. arrival [əˋraɪv!] *n.* 入境；到達

6. stop [stɑp] *n.* （巴士等的）站

35

FYI 好用資訊

**trolley**
手推車

**carousel**
行李轉盤

**duffel bag**
簡便行李袋

**luggage tag**
行李牌

Travel Tips 旅遊撇步一起走

　　明智地打包行李可以免除很多旅遊時的壓力。在某些行程中，假如你真的肯花心思且很有效率，可以考慮把一切需要的東西塞在一、兩個袋子裡，以便帶上飛機。其實一般人很難把東西減少到這種程度，不過輕裝旅遊確實會讓你覺得很自由，並有助於增加你行程上的自主性與冒險性。

# CHAPTER 3

# CHECKING IN TO THE HOTEL

## 住進旅館

# David
## 大衛

 Dialogue 對話

CD 1-20

**David has taken a bus to the KhaoSan road, the center for <u>budget</u><sup>1</sup> <u>backpacking</u><sup>2</sup>. He finds a <u>hostel</u><sup>3</sup> and goes inside.**

*David* : Hi, do you have any <u>free</u><sup>4</sup> rooms?

*Pinachorn* : Not free, but cheap!

*David* : Ha ha! Yes, I mean <u>empty</u><sup>5</sup> rooms.

*Pinachorn* : Do you want a <u>single</u><sup>6</sup>, a <u>double</u><sup>7</sup> or a <u>dorm bed</u><sup>8</sup>?

*David* : How much are they?

*Pinachorn* : A single is 200 <u>baht</u><sup>9</sup>, a double is 120 baht and a dorm bed is 50 baht.

*David* : I guess I'm not that <u>keen</u><sup>10</sup> on sharing so I'll have a single. I'll be here for three nights.

*Pinachorn* : If you want <u>aircon</u><sup>11</sup> that's an extra 20 baht a day.

*David* : What about a bathroom?

*Pinachorn* : There's a <u>private</u><sup>12</sup> shower <u>surcharge</u><sup>13</sup> of another 10 baht a night.

*David* : So, <u>let me get this straight</u><sup>14</sup>—a single room with aircon and a private shower is 230 baht a night?

*Pinachorn* : That's right—<u>plus</u><sup>15</sup> another 10 baht for hot water.

*David* : So, 240 baht a night?

*Pinachorn* : Minus 10% if you pay for 3 nights or more.

*David* : <u>I'll tell you what</u><sup>16</sup>. Here's 1,000 baht. <u>Take out</u><sup>17</sup> what I <u>owe</u><sup>18</sup> you for 3 nights and give me the change!

*Pinachorn* : You want dinner? Only 50 baht on Wednesdays, plus 10 baht for...?

*David* : No, thanks! I'll get some food outside.

*Pinachorn* : OK, here is your change of 352 baht.

*David* : All right! Thanks!

大衛搭了公車到考山路，那裡是平價自助旅遊的中心。他找了一家旅舍，並走了進去。

大衛 ：嗨，你們有沒有空／免費（雙關語）的房間？

普林納瓊：不是免費的，但是很便宜！

大衛 ：哈哈！是的，我的意思是空的房間。

普林納瓊：您要單人房、雙人房，還是宿舍床位？

大衛 ：它們分別是多少錢？

普林納瓊：單人房二百銖，雙人房一百二十銖，宿舍床位五十銖。

大衛 ：我想我不是麼喜歡與人共用一房的人，所以我住單人房好了。我會在這邊待三個晚上。

普林納瓊：假如您要空調，那一天要多加二十銖。

大衛 ：那浴室呢？

普林納瓊：私人淋浴的話一個晚上再加收十銖的費用。

大衛 ：那，讓我搞清楚──單人房加上空調和私人淋浴一晚是二百三十銖嗎？

普林納瓊：沒錯──熱水再加十銖。

大衛 ：所以一晚是二百四十銖嘍？

普林納瓊：假如您付三個晚上以上的費用，可以打九折。

大衛 ：這樣吧，這裡是一千銖。扣掉我要給你的三個晚上的費用，然後找零錢給我。

普林納瓊：您要吃晚餐嗎？星期三只要五十銖，再加十銖就……

大衛 ：不用了，謝謝！我會在外面吃。

普林納瓊：好的，這是三百五十二銖找您。

大衛 ：好！謝謝！

## Words and Phrases

1. budget [`bʌdʒɪt] *adj.* 省錢的

2. backpacking [`bæk͵pækɪŋ] *n.* 背著背包到處遠行

3. hostel [`hɑstl] *n.* 招待所；小旅館（招待開著汽車、騎自行車或步行的青年旅遊者）

4. free [fri] *adj.* （房屋等）未被佔用的；免費的

5. empty [`ɛmptɪ] *adj.* 空的；無人居住的

6. single [`sɪŋgl] *n.* 單人房

7. double [`dʌbl] *n.* 雙人房

8. dorm bed [`dɔrm͵bɛd] 宿舍床位

9. baht [bɑt] *n.* 銖（泰國貨幣單位）

10. keen [kin] *adj.* 熱中於；著迷於

11. aircon [`ɛr͵kɑn] *n.* 空調設備（air-conditioning 的簡稱；美國較常稱AC）

12. private [`praɪvɪt] *adj.* 私人的；個人的

13. surcharge [`sɝ͵tʃɑrdʒ] *n.* 額外費用；附加費用

14. Let me get this straight. 讓我把這狀況搞清楚。

15. plus [plʌs] *prep.* 加上

16. I'll tell you what. 這樣好了。

17. take out 扣除；去除

18. owe [o] *v.* 欠；欠（某人）債，對……負有（債務、義務）

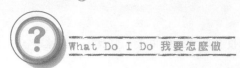

What Do I Do 我要怎麼做

CD 1-21

# No, Thanks 不用了，謝謝

**①** Clerk     : Will you have your dinner here at the hotel this evening?

You      : No, thank you. I've already made other plans for the evening.

櫃台人員：您今晚要在旅館裡用餐嗎？

你         : 不了，謝謝。我今晚已經有其他的打算。

---

**②** Clerk     : Will you be staying another night?

You      : No. I'll be ¹checking out today.

櫃台人員：您還會再待一個晚上嗎？

你         : 不，我今天會退房。

---

**③** Clerk     : We'll be happy to do your ²laundry for a small ³fee.

You      : No thanks, not today. But I might ⁴take you up on that offer tomorrow.

櫃台人員：您只要付一點點錢，我們很樂意幫您送洗衣服。

你         : 不用了，謝謝，今天不用。但明天可能就要有勞你了。

*Words and Phrases*

1. check out 退房

2. laundry [`lɔndrɪ] *n.* 要洗的衣物或是洗好的衣物的總稱

3. fee [fi] *n.* 費用

4. take sb. up on sth. 接受某人提出的提議、賭注、挑戰等

CD 1-22

# Something Is Not Quite Right 有些事不太對勁

**1** You : There is never any hot water in my room. Would you ¹check on it for me?

Clerk : Hot water is ²available only between the hours of 7:30 p.m. and 7:45 a.m.

你 ：我的房間裡一直都沒有熱水。你可以幫我看看嗎？

櫃台人員：有熱水的時間只從晚上七點半到早上七點四十五分。

---

**2** You : I saw a mouse in my room last night. Can you do something about that?

Clerk : Mouse? It was probably a ³rat. Here, take this stick for when you see it again.

你 ：我昨晚在房裡看到小老鼠，你能幫我處理嗎？

櫃台人員：小老鼠？大概是大老鼠吧。喏，等你再看到的時候就用這根棍子。

---

**3** You : I ⁴barely slept last night. What was all that noise?

Clerk : That was our ⁵house band. They play in the ⁶bar Tuesday through Friday.

你 ：我昨天晚上幾乎沒睡。那些噪音是怎麼回事？

櫃台人員：那是我們的駐唱樂團。他們從星期二到星期五都會在酒吧裡表演。

📖 *Words and Phrases*

1. check on 檢查

2. available [ə`veləbl] *adj.* 可獲得的

3. rat [ræt] *n.* 老鼠（mouse指的是體型較小、較可愛的鼠科）

4. barely [`bɛrlɪ] *adv.* 幾乎不能

5. house band 駐唱樂團（house可指旅館、飯店）

6. bar [bɑr] *n.* 酒吧

41

**FYI 好用資訊**

**bunk bed**

上下鋪

**single bed**

單人床

**double bed**

雙人床

**twin bed**

一對單人床

**Travel Tips 旅遊撇步一起走**

　　住旅館時，有時候真的是便宜沒好貨。如果要確保自己住到舒適、安全的房間，最好的辦法就是先看房間再付錢。檢查看看門鎖鎖不鎖得緊；確定浴室夠乾淨，床上有新床單；四下看看會不會有野生動物入侵。如此，你就可以對要不要住下來做出明智的決定。

```
Notes
```

# Marie & Celeste

## 瑪莉&賽麗絲特

 Dialogue 對話

CD 1-23

**Marie and Celeste check into their ¹pension.**

*²Mme Fourlain*: Hello, come in. You must be Marie and Celeste. I'm Madame Fourlain, the owner.

*Marie* : Hi. I'm glad you received our email ³booking. Our friends Sylvie and Paul told us that they really enjoyed their ⁴stay here last year.

*Mme Fourlain* : Yes, I remember them well. Such a nice young couple.

*Celeste* : Should we take our bags to our room?

*Mme Fourlain* : Yes, please follow me. It's just up one ⁵flight of stairs.

*Marie* : What a lovely room!

*Celeste* : And a ⁶fantastic view! Is that ⁷Notre Dame?

*Mme Fourlain* : Yes, it is. If you look the other way you can see the top of the ⁸Eiffel Tower.

*Marie* : Cool. If I weren't so hungry I'd want to go ⁹exploring immediately.

*Mme Fourlain* : Oh, I'm so sorry. I forgot you came ¹⁰straight from the airport. I'll go down and make breakfast.

*Celeste* : That's very kind of you. I'd just like some bread and a cup of coffee.

*Marie* : Me too.

*Mme Fourlain* : No problem. It'll be ready in ten minutes.

瑪莉與賽麗絲特住進了民宿。

佛蘭太太：哈囉，請進。你們一定是瑪莉和賽麗絲特，我是屋主佛蘭太太。

瑪莉　　：嗨，很高興您收到了我們的電子郵件預約。我們的朋友席薇和保羅告訴
　　　　　我們說，他們去年在這裡住得很盡興。

佛蘭太太：是的，我還記得他們。很不錯的一對年輕夫妻。

賽麗絲特：我們是不是應該把袋子拿到房間去？

佛蘭太太：好的，請跟我來。只要走一段樓梯就到了。

瑪莉　　：真是個迷人的房間！

賽麗絲特：景觀也棒透了！那是聖母院嗎？

佛蘭太太：是的。假如你們看另外一邊，還可以看到艾菲爾鐵塔的頂端。

瑪莉　　：酷。假如我不是那麼餓的話，我真想馬上去一探究竟。

佛蘭太太：喔，真是抱歉，我忘了你們是直接從機場來的。我下樓去弄早餐。

賽麗絲特：您真是太好了。我想要些麵包和一杯咖啡。

瑪莉　　：我也是。

佛蘭太太：沒問題，十分鐘就好。

## Words and Phrases

1. pension [`pɛnʃən] n. （歐洲，尤其是法國、比利時等地的）膳宿公寓；小旅社；民宿

2. Mme [mə`dəm] n. 夫人；太太；女士（Madame 的縮寫，用於非英美地區、尤其是法國已婚婦女姓名前的尊稱，相當於美語中的 Mrs.，有時也用作對年長未婚女子的尊稱）

3. booking [`bukɪŋ] n. （席位等的）預定

4. stay [ste] n. 居留；停留

5. flight [flaɪt] n. 樓梯（兩個休息平台之間的一段樓梯）

6. fantastic [fæn`tæstɪk] adj. 極好的；了不起的

7. Notre Dame [ˌnotɚ`dem; ˌnotrə`dɑm] （巴黎）聖母院

8. Eiffel Tower [`aɪfḷ`tauɚ] 艾菲爾鐵塔

9. explore [ɪk`splor] v. 勘查，探險

10. straight from... 直接從……

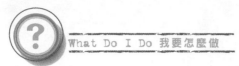

What Do I Do 我要怎麼做

CD 1-24

# You Did Something Wrong 你做錯事了

**①** Host: I'd ¹appreciate it if you keep the noise level down at night.

You : I'm sorry about the noise last night. It won't happen again.

老闆 ：若您在晚間把音量降低，我將會很感激。

你　　：對於昨晚的噪音我很抱歉。不會再有第二次。

---

**②** Host: Please don't use the ²bath towels to clean your shoes.

You : I ³apologize. Please ⁴allow me to pay for a new set of towels.

老闆 ：請不要用浴巾來擦鞋子。

你　　：我道歉。請讓我賠你一組新的浴巾。

---

**③** Host: Excuse me, but there's only $45 here. You still owe $10.

You : Sorry, my ⁵mistake. Here's the other ten.

老闆 ：對不起，這裡只有四十五元，您還欠十元。

你　　：抱歉，是我的錯。另外的十元在這裡。

## Words and Phrases

1. appreciate [ə`priʃɪˌet] v. 對（人的好意
   等）表示感謝、感激

2. bath towel 洗澡用的浴巾

3. apologize [ə`pɑləˌdʒaɪz] v. 道歉

4. allow [ə`lau] v. 准許；允許

5. mistake [mə`stek] n. 錯誤；過錯

Getting What You Want 解決你的需求

CD 1-25

# Asking Your [1]Host for [2]Advice 請教老闆

**① You :** Would you mind giving me [3]<u>directions</u> to the nearest [4]<u>Metro</u> stop?

**Host:** It's a little [5]<u>complicated</u>. Let me draw you a map.

你　：可不可以麻煩你告訴我，最近的地鐵站要怎麼去？

老闆：這有點複雜。讓我畫張地圖給你。

**② You :** Where is a good place for lunch—something tasty and [6]<u>inexpensive</u>?

**Host:** I know just the place—a little [7]<u>bistro</u> right [8]<u>around the corner</u>.

你　：哪裡有吃午餐的好地方——好吃又不貴的地方？

老闆：我知道有個好地方——拐角的一家小餐館。

**③ You :** Is it safe to visit Rue St. Denis at night?

**Host:** You should be okay. Just be careful.

你　：晚上去逛聖德尼街安全嗎？

老闆：你應該不會有問題。小心點就是了。

## *Words and Phrases*

1. host [host] *n.* （旅館等的）主人

2. advice [əd`vaɪs] *n.* 建議

3. direction [də`rɛkʃən] *n.* 行進路線；方向；指引

4. metro [`mɛtro] *n.* 地下鐵、捷運等交通設施

5. complicated [`kɑmpləˌketɪd] *adj.* 複雜的

6. inexpensive [ˌɪnɪks`pɛnsɪv] *adj.* 花費不多的

7. bistro [`bistro] *n.* （特指法國非正式的）小酒店、小餐館

8. around the corner 在拐角處

FYI 好用資訊

每間民宿或寄宿公寓都有它特有的住宿注意事項，而且它們往往比普通旅館所定的規矩要怪異得多。

1. Breakfast at 8:00. Coffee, bread, jam, eggs available on request.

2. No visitors after 10 p.m.

3. Please do not feed my cat, Simone.

4. No TV is available here. No TV!

5. Please keep the noise down after 10 p.m.

6. If there is a problem while I'm gone, please contact me at my cell 392-7771.

7. Enjoy your stay!

   Also: The handle on the toilet in #4 sticks. Be sure to release it before leaving the room so we don't have another $300 water bill.

Travel Tips 旅遊撇步一起走

　　假如你有機會住到歐洲或美國的民宿，記住你的房間裡面可能擺飾著珍貴的骨董家具。因此，千萬不要把你的濕毛巾隨意亂丟，搞不好你一不小心就丟在十八世紀路易十五時代的桃木衣櫃上。

Notes

# Kevin & Sarah

### 凱文 & 莎拉

Dialogue 對話

CD 1-26

**Sarah and Kevin check into their hotel and ask about the** [1]facilities **that are available to them.**

*Clerk* : Here is your [2]cardkey. Your room is 1209. Turn left when you come out of the elevator and walk to the end of the [3]corridor.

*Kevin* : Thanks. Can we get something to eat at this time of day?

*Clerk* : Certainly, sir. Here at the Four Seasons, you can eat [4]at any time. There is a Mexican restaurant on the 2nd floor [5]mezzanine, which is open 24 hours. The Vivaldi coffee shop is just over there through the [6]lobby. They serve a wide [7]range of [8]beverages and snacks, [9]24/7.

*Sarah* : Could you also tell us where the [10]gym is? If I can buy cakes 24/7, I'm going to need some exercise.

*Clerk* : The gym is in the basement. The [11]spa and swimming pool are on the [12]roof. Everything is free for guests except for massages.

*Sarah* : That sounds great. Is there anything else that we should know about?

*Clerk* : There's [13]a whole bunch of brochures over there [14]detailing many of the things that you can do in this part of Florida. Please [15]don't hesitate to ask if you'd like me to book any [16]tours for you.

*Kevin* : We will. You've been very helpful.

凱文與莎拉登記住進了旅館，並詢問他們可使用哪些設施。

櫃台人員：這是你們的卡片鑰匙，你們的房間是一二○九。出電梯後左轉，走廊走
到底就到了。

凱文　　：謝謝。這個時間找得到地方吃東西嗎？

櫃台人員：當然了，先生。在我們四季飯店，您可以在任何時間用餐。在一、二樓
間的夾層有一家墨西哥餐廳，二十四小時營業。韋瓦第咖啡店就在大廳
的那一頭，他們有賣各種飲料和點心，而且全年無休。

莎拉　　：可不可以再告訴我們健身房在哪裡？假如我隨時都買得到蛋糕，我就必
須得做些運動才行。

櫃台人員：健身房在地下室，水療和游泳池在頂樓。除了按摩以外，所有的都是免
費的。

莎拉　　：聽起來真棒。還有沒有什麼是我們該知道的？

櫃台人員：那裡有一整疊手冊，裡面詳述了兩位在佛羅里達州的這個地區所能做的
許多事。假如兩位要我幫忙訂任何行程，請隨時吩咐。

凱文　　：我們會的。你幫了大忙。

## 🎧 Words and Phrases

1. facilities [fə`sɪlətɪz] *n.* 設備；設施

2. cardkey [`kɑrd͵ki] *n.* 鑰匙卡

3. corridor [`kɔrədɚ] *n.* 走廊

4. at any time 任何時候

5. mezzanine [`mɛzə͵nin] *n.* 閣樓；夾層
（指上下樓層之間的一個局部樓層）

6. lobby [`lɑbɪ] *n.* （旅館、劇場等靠近大
門入口的）廳堂；門廳

7. range [rendʒ] *n.* 範圍；一批、一組、
一套

8. beverage [`bɛvrɪdʒ] *n.* （通常指水以
外的）飲料

9. 24/7 [`twɛntɪ`for`sɛvən] *adv.* 全天無休
地；永不打烊地

10. gym [dʒɪm] *n.* 健身中心

11. spa [spɑ] *n.* （可供多人使用的）
礦、溫泉療養池

12. roof [ruf] *n.* 屋頂

13. a whole bunch of... 一整疊的……

14. detail [`ditel] *v.* 詳細說明

15. don't hesitate to... 不必猶豫……

16. tour [tur] *n.* （景點等的）遊歷；參觀

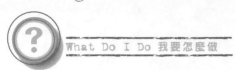
**What Do I Do** 我要怎麼做

CD 1-27

# ¹**Business** at the ²**Front Desk** 櫃台服務

**①** Clerk　: Do you have a smoking or non-smoking preference?

　　You　　: Non-smoking, please. I hate it when the room smells like smoke.

　　櫃台人員：請問您有吸菸或不吸菸的優先選擇嗎？

　　你　　　：請給我不吸菸房。我無法忍受房間裡聞起來都是菸味。

---

**②** Clerk　: Shall I call someone to help you with your bags?

　　You　　: No, thank you. I can manage.

　　櫃台人員：要不要我叫人幫您提行李？

　　你　　　：不用了，謝謝。我可以應付得來。

---

**③** Clerk　: If you need anything at all, just dial 9 to ³reach the front desk.

　　You　　: Thank you very much. I'll remember that.

　　櫃台人員：假如您需要任何東西，只要撥九聯絡櫃台即可。

　　你　　　：多謝，我會記住的。

📖*Words and Phrases*

1. business [ˋbɪznɪs] *n.* 事；事情

2. front desk [ˋfrʌntˋdɛsk] （旅館等的）接待處

3. reach [ritʃ] *v.* 與……取得聯繫

Getting What You Want 解決你的需求

CD 1-28

# More Front Desk Business 更多櫃台服務

**(1) You** : Is there a ¹charge to ²connect to the Internet from my room?

**Clerk** : Yes. Internet fees are 50 cents per minute.

你 ：從我的房間連上網路要收費嗎？

櫃台人員：要的。上網費是每分鐘五毛錢。

**(2) You** : I would like a ³wake-up call at 6 a.m. tomorrow.

**Clerk** : No problem, sir. Good night.

你 ：我在明早六點需要一通起床呼叫電話。

櫃台人員：沒問題，先生。晚安。

**(3) You** : I'm going to be out late tonight. Would it be okay if I check out at noon tomorrow, ⁴rather than eleven?

**Clerk** : No problem, sir.

你 ：我今晚會在外待到很晚，我可以在明早十二點而不是十一點退房嗎？

櫃台人員：沒問題，先生。

## Words and Phrases

1. charge [tʃɑrdʒ] *n.* 索價；收費

2. connect to... 連接到⋯⋯

3. wake-up call 起床呼叫電話（=morning call）

4. rather than... 而不是⋯⋯

FYI 好用資訊

最近有很多高級旅館都設有旅館業務專用的特殊電視頻道。你可以利用遙控器來訂閱電影、查看旅館所提供的服務以及檢視帳單。

WELCOME TO FOUR SEASONS

Please select from the following menu:

1. MOVIES/ENTERTAINMENT

2. HOTEL SERVICES

3. REVIEW YOUR BILL

4. RETURN TO THE PREVIOUS MENU

BETATEK

Travel Tips 旅遊撇步一起走

　　近來邁阿密最酷的地方就是邁阿密海灘上的裝飾藝術歷史區。當地有幾十家裝飾藝術旅館與公寓建築，大部分都是在一九二〇和一九三〇年代所建造的。裝飾藝術的建築皆為粉彩色，圓角和獨特的幾何設計則是它的特色。這些建築都細心地被保存了下來，當地也擺脫了過去的犯罪與腐敗形象，如今這個地方已成為觀光客、爵士樂迷與邁阿密可愛居民的聚集中心。

# CHAPTER 4

# GETTING
# INFORMATION

# 打聽消息

# David
## 大衛

 Dialogue 對話

CD 1-29

**David has spent a night in the hostel in Bangkok. He's now discussing interesting places to go with another guest.**

*David* : Morning, I'm David. [1]What's up?

*Rick* : Hey David, I'm Rick.

*David* : It's pretty noisy here. [2]How was your sleep?

*Rick* : Great. In the dormitory, the noise is the least of your [3]concerns. The smell of six pairs of sweaty feet in a non-aircon room will put you [4]out just like that!

*David* : Year, right. Have you been here long?

*Rick* : A couple of months. I love this city. There's always so much [5]going on.

*David* : Well, I've only got a [6]fortnight for the whole country, so give me the [7]highlights.

*Rick* : OK. A Bangkok [8]roundup. For old buildings, try the Grand Palace, the [9]Vimanmek Palace and the [10]Wat Arun. The National Museum is interesting, as is the Royal Barges museum. For shopping, you have to go to the [11]Chatuchak weekend market; and for girls, drinks and [12]nightlife, there is nowhere better than Patpong road.

*David* : How about outside Bangkok?

*Rick* : For [13]trekking, go north to Chiangmai. The train is the easiest way to get there. If you want beaches, [14]head south to [15]Ko Samui or Hua Hin.

*David* : You seem to know what's going on.... .

*Rick* : Nah, not really. The places I've told you about are all [16]well-known; you can find them in any guidebook. The only [17]non-touristy place I've been to was somewhere on the Burmese [18]border.

*David* : Thanks for the [19]tips. I'm going to [20]head out before I get caught by the desk clerk and his [21]figures!

大衛在曼谷的旅社中待了一晚。他現在正在和另一位遊客討論要去哪些好玩的地方。

大衛：早，我是大衛。你好嗎？

瑞克：嗨，大衛，我是瑞克。

大衛：這裡好吵。你睡得如何？

瑞克：挺不錯的。在宿舍裡，噪音是最不值得煩惱的事了。六雙流汗的腳丫子在沒有空調的房間裡會讓你馬上昏過去！

大衛：是啊，沒錯。你在這已經待很久了嗎？

瑞克：兩個月左右。我喜歡這城市，總是有一大堆好玩的事。

大衛：嗯，我只有兩個星期的時間玩遍全國，所以告訴我重點吧。

瑞克：好，曼谷的重點介紹。如果想看古建築物，可以去大王宮、威瑪曼宮和黎明寺。國家博物館很好玩，御舟博物館也是。如果要購物，就一定得去乍都節週末市場；如果要女人、酒和夜生活，則沒有一個地方比得上帕彭路。

大衛：那出了曼谷呢？

瑞克：如果要徒步旅行，就朝北往清邁去，搭火車是到那裡最簡便的方式。假如你想要去海邊，就往南去蘇梅島或是華欣。

大衛：你似乎都瞭若指掌……

瑞克：不，其實並沒有，我告訴你的都是眾所皆知的地方，任何一本旅遊導覽上都找得到。我唯一去過的非觀光地點是緬甸的邊界附近。

大衛：多謝指教。我要在被櫃台人員抓去算帳之前先閃囉！

## Words and Phrases

1. What's up? 近來如何？
2. How was your sleep? 睡得怎麼樣？
3. concern [kən`sɜn] n. 擔心；利害關係
4. out [aʊt] adv. 失去知覺
5. going on adj. 在進行；在發生
6. fortnight [`fɔrtnaɪt] n. 兩週
7. highlight [`haɪlaɪt] n. 壓軸；最有趣之處
8. roundup [`raʊndʌp] n. 綜述；摘要
9. Vimanmek Palace 威瑪曼宮（又稱為雲天石宮）
10. Wat Arun 黎明寺（又稱為鄭皇廟）
11. Chatuchak weekend market 乍都節週末市場
12. nightlife [`naɪtˌlaɪf] n. 夜生活
13. trekking [`trɛkɪŋ] n. 徒步旅行；長途跋涉
14. head [hɛd] v. 朝……前往
15. Ko Samui 蘇梅島
16. well-known [`wɛl`non] adj. 知名的
17. non-touristy [nɑn`tʊrəstɪ] adj. 非觀光的
18. border [`bɔrdɚ] n. 邊界
19. tip [tɪp] n. 提醒；建議；暗示
20. head out 出發
21. figure [`fɪgjɚ] n. 數字；金額

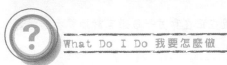

What Do I Do 我要怎麼做

CD 1-30

# Tourist ¹Q and A 觀光客問答

**①** Stranger : I'm lost. How do I get to Patpong road?

    You : I'm not sure. I'm a tourist just like you.

    陌生人 ：我迷路了。帕彭路要怎麼走？

    你 ：我不知道。我跟你一樣是觀光客。

---

**②** Taxi Driver : If you'd like, I can ²show you around the whole city.

    You : How much would that cost me?

    計程車司機：假如你願意的話，我可以帶你參觀整個城市。

    你 ：那樣要花我多少錢？

---

**③** New Friend : Who told you that was a good hostel?

    You : It was ³recommended in a guidebook I read.

    新朋友 ：是誰告訴你那間旅舍不錯的？

    你 ：我看的一本旅遊指南推薦的。

*Words and Phrases*

1. Q and A  問答

2. show sb. around  帶某人參觀

3. recommend [ˌrɛkənˋmɛnd] *v.* 建議；推薦

Getting What You Want 解決你的需求

CD 1-31

# The Whole Truth 完整的事實

**①** **You** : If I hire you as a guide, will there be any ¹extra charges?

**Guide** : No! Price is for one day—no extra charges!

你 ：假如我請你當導遊，要不要收什麼額外費用？

導遊 ：不用！就是一天的價錢——不需額外費用！

---

**②** **You** : Where can I find some good Thai food?

**Guide** : Most restaurants in downtown Bangkok are pretty good.

你 ：哪裡有美味的泰國菜？

導遊 ：大部分位於曼谷市中心的餐廳都不錯。

---

**③** **You** : Is this price ²negotiable? It seems too high to me.

**Vendor** : I might be able to ³come down a little. What price range did you have in mind?

你 ：這個價錢可以商量嗎？對我而言似乎太貴了。

商家 ：我也許可以算便宜一點。你想的價格大概是多少？

*Words and Phrases*

1. extra [`ɛkstrə] *adj.* 額外的

2. negotiable [nɪ`goʃɪəb] *adj.* 有商量餘地的

3. come down 降價

59

**trekking**
徒步旅行

**palace**
皇宮

**hostel**
青年旅館

**nightlife**
夜生活

Travel Tips 旅遊撇步一起走

　　去國外旅遊時，記得把所有的文件備齊。你需要護照，很可能還需要簽證。你可能還需要檢疫卡（vaccination card）和國際駕照。遺失這些東西會很麻煩。出發之前，不妨把文件掃瞄一下，然後用電子郵件寄給自己。如此一來，假如你在旅行時不幸遺失了這些文件，就可以找一家網咖把它們列印出來。

## Notes

# Marie & Celeste

瑪莉 & 賽麗絲特

Dialogue 對話

CD 1-32

**Marie and Celeste have finished their breakfast and can't wait to get out and explore Paris.**

*Marie* : Mme Fourlain said that the [1]Tourist Information Bureau was on the [2]Champs Elysees.

*Celeste*: I don't think even *we* can miss that.

*Marie* : There, #137: the big green "I."

(*Marie steps up to the counter*)

*Clerk* : How can I help you?

*Marie* : [3]Nothing in particular. We'd just like a few maps of Paris, Metro [4]routes, [5]places of interest, things like that.

*Clerk* : No problem. All the basic information is in these three [6]brochures. Everything you need to know about museum, [7]galleries, [8]malls and parks. There's a special section on the Metro and lots of information about [9]sites within 75 kilometers of Paris.

*Celeste*: There is one more thing. We are in Paris for two weeks and we thought it might be fun to rent some [10]scooters. Is that possible?

*Clerk* : Of course. You have International Driver's Licenses, yes?

*Celeste*: Yes, and we came from Taiwan so we [11]are used to riding scooters.

*Clerk* : In that case I'll call [12]Monsieur Roncart, who I know has scooters [13]for hire.

*Marie* : That you. You're very kind.

瑪莉與賽麗絲特用畢早餐，迫不及待地要出去探索巴黎。

瑪莉　　：佛蘭太太說，旅遊服務局在香榭麗舍大道上面。

賽麗絲特：那我想連我們都不可能找不到的。

瑪莉　　：在那裡，一三七號，有個綠色的大「I」。

（瑪莉走到櫃台前。）

櫃台人員：有什麼可以替兩位效勞的嗎？

瑪莉　　：沒什麼特別要緊的事。我們只是要幾份介紹巴黎、地鐵路線和遊樂地點之類的地圖。

櫃台人員：沒問題，所有的基本資料都在這三本小冊子裡。裡面有你們需要知道的博物館、畫廊、購物中心和公園的相關事宜，另外還有專門單元介紹地鐵以及巴黎方圓七十五公里之內各個景點的許多相關資料。

賽麗絲特：還有一件事。我們在巴黎要待兩個星期，所以我們覺得租機車來騎可能會滿好玩的。這可行嗎？

櫃台人員：當然。你們有國際駕照，對吧？

賽麗絲特：有。我們來自台灣，所以都習慣騎機車。

櫃台人員：這樣的話，我打電話給朗卡特先生，我知道他有機車出租。

瑪莉　　：謝謝，你真好。

## (🚌)Words and Phrases

1. Tourist Information Bureau  旅遊局

2. Champs Elysees [ˌʃɑnzeliˋze] 香榭麗舍大道

3. Nothing in particular. 沒什麼特別的事。

4. route [rut] *n.* 路線

5. places of interest  名勝

6. brochure [broˋʃʊr] *n.* 小冊子

7. gallery [ˋgælərɪ] *n.* 畫廊；美術館

8. mall [mɔl] *n.* （車子不得入內的）商店區、商業大街

9. site [saɪt] *n.* 景點

10. scooter [ˋskutɚ] *n.* 小型摩托車

11. be used to... 習慣了（做）……

12. monsieur [məˋsjɚ] *n.* 【法文】先生（相當於美語中的 Mr. 或 Sir）

13. for hire 出租；供租用

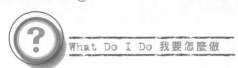

What Do I Do 我要怎麼做

 CD 1-33

# Talking with the ¹Ticket Taker 和收票員對話

① Ticket taker : Are you a student? Students ²enter for ³half price today.

　You　　　 : Yes! Thanks for ⁴reminding me. Here's my ⁵student ID.

　收票員　 : 你是學生嗎？今天學生可以半價入場。

　你　　　 : 是！謝謝你提醒我。這是我的學生證。

---

② Ticket taker : Is the address on your ID ⁶current?

　You　　　 : No, it's not. I'll write down my new address for you.

　收票員　 : 你學生證上的地址是現址嗎？

　你　　　 : 不，不是。我把我新的地址寫給你。

---

③ Ticket taker : I see you're from Taipei. How interesting!

　You　　　 : Yes. Have you ever been there?

　收票員　 : 我知道你是從台北來的。真有趣！

　你　　　 : 是的。你去過那裡嗎？

📶 *Words and Phrases*

1. ticket taker 收票員

2. enter [`ɛntɚ] *v.* 入場；進入

3. half price 半價

4. remind [rɪ`maɪnd] *v.* 提醒

5. student ID 學生證

6. current [`kɝənt] *adj.* 當下的；最新的

CD 1-34

# To the Tower 去艾菲爾鐵塔

**(1) You** : How long would it take to walk to the Eiffel Tower?
**Frenchman** : Too long. Hours. Take the bus. Or a taxi.
你　　　 ：走路去艾菲爾鐵塔要多久？
法國人　 ：很久喔。要好幾個小時。搭公車或搭計程車吧。

- - - - - - - - - - - - - - - - - - - - - - - - - - - - - - -

**(2) You** : When will the ¹next bus come?
**Frenchman** : They come ²every fifteen minutes.
你　　　 ：下一班公車什麼時候來？
法國人　 ：公車每十五分鐘一班。

- - - - - - - - - - - - - - - - - - - - - - - - - - - - - - -

**(3) You** : Will this bus take me to the Eiffel Tower?
**Driver** : Yes. There's a stop right near the Tower.
你　　　 ：這班公車到不到艾菲爾鐵塔？
司機　　 ：到，鐵塔旁邊就有一站。

## Words and Phrases

1. next [nɛkst] *adj.* 接下來的；下一個的

2. every [ˋɛvrɪ] *adj.* 每隔……的

巴黎地鐵系統的主要路線圖請參考下面這個網址：
http://www.webscapades.com/france/paris/metro.htm

Travel Tips 旅遊撇步一起走

　　帶有合格身分證的學生在旅遊時，可以享有很多折扣，比方說飛機票、博物館、租車、旅館、餐廳、商店等等。假如你是學生（或青年），而且想要利用這些折扣以及其他為學生所提供的便宜機會，那麼你可以上網到isic-card.com申請國際學生證。申請手續既簡單又不貴（大概七英鎊左右）。另一種學生的折扣卡是ISE（International Student Exchange）卡，任何年紀的學生，以及十二到二十六歲之間的年輕人都可申請。請上isecard.com網站查詢，http://www.edu-fair.com/Fair/ISIC.html也提供了實用資訊。

# Notes

# Kevin & Sarah

## 凱文&莎拉

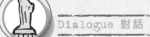

CD 1-35

**Kevin and Sarah are asking the hotel** [1]**concierge to tell them about places of interest in the area.**

| | |
|---|---|
| *Clerk* | : Good afternoon. I hope your [2]jet lag isn't too bad? |
| *Sarah* | : No, we're both feeling good. We can't wait to get out and do some [3]sightseeing. Where would you recommend? |
| *Clerk* | : Well, [4]apart from the beach, I would say that you should definitely [5]check out the Art [6]Deco [7]Historical [8]District. If you are [9]into museum type things, then the Metro Dade [10]Cultural Center is pretty good. |
| *Kevin* | : Oh no, please. I hate museums! |
| *Clerk* | : OK, how about the Parrot Jungle and Gardens? |
| *Kevin* | : That sounds more [11]up my alley but I think we want to do something more [12]active. |
| *Clerk* | : How about an [13]alligator tour in the Everglades [14]National Park? |
| *Kevin* | : Yes! That sounds perfect. |
| *Sarah* | : But that'll take a full day and it's after 2:00 now. How about we just [15]wander around the Art Deco area this afternoon, [16]grab some dinner, [17]hit the sack early and [18]do the Everglades tomorrow? |
| *Kevin* | : OK. Can you book us on a tour tomorrow? |
| *Clerk* | : I sure can. Bus leaves at 6:30 a.m. Is that OK for you [19]folks? |
| *Kevin & Sarah* | : Urgh! We'll try. |

凱文與莎拉請旅館的櫃台人員告訴他們，當地有什麼旅遊勝地。

櫃台人員　：午安。希望你們的時差不會太嚴重？

莎拉　　　：不會，我們都覺得很好。我們等不及要出去觀光了。你建議什麼地方呢？

櫃台人員　：這個嘛，除了海邊，我建議你們一定得去看看裝飾藝術歷史區。假如你們喜愛博物館之類的東西，那麼梅卓達德文化中心相當不錯。

凱文　　　：噢，拜託不要。我討厭博物館！

櫃台人員　：好吧，那麼鸚鵡叢林園怎麼樣？

凱文　　　：這聽起來比較合我的意，可是我想我們還是希望從事比較動態的活動。

櫃台人員　：那麼沼澤國家公園的鱷魚之旅怎麼樣？

凱文　　　：好！聽起來再理想不過了。

莎拉　　　：可是那要花一整天，而現在已經過兩點了。我們乾脆下午去裝飾藝術區走一走，隨意吃頓晚餐，晚上早點上床睡覺，然後明天再從事沼澤之旅，怎麼樣？

凱文　　　：好。你能幫我們訂明天的行程嗎？

櫃台人員　：當然可以。巴士早上六點半出發，你們兩位起得來嗎？

凱文與莎拉：呃，我們盡量。

## Words and Phrases

1. concierge [ˌkɑnsɪˋɛrʒ] *n.* （尤指歐洲各國旅館的）服務台職員

2. jet lag [ˋdʒɛtˌlæg] 時差

3. sightseeing [ˋsaɪtˌsiɪŋ] *n.* 觀光；遊覽

4. apart from... ……之外

5. check out 看看；得到證實

6. deco [ˋdɛko] *n.* 裝飾（decoration的略式）

7. historical [hɪsˋtɔrɪkl] *adj.* 歷史的；歷史上著名的

8. district [ˋdɪstrɪkt] *n.* 泛指地方、區域

9. into [ˋɪntu] *prep.* 對於……熱中

10. cultural center [ˋkʌltʃərəlˋsɛntə] 文化中心

11. up my alley 合我的胃口、能力

12. active [ˋæktɪv] *adj.* 激烈的；需付出體力的

13. alligator [ˋæləˌgetə] *n.* （美洲產）短吻鱷魚

14. national park 國家公園

15. wander [ˋwɑndə] *v.* 漫遊

16. grab [græb] *v.* 隨意選取

17. hit the sack 就寢；上床睡覺

18. do [du] *v.* 做；從事

19. folks [foks] *n.* 各位

What Do I Do 我要怎麼做

CD 1-36

# Talking to Your Guide 和導遊對話

(1) Tour Guide : Sir, please do not ¹pet the alligator. It's not safe.

You : Yeah, ²I should know better. That was stupid.

導遊 :先生，請不要摸鱷魚。那樣不安全。

你 :是的，我本該知道的。那真蠢。

---

(2) Uuseum Guide : Would you like to wait for the next ³guided tour?

You : No, I think I'll just walk through on my own.

博物館導覽員：您要等下一梯次的導覽嗎？

你 :不了，我想我就自己去逛好了。

---

(3) Tour Guide : I'm sorry, sir. You ⁴missed the 6:30 bus.

You : Is there another bus anytime soon?

導遊 :抱歉，先生。您錯過了六點半的巴士。

你 :下一班很快就會來嗎？

---

📖 *Words and Phrases*

1. pet [pɛt] *v.* 撫摸

2. I should know better. 我本該知道的。

3. guided tour 導覽

4. miss [mɪs] *v.* 錯過

Getting What You Want 解決你的需求

CD 1-37

# Please ¹Clarify 請說明

**①** You : Is this ²pass good for the whole week, or just today?

Museum Clerk : It's good from Monday to Friday.

你 :這張通行證整個星期都能用，還是只有今天而已？

博物館人員 :從週一到週五都能用。

---

**②** You : Would it be cheaper for me to pay the ³daily rate?

Vender : For four days or more, the ⁴weekly rate is cheaper.

你 :我按日付費會不會比較便宜？

商家 :如果是四天以上，按週付費會比較划算。

---

**③** You : You charged us for using the phone. I thought ⁵local calls were free.

Hotel Clerk : Local calls are free, but you made several ⁶long-distance calls.

你 :我們用電話你們有算錢，我以為打市內電話是免費的。

飯店櫃台人員:市內電話是不用錢，可是你們打了幾通長途電話。

*Words and Phrases*

1. clarify [`klærə‚faɪ] *v.* 解釋清楚；澄清

2. pass [pæs] *n.* 免費入場證；通行證

3. daily [`delɪ] *adj.* 按日的

4. weekly [`wiklɪ] *adj.* 按週的

5. local call 市內電話

6. long-distance call 長途電話

「赤裸鸚鵡坊」酒吧傳單

Naked Parrot Lounge

The Naked Parrot will sing for you!
More Sugar - Wednesdays and Fridays
More Spice - Fridays and Saturdays
More Satin - Thursdays and Thursdays
More Lacy - Thursdays and Saturdays
Saturday Night Special
Double D Candee from Houston!
Happy Hour every weekday form 3 to 6.
No cover change before 8
Bump and Grind, Blow Your Mind!
183 West Belmont, B1

Travel Tips 旅遊撇步一起走

在遊覽像遊樂園這種人多擁擠的觀光地點時，你會發現大部分的人在通過大門之後都會往右走，而且大多都會跟著人潮前進。所以，如果你想在迪士尼樂園這類地方避開人群，一開始就要往左走，而不應往右走。所以，記得下回逆向繞行遊樂園，就能搶在人群之前玩到你最喜歡的設施。

Notes

## Notes

# CHAPTER 5

# TRANSPORTATION

## 交通工具

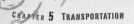

# David
大衛

Dialogue 對話

CD 1-38

**David is buying a train ticket from Bangkok to Chiangmai.**

*David* : Good morning. I'd like a ¹return ticket to Chiangmai, leaving on Friday evening, please. That's the 22$^{nd}$.

*Clerk* : Do you want a ²regular ticket or a ³sleeper?

*David* : I think a sleeper.

*Clerk* : First or second ⁴class?

*David* : Is there a big difference in price?

*Clerk* : First is 2,300 baht, second is 1,450 baht.

*David* : Definitely second class then.

*Clerk* : Would you like a ⁵compartment with aircon or ⁶fan?

*David* : This reminds me of my hostel! Aircon, please.

*Clerk* : So that's 1,600 baht.

*David* : I thought you just said it was 1,450 baht.

*Clerk* : This is Friday night so there is a weekend ⁷supplement.

*David* : OK. That's fine. Thanks.

*Clerk* : The train leaves at 9:30 p.m. from ⁸Platform 7. You are in ⁹Carriage D, ¹⁰Berth 30A. Please try to get here 30 minutes before ¹¹departure. Here's your change. Next please!

*David* : Sorry, one more thing. Can I buy food on the train?

*Clerk* : Yes, there is a trolley serving snacks and drinks. Next please!

大衛正在買從曼谷到清邁的火車票。

大衛　：早安，我要買星期五晚上出發到清邁的來回票，麻煩你。那天是二十二號。

售票員：您要普通票還是臥舖？

大衛　：臥舖好了。

售票員：頭等還是次等？

大衛　：價錢上的差別有很大嗎？

售票員：頭等是二千三百銖，次等是一千四百五十銖。

大衛　：那當然是要次等的囉。

售票員：您要有空調的還是有風扇的隔間？

大衛　：這讓我想起了我住的旅舍。麻煩你，有空調的。

售票員：這樣是一千六百銖。

大衛　：我以為你剛說是一千四百五十銖。

售票員：您買的是星期五晚上的票，所以有加收週末的額外費用。

大衛　：好，那就這樣吧，謝謝。

售票員：這班車晚上九點半從第七月台出發。您是D車廂30A舖。請盡量在發車前半小時到這裡。這是您的找零。麻煩下一位！

大衛　：抱歉，還有一件事。車上有賣吃的嗎？

售票員：有，車上有餐車販賣餐點和飲料。麻煩下一位！

註：查詢泰國的火車車資請參照 http://www.railway.co.th/httpEng/farerate.html

## 🚌 Words and Phrases

1. return ticket　回程票

2. regular [ˋrɛgjələ] *adj.* 普通的

3. sleeper [ˋslipə] *n.* 臥車車廂；臥舖

4. class [klæs] *n.* 等級

5. compartment [kəmˋpɑrtmənt] *n.*（客車、船艙、臥車車廂等的）隔間、車室

6. fan [fæn] *n.* 風扇

7. supplement [ˋsʌpləmənt] *n.* 補足；增補；補充

8. platform [ˋplætfɔrm] *n.* 月台

9. carriage [ˋkærɪdʒ] *n.*（鐵路）客車車廂

10. berth [bɝθ] *n.*（船、火車的）臥舖、舖位

11. departure [dɪˋpɑrtʃə] *n.* 啟程；出發

What Do I Do 我要怎麼做

# [1]**Mano a Mano** with the Clerk 面對售票員

**1** Clerk : I'm sorry, sir. No seats are available on this train.

You : Would you please check again? I'm willing to pay extra.

售票員：抱歉，先生。這班車沒有位子了。

你　　：能不能請你再查查看？我願意多付一點錢。

---

**2** Clerk : Adding in the [2]foreigner surcharge, your [3]total [4]comes to 3,700 baht.

You : That can't be right. There must be some mistake.

售票員：加上外籍乘客加收的費用，您的金額總共是三千七百銖。

你　　：這不可能是正確的，其中一定有錯。

---

**3** Clerk : Pay attention. I told you once already: 7:30 p.m.

You : There's no need to be [5]rude. I didn't hear you the first time.

售票員：注意聽，我已經跟你說過一次了，是晚上七點半。

你　　：不用那麼衝吧，我剛才沒聽到你說的話。

🚌 *Words and Phrases*

1. mano a mano *adj.* 單挑的；獨自面對面的

2. foreigner [ˈfɔrɪnɚ] *n.* 外地人；外國人

3. total [ˈtotḷ] *n.* 全額；總數

4. come to... *v.* 總計為……

5. rude [rud] *adj.* 無理的；粗暴的

CD 1-40

# Requesting a ¹Change 要求更動

**1** You : The air conditioning isn't ²working. Could I move to another compartment?

Attendant : Let me check and see if one is available.

你 ：空調壞了，我可以換到另一個隔間去嗎？

服務人員 ：讓我看看還有沒有空的隔間。

---

**2** You : I'd like to move to another seat, please. Somebody made a terrible ³mess here.

Attendant : Oh, dear. I see what you mean. Come with me.

你 ：我想換到另一個位子去，麻煩你。有人把這裡搞得一團亂。

服務人員 ：噢，真的。我知道你的意思。請跟我來。

---

**3** You : Would you please ask those kids ⁴in the back to be quiet?

Attendant : Yes, I'll ⁵take care of it.

你 ：可不可以麻煩你請後面的那些小孩子安靜一點？

服務人員 ：好，我會處理的。

## 🚌 Words and Phrases

1. change [tʃendʒ] *n.* 變更；更動

2. working [`wɝkɪŋ] *adj.* 運作的；運轉的

3. mess [mɛs] *n.* 髒亂；凌亂

4. in the back 在後方的

5. take care of sth. *v.* 處理某事

FYI 好用資訊

從曼谷至清邁的車票。

SRT

Departure:
6/15/05 / Bangkok / Main Station / Platform 7 / 9:30 p.m.
Arrival: 6/16/05 / Chiangmai / 0:00 p.m.
Status: Second Class Sleeper Carriage D, Berth 30A
Price: 1600 Baht

Travel Tips 旅遊撇步一起走

　　搭火車旅遊既浪漫、輕鬆又划算，但前提是你不必坐在荒涼的月台上等待誤點的車子。各國的鐵路服務效率有很大的差異，但有一個地方的列車幾乎從來不誤點，那就是瑞士。最近有一項調查發現，瑞士的火車有八一％是在表訂時間的一分鐘內抵達，而且幾乎有九五％的火車都不會誤點超過四分鐘。假如那個瑞士的車掌誤點六分鐘，他大概就會覺得自己完全不及格。這才叫服務。

# Notes

# Marie & Celeste

## 瑪莉＆賽麗絲特

Dialogue 對話

CD 1-41

**Marie and Celeste are meeting Monsieur Roncart in order to rent a scooter from him.**

*Marie* : Monsieur Roncart?

*M. Roncart* : Yes. [1]How can I be of assistance to you two beautiful young ladies?

*Marie* : We'd like to [2]rent two scooters.

*M. Roncart* : Oh, no! Scooters? They are much too dangerous for lovely young girls [3]like yourselves. I will take you in my car. Come, come!

*Celeste* : No really. That's very [4]generous of you, but we want scooters. We ride them all the time at home; we're used to them.

*M. Roncart* : My car is very comfortable!

*Marie* : I'm sure it is, but we want scooters.

*M. Roncart* : Oh well, if you insist. I can never say "no" to a pretty girl. 31 euros a day plus a 150-euro [5]refundable [6]deposit.

*Celeste* : OK, we'll pay for five days [7]in advance.

瑪莉與賽麗絲特來找朗卡特先生，以便向他租機車。

瑪莉　　　　：朗卡特先生嗎？

朗卡特先生：是的。有什麼事可以為你們兩位年輕美麗的小姐效勞嗎？

瑪莉　　　　：我們想租兩台機車。

朗卡特先生：噢，不！機車？像你們這麼可愛的年輕女孩子騎機車太危險了。我開
　　　　　　車載你。來，來！

賽麗絲特　　：不用了。您太客氣了，可是我們想騎機車。我們在家的時候天天都在
　　　　　　騎，我們已經習慣了。

朗卡特先生：我的車很舒服喔！

瑪莉　　　　：我想一定是，可是我們想騎機車。

朗卡特先生：哦，好吧，假如你們堅持的話。我從來都無法對美女說「不」。一天
　　　　　　三十一歐元外加上一百五十歐元的押金。

賽麗絲特　　：好，我們要先預付五天的金額。

## 🚌 Words and Phrases

1. How can I be of assistance? 我能夠幫得上忙嗎？

2. rent [rɛnt] v. 租用

3. like yourselves 像你們一樣

4. generous [`dʒɛnərəs] adj. 慷慨的；大方的

5. refundable [rɪ`fʌndəbl] adj. 可退還的

6. deposit [dɪ`pɑzɪt] n. 訂金；保證金

7. in advance 事前地；預先地

**What Do I Do** 我要怎麼做

CD 1-42

## ¹Negotiating 談判

**(1)** Clerk : For a week, it'll come to 308 euros.

You : Do you have anything more ²<u>economical</u>?

店員 ：一星期的話，是三百零八歐元。

你 ：你們有沒有比較便宜的？

---

**(2)** Clerk : Will you be needing a ³<u>helmet</u> and driving gloves?

You : I'd like a helmet, but I hope you won't be charging extra for that.

店員 ：你會需要安全帽和騎車手套嗎？

你 ：我要個安全帽，可是我希望你不會要另外算錢。

---

**(3)** Clerk : We have a weekend ⁴<u>special</u> that starts tomorrow.

You : Can I take advantage of the special and also get the ⁵<u>student discount</u>?

店員 ：我們明天起有週末特價。

你 ：我可不可以享受特價並同時獲得學生優惠？

## Words and Phrases

1. negotiate [nɪˋgoʃɪˌet] *v.* 協商；講條件

2. economical [ˌikəˋnɑmɪkl] *adj.* 節省的；省錢的

3. helmet [ˋhɛlmɪt] *n.* 頭盔；安全帽

4. special [ˋspɛʃəl] *n.* 優待；特價

5. student discount 學生優待

**Getting What You Want 解決你的需求**

CD 1-43

# Renting a ¹Vehicle 租車

**(1)** You : Is ²insurance ³included in the price?

**Clerk** : No. Insurance is extra.

你 ：這個價錢有沒有含保險？

店員 ：沒有，保險要另外算。

---

**(2)** You : Will I have to pay extra for ⁴mileage?

**Clerk** : Only if you drive more than 500 kilometers.

你 ：里程數要另外算錢嗎？

店員 ：除非你騎到五百公里以上，否則不用。

---

**(3)** You : So, I have to return the car by this time a week ⁵from now?

**Clerk** : Actually, you have ⁶until 5 p.m. next Friday.

你 ：那，我必須在一星期後的這個時間還車嗎？

店員 ：事實上你能用到下週五的下午五點為止。

📖 *Words and Phrases*

1. vehicle [ˋviəkl̩] *n.* 車輛

2. insurance [ɪnˋʃurəns] *n.* 保險

3. included [ɪnˋkludɪd] *adj.* 有包含在內的

4. mileage [ˋmaɪlɪdʒ] *n.* 英里里程

5. from now 從現在算起

6. until [ənˋtɪl] *prep.* 直到

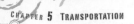

FYI 好用資訊

朗卡特機車出租價目表
# Les Scooters de Roncart

| C.C. \ time / cost | 5 hours | 1 day | 3 days | 5 days |
|---|---|---|---|---|
| **Honda Sky Scooter 50 cc.**<br>Catalytic<br>Automatic shifting<br>One person allowed<br>Driving experience required. | 23 | 31 | 81 | 150 |
| **Scooter 125 cc.**<br>4-stroke engine<br>Automatic shifting<br>Two persons allowed<br>Driving experience required. | 40 | 65 | 183 | 308 |
| **Honda Transalp 650cc.**<br>Big wheels<br>4-stroke engine<br>Comfortable and reliable<br>Driving experience and motorcycle<br>Driver's license required. | 95 | 274 | 440 | 594 |

Note: Price includes mileage, liability insurance and helmets.

**For safety reasons, we strongly recommend not renting a scooter without prior experience. Novice drivers can be extremely dangerous to themselves and to others.**

Travel Tips 旅遊撇步一起走

　　當你在國外決定租車前，一定要多加考慮，因為路況和國內的習慣可能會有很大的差異。或許可以學著適應，但駕駛本來就是一件危險的事。在許多國家，不管你想去哪裡，搭乘大眾交通工具都到得了，而且也比租用交通工具便宜許多。公車和火車上都是認識人的好地方。等你到了目的地時，你可能就會已經認識了一些新朋友，而且還不必去擔心停車的問題。

Notes

# Kevin & Sarah

## 凱文＆莎拉

Dialogue 對話

CD 1-44

**Kevin and Sarah are waiting for the bus to take them back from the Art Deco Historical District in South Beach to their hotel.**

*Sarah* : This wasn't one of your better ideas, Kevin.

*Kevin* : What do you mean?

*Sarah* : Well, we've been waiting an [1]eternity. Walking [2]would have been quicker.

*Kevin* : I'm [3]positive this is the right stop. I'll ask this guy. Excuse me, do you know when the bus is [4]due?

*Man* : [5]Por favor?

*Kevin* : (*To Sarah*) Either he's speaking Spanish or he's [6]drunk!

*Sarah* : Let me try. Sir, bus...come when?

*Man* : Is 4 p.m. happy time. Yes, please!

*Sarah* : (*To Kevin*) I think he doesn't speak much English *and* he's drunk.

*Man* : You drink. [7]Whisky...good!

*Sarah* : No, thank you. Oh, [8]thank goodness, the bus is coming. [9]Flag it down, Kevin, quickly.

*Kevin* : Is this the bus going back to the Four Seasons Hotel?

*Bus Driver* : Sure is, [10]buddy. Hey Raul, you drinking again?

*Man* : Whisky...good!

*Sarah* : Next time, I [11]swear, we take taxi.

*Kevin* : I wonder what kind of whisky that is?

凱文與莎拉正在等公車，好把他們從南灘的裝飾藝術歷史區載回旅館。

莎拉　　：凱文，你這主意可不怎麼高明。

凱文　　：什麼意思？

莎拉　　：嗯，我們已經等了那麼久了，走路搞不好會比較快的。

凱文　　：我確定是這個站牌沒錯。我來問這個人。抱歉，你知道公車什麼時候會來嗎？

男子　　：Por favor？

凱文　　：（對莎拉說）他不是在說西班牙文就是喝醉了！

莎拉　　：讓我試試看。先生，公車……什麼時候來？

男子　　：是下午四點。快樂時光。是的，請！

莎拉　　：（對凱文說）我想他不太會說英語，「而且」也醉了。

男子　　：你們喝。威士忌……好喝！

莎拉　　：不用了，謝謝。噢，謝天謝地，公車來了。凱文，把它招下來，快點。

凱文　　：這班公車是回四季飯店的嗎？

公車司機：當然是，老兄。嘿，勞烏爾，你又喝酒啦？

男子　　：威士忌……好喝！

莎拉　　：下一次，我發誓，我們坐計程車。

凱文　　：不知道那究竟是哪一種威士忌？

## Words and Phrases

1. eternity [ɪˈtɝnətɪ] *n.* 永恆（在此是強調等了非常久的一段時間）

2. would have been... 可能早就……

3. positive [ˈpɑzətɪv] *adj.* 確定的；確信的

4. due [du] *adj.* 預計到達

5. por favor [ˈpor͵fɑˈbor]【西班牙文】請（相當於英文的please）

6. drunk [drʌŋk] *adj.* 酒醉的

7. whisky [ˈhwɪskɪ] *n.* 威士忌

8. thank goodness 謝天謝地

9. flag sth. down 把……招下來

10. buddy [ˈbʌdɪ] *n.* 夥伴；老兄

11. swear [swɛr] *v.* 發誓

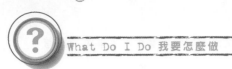

What Do I Do 我要怎麼做

CD 1-45

# Dealing With Unwanted Attention
## 應付惱人的騷擾

**(1)** Stranger : C'mon! Have a drink with me!

You : No, thank you. I have to go. Someone is waiting for me.

陌生人 ：來吧！跟我喝一杯！

你 ：不了，謝謝。我必須走了，有人在等我。

---

**(2)** Stranger : Psst. Do you need a watch? I'll give you a ²<u>deal</u>.

You : How about I sell you mine instead? I'll take $300 for it.

陌生人 ：噗呲，你需要錶嗎？我可以賣你便宜。

你 ：我把我的錶賣給你怎麼樣？賣你三百美元就好。

---

**(3)** Stranger : ³<u>Spare change</u>?

You : No, sorry.

陌生人 ：有多餘的零錢嗎？

你 ：沒有，對不起。

## Words and Phrases

1. deal [dil] *v.* 打交道；對待；應付

2. deal [dil] *n.* 有利的交易

3. spare change [ˋspɛrˋtʃendʒ] 多餘的零錢（是路旁乞丐要錢時常說的話）

Getting What You Want 解決你的需求

 CD 1-46

# Public Transportation 大眾運輸

**(1)** You      : Stop! I missed my stop. I need to ²get off the bus.

Driver   : The next stop is just ³ahead.

你       ：停車！我過站了。我必須下車。

司機      ：下一站就在前面。

---

**(2)** You      : Is this ticket good for a ⁴round trip, or just ⁵one-way?

Driver   : Round trip.

你       ：這張票是可以坐來回的，還是只是單程而已？

司機      ：來回。

---

You      : Will I be able to bring my drink onto the bus?

**(3)** Stranger : You might not be able to. They might ask you to ⁶dispose of it first.

你       ：我可以把我的飲料帶上公車嗎？

陌生人    ：你可能不行。他們可能會要你把它丟掉。

Words and Phrases

1. public transportation  大眾運輸

2. get off  下車

3. ahead [əˋhɛd] *adj.* 在前面；在前方

4. round trip [ˋraʊndˋtrɪp] 來回；全程

5. one-way [ˋwʌnˋwe] *adj.* 單程

6. dispose [dɪˋspoz] *v.* 丟棄（注意後接介係詞 of）

FYI 好用資訊

邁阿密裝飾藝術區的範圍囊括了十六個街區(**city block**)，最具特色的所在地集中在三條平行的街道上，各為**Ocean Drive**、**Collins Avenue**和**Washington Avenue**。裝飾藝術區之所以成為勝地，原因在於它那粉彩色的外牆、俐落的線條設計、水磨石的地板、霓虹裝飾燈與航海主題的建築物反映出了二〇、三〇與四〇年代的思想與風情（打星號的地方為邁阿密裝飾藝術區的所在地）。

地圖來源：**http://www.mapquest.com/**

Travel Tips 旅遊撇步一起走

　　在大城市之中很容易迷路。假如你是抱著冒險的心情到具有異國風情的國外城市從事旅遊，那麼閒逛、探險以及故意迷路就會變得很有趣。你可以逛到累又找不到回旅館的路為止。萬一遇到這種情況，尤其是如果你的語言能力不怎麼樣的話，切記要把寫有旅館地址與電話的名片帶在身上。如此一來，只要輕鬆地招一輛計程車，你就不用怕迷路了。

CHAPTER **6**

# MEETING THE LOCALS

認識當地人

# David
## 大衛

 Dialogue 對話

CD 1-47

**David is out shopping in the Chatuchak Market when a ¹local girl talks to him.**

| | |
|---|---|
| *David* | : How much is this ²material? |
| ³*Shopkeeper* | : For you, special price, only 5,000 baht. |
| *David* | : That's expensive. I don't think I have that much cash ⁴on me. |
| *Girl* | : Excuse me, where are you from? |
| *David* | : Taiwan. I'm just here on vacation. You know, ⁵see the sights for a couple of weeks. |
| *Girl* | : Well, let me give you some advice. In a market like this you must ⁶haggle. If you don't, the shopkeepers will think you're a fool. |
| *David* | : Well, I feel a bit ⁷ashamed to ⁸bargain too much, you know? |
| *Girl* | : It's part of the fun. If you don't want to negotiate you might as well just go to a department store. |
| *David* | : I guess so, but ⁹my heart isn't really in it. Most things here seem cheap anyway. |
| *Girl* | : Anyway, I will help you with your shopping and ¹⁰afterwards you can buy me a cup of coffee. I like to practice my English. |
| *David* | : OK. That would be great. I promised a whole bunch of people I'd bring them ¹¹souvenirs. |

大衛外出到卡都節市場買東西，有一個當地的女孩子跟他聊了起來。

大衛：這塊布料多少錢？

店員：你的話，特價，五千銖就好。

大衛：太貴了。我想我身上沒帶那麼多現金。

女孩：抱歉，請問你從哪裡來？

大衛：台灣。我只是來這裡度假。你知道的，就是觀光幾個星期。

女孩：嗯，讓我給你一點忠告。在這樣的市場，你必須討價還價。假如你不討還價，店員就會把你當傻瓜。

大衛：嗯，你知道嗎？我不太好意思殺價殺得太兇。

女孩：這也是一種樂趣。假如你不想講價，那乾脆直接去百貨公司好了。

大衛：我想也是，可是我真的不是很想。反正這裡大部分的東西看起來都很便宜。

女孩：不管怎麼說，我來當你的購物幫手，之後你可以請我喝杯咖啡。我喜歡練習我的英文。

大衛：沒問題，那真是太好了。我答應了一堆人要買紀念品給他們。

## 🚌 Words and Phrases

1. local [`lokl] *adj. n.* 1. 當地的 2. 當地居民；本地人

2. material [mə`tɪrɪəl] *n.* 衣料；材料

3. shopkeeper [`ʃɑpˌkipɚ] *n.* 店主

4. on me 我身上

5. see the sights 瀏覽風光

6. haggle [`hægl] *v.* （就條件、價格等）爭論、討價還價

7. ashamed [ə`ʃemd] *adj.* 覺得丟臉的；不好意思的

8. bargain [`bɑrgɪn] *v.* 討價還價；就價格進行談判

9. have one's heart in... 對……感濃厚興趣

10. afterwards [`æftɚwɚdz] *adv.* ……之後

11. souvenir [ˌsuvə`nɪr] *n.* 紀念品

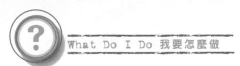 **What Do I Do** 我要怎麼做

CD 1-48

# Thanks for the Advice 謝謝忠告

**①** New Friend : If you don't haggle, they'll ¹take advantage of you.

You : Thanks. I appreciate the advice.

新朋友 ：假如你不討價還價的話，他們就會坑你。

你 ：謝了。謝謝你的忠告。

---

**②** New Friend : This is an interesting neighborhood, but it isn't safe at night.

You : OK. Thanks for the warning. I won't stay here ²after dark.

新朋友 ：這附近是個好玩的地方，可是晚上不太安全。

你 ：好，謝謝提醒。我不會在天黑後來這裡。

---

**③**

New Friend : Why do you want to go to a Mexican restaurant? We're in Thailand!

You : ³Good point. Take me to an ⁴authentic Thai restaurant then.

新朋友 ：你為什麼想去墨西哥餐館？我們在泰國耶！

你 ：說得對。那麼帶我去一家道地的泰國餐館吧。

*Words and Phrases*

1. take advantage *v.* 佔便宜

2. after dark 天黑以後

3. Good point. 說得沒錯。

4. authentic [ɔ`θɛntɪk] *adj.* 道地的

Getting What You Want 解決你的需求

CD 1-49

# ¹Getting Rid of a ²Pest 擺脫討厭的傢伙

**(1)** You : That's enough. I am NOT going to buy that flower. Now please go away.

Vendor: I'll be back to see if you change your mind.

你 ：夠了。那朵花我是不會買的。現在請你走開。

小販 ：我會再回來看看你是不是會改變主意。

---

**(2)** You : No, I do NOT want you to wait for me. I plan to **walk home**.

Driver : Walk? No! Too far. I wait for you. No charge, small charge.

你 ：不用，我不需要你等我。我打算走路回家。

司機 ：走路!?不會吧！太遠了。我等你，不收費，只收一點點。

---

**(3)** You : Look, I'm sorry, but I'm not interested. I'd like to be alone now.

Suitor : OK, OK. Well, it was nice to meet you at least.

你 ：聽好，我很抱歉，可是我沒有興趣。我現在只想一個人。

追求者 ：好，好。好吧，至少很高興認識你。

## Words and Phrases

1. get rid of... 擺脫掉……

2. pest [pɛst] *n.* 討厭、難纏的人

FYI 好用資訊

**handicraft**

手工藝品

**necklace**

項鍊

**utensils**

餐具

**stand**

攤子

Travel Tips 旅遊撇步一起走

　　假如你常常旅遊，就會遇到很多人，包括一些你希望永遠不要遇到的人，比如說，搶匪。假如你必須帶很多錢在身上，不妨分兩個（甚至三個）不同的地方來擺，而且要把大部分的錢藏好。你可以在褲子裡面縫暗袋，或者假如你是穿牛仔褲的話，也可以在褲腰開個小洞，然後把錢塞在裡面。身上帶的錢要足以應付正常的花費，可以就擺在口袋、錢包或安全錢袋裡。假如不幸遇到搶匪，也許他拿了這些錢就會放你一馬，而不會發現你其他藏起來的錢。

# Notes

# Marie & Celeste

瑪莉 & 賽麗絲特

 Dialogue 對話

CD 1-50

**Marie and Celeste are in a busy coffee shop when a man comes over to their table.**

*Marie*     : I think riding scooters here is even more fun than in Taipei.

*Celeste*   : It's a lot less ¹congested. Ah, here comes the waiter.

*Marie*     : Two ²espressos, please.

*Raymond* : I'm sorry. You're ³mistaken. I don't work here. There is ⁴nowhere else to sit so I wondered if I might join you?

*Celeste*   : Of course. Sit down.

*Raymond* : I am Raymond, and you are?

*Marie*     : I'm Marie, and this is Celeste.

*Raymond* : Such beautiful French names, but you are, I think, from Japan?

*Celeste*   : No, we're Taiwanese, but lots of people ⁵mistake us for Japanese.

*Raymond* : A thousand apologies. So, have you seen much of Paris?

*Marie*     : Well, yesterday we ⁶took in the ⁷Louvre and Notre Dame. The day before we ⁸did the boat trip on the Seine...

*Celeste*   : ...and the day after tomorrow we plan to ride out to ⁹Versailles.

*Raymond* : And this evening? You have other plans?

*Marie*     : I think we are...

*Celeste*   : ...no, nothing. ¹⁰What do you have in mind?

*Raymond* : Well, my brother owns a small bistro, which offers some of the finest in French ¹¹cuisine. I would be delighted to buy you both dinner. Here is the ¹²card.

*Celeste*   : Fine. How does 7:30 sound?

*Raymond* : Perfect. Ah, the waiter. Three espressos, please!

瑪莉與賽麗絲特在一家生意很好的咖啡店裡，有一個男子來到她們的桌前。

瑪莉　　：我覺得在這裡騎機車甚至比在台北騎還好玩。

賽麗絲特：這裡壅塞的情況好得多了。啊，服務生來了。

瑪莉　　：麻煩來兩杯濃縮咖啡。

雷蒙　　：抱歉，你們搞錯了，我不在這裡工作。因為沒有其他的地方了，所以我在想是不是可以跟你們一起坐？

賽麗絲特：當然可以，坐吧。

雷蒙　　：我叫雷蒙，你們是？

瑪莉　　：我叫瑪莉，她叫賽麗絲特。

雷蒙　　：真好聽的法國名字，但你們，我猜是從日本來的吧？

賽麗絲特：不是，我們是台灣人，不過有很多人都把我們誤認為日本人。

雷蒙　　：萬分抱歉。那麼，你們逛過巴黎很多地方了吧？

瑪莉　　：嗯，昨天我們看了羅浮宮和聖母院，前天我們去塞納河遊船……

賽麗絲特：……而後天我們打算騎車去凡爾賽。

雷蒙　　：那今天晚上呢？你們有其他的計劃嗎？

瑪莉　　：我想我們會……

賽麗絲特：……沒有，沒事。你有什麼主意呢？

雷蒙　　：嗯，我哥哥開了一家小餐館，賣的是最最好吃的法國菜。我很樂意請你們兩位吃晚餐。這是名片。

賽麗絲特：好啊。你覺得七點半怎麼樣？

雷蒙　　：太好了。啊，服務生來了。麻煩給我們三杯濃縮咖啡。

## 🚌 Words and Phrases

1. congested [kənˋdʒɛstɪd] adj. 壅塞的

2. espresso [ɛsˋprɛso] n. 濃縮咖啡

3. mistaken [məˋstekən] adj. 弄錯的

4. nowhere else 沒有別的地方

5. mistake sb. for... 誤認某人為……

6. take in 觀看；盡收眼底

7. Louvre [ˋluv; ˋluvrə] n. 羅浮宮

8. do [du] v. 從事

9. Versailles [vɛrˋsaɪ; vəˋselz] n. 凡爾賽宮

10. What do you have in mind? 你有什麼盤算？

11. cuisine [kwɪˋzin] n. 烹調；料理

12. card [kɑrd] n. 名片

What Do I Do 我要怎麼做

CD 1-51

# Accepting an [1]Invitation 接受邀約

**(1)** New Friend : Will you have dinner with me?

You     : I'd be delighted.

新朋友    :你願意和我共進晚餐嗎？

你       :我很樂意。

---

**(2)** New Friend : Are you busy tomorrow?

You     : No, no plans at all. [2]Would you like to do something?

新朋友    :你明天會很忙嗎？

你       :不會，完全沒計畫。你想做些什麼嗎？

---

**(3)** New Friend : If you want, I can show you around the city.

You     : Really? I'd love that.

新朋友    :假如你願意的話，我可以帶你在城內逛逛。

你       :真的嗎？那正合我意。

## Words and Phrases

1. invitation [ˌɪnvəˋteʃən] *n.* 邀請；邀約

2. Would you like to do something? 你想做些什麼嗎？

CD 1-52

# ¹Extending an Invitation 提出邀約

**①** You : If you'd like, we can ²share a taxi.

New Friend : Good idea.

你 ：假如你願意的話，我們可以共搭一部計程車。

新朋友 ：好主意。

---

**②** You : If you're not busy, would you like to go shopping with me?

New Friend : What are we shopping for?

你 ：假如你不忙的話，願意陪我去買東西嗎？

新朋友 ：我們要買什麼呢？

---

**③** You : If you're ever in Taiwan, give me a call and I'll show you around.

New Friend : Thanks a lot. I might just do that.

你 ：假如哪天你到台灣來的話，打通電話給我，我會帶你到處逛逛。

新朋友 ：多謝。我可能真的會這麼做。

---

📖 *Words and Phrases*

1. **extend** [ɪk`stɛnd] *v.* 延長；提供

2. **share** [ʃɛr] *v.* 分享；共用

103

某餐廳酒品一覽表

### Grand Millésimé Brut 1996  $15.00
### Gosset
Gosset is one of the oldest champagne firms and it has quite a reputation for high-quality vintage wines. 1996 produced champagnes with green apple crispness and delicate, floral tones.

### Puligny-Montrachet 1er Cru 1999 $14.00
### Les Folatiéres, Gérard Chavy
This full-bodied chardonnay from Burgundy offers powerful buttery and citrus characters on the nose and a palate of intense nuts, vanilla spices and quince pears, with a very classy and long finish.

### Côte-Rotie 1997  $12.00
### Robert & Patrick Jasmin, Rhône Valley
Jasmin's modern style of winemaking shows the classic syrah flavours of redcurrant and black pepper, but is enhanced by characters of tobacco, suede and vanilla on the nose and a stalky finish.

Travel Tips 旅遊撇步一起走

　　到底哪裡才是認識新朋友的最佳地點呢？假如你正在國外旅遊的話，那你就已經置身其中了。在國外很容易認識新朋友，因為有很多當地人會對你產生好奇心，而且會特地停下腳步跟你聊天。你在路上的體驗可以讓你和其他遊客產生交集，而且你也許會發現自己在旅行時變得比較活潑大方。旅行這項活動之所以這麼有意義，其中一個原因就在於此。

Notes

# Kevin & Sarah

凱文＆莎拉

Dialogue 對話

CD 1-53

**Sarah and Kevin are by the pool in their hotel talking to the man behind the bar.**

*Sarah* : So, we were on the bus and this ¹<u>drunken</u> guy kept offering us whiskey all the way back to the hotel.

*Kevin* : Sarah wouldn't even let me touch a ²<u>drop</u>!

³<u>Barman</u> : Well, I've lived in Miami my whole life and I haven't ⁴<u>caught</u> a city bus for the last twenty years. My advice to you folks is to rent a car.

*Sarah* : We don't have driver's licenses. Do people ride scooters here?

*Barman* : Plenty of scooters in Miami Beach. ⁵<u>I've got no idea</u> where to rent them though. Another drink?

*Kevin* : Yeah, another beer for me. It'll help me sleep. We've got an ⁶<u>early start</u> tomorrow.

*Barman* : You going on the alligator tour?

*Sarah* : Yes. Kevin's probably going to try to ⁷<u>wrestle</u> one of them!

*Barman* : Ha! I knew a Japanese tourist that tried that once. Alligator bit his arm ⁸<u>clean</u> off!

*Sarah* : Hmm. You hear that Kevin? If you want to wrestle the alligators, take that nice watch you bought on the airplane off first–it was expensive!

*Kevin* : Don't laugh. If I lose my arm, who's going to carry all your luggage?

莎拉與凱文在旅館的游泳池畔和酒保聊天。

莎拉：那，我們坐在公車上，這個醉漢不停地要我們喝威士忌，直到我們回到旅館。

凱文：莎拉連一滴都不讓我喝！

酒保：我一輩子都住在邁阿密，不過過去二十年來從未搭過市內公車。我給兩位的建議是租一輛車。

莎拉：我們沒有駕照。這裡的人騎不騎摩托車？

酒保：邁阿密海灘上有一大堆摩托車，可是我不知道要去哪裡租。要再來一杯嗎？

凱文：要，再給我一杯啤酒，這樣可以幫助我入睡。我們明天一早就得動身。

酒保：你們要參加鱷魚之旅嗎？

莎拉：是的。凱文可能會找一隻鱷魚摔角，較量較量。

酒保：哈，我認識一位日本觀光客，他就試過一次，結果鱷魚一口就把他的手臂整隻咬了下來！

莎拉：嗯。你聽見了嗎，凱文？假如你想要跟鱷魚摔角，先把你在飛機上買的那支好錶拿下來，它可是很貴的！

凱文：別笑。假如我沒了手臂，誰來幫妳提那些行李啊？

## Words and Phrases

1. drunken [ˋdrʌŋkən] *adj.* 醉酒的；喝醉了的

2. drop [drɑp] *n.* 滴

3. barman [ˋbɑrmən] *n.*【英】酒保（美國多用 bartender）

4. catch [kætʃ] *v.* 追上；趕上；搭上

5. I've got no idea. 我不知道。

6. early start 早早動身

7. wrestle [ˋrɛsl] *v.* 摔角；角力

8. clean [klin] *adv.* 完全地

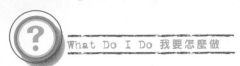 What Do I Do 我要怎麼做

 CD 1-54

## Small Talk 閒聊

---

① Guy at the Bar : You're not from around here, are you?

　　You　　　　: No. I'm traveling. I'm from Taiwan.

　　吧台客人　　：你不是本地人，對吧？

　　你　　　　　：不是，我正在旅遊。我是台灣來的。

---

② Kid by the Pool : Can you speak Chinese?

　　You　　　　: Yes, I can. Would you like to hear me say something?

　　游泳池邊的小孩 ：你會說中文嗎？

　　你　　　　　：會，我會。你想聽我說兩句嗎？

---

③ ²Bartender : What do they like to drink where you come from?

　　You　　　　: Mostly the same stuff they like around here.

　　酒保　　　　：你們那裡的人都喜歡喝什麼？

　　你　　　　　：大體上跟這裡的人喜歡的差不多。

---

🚌 *Words and Phrases*

1. small talk　閒聊

2. bartender [ˋbɑrˌtɛndɚ] *n.* 【美】酒保（=barman）

Getting What You Want 解決你的需求

 CD 1-55

# **Initiating a Conversation 打開話匣子**

**①** You : Hi. I see you're watching the game. Which team do you like?

Guy at the Bar : I like any team that's not the ²Yankees. I hate the Yankees.

你 ：嗨。我看你在觀看這場比賽。你喜歡哪一隊？

吧台客人 ：除了洋基以外，任何一隊都喜歡。我討厭洋基隊。

---

**②** You : Are you on vacation with your family?

Kid by the Pool : Yes. And we're going to Disney World in two days.

你 ：你跟家人在度假嗎？

游泳池邊的小孩 ：是啊。而且我們過兩天要去迪士尼樂園。

---

**③** You : Florida is an interesting place. Have you lived here all your life?

Bartender : No. I moved down here from Minnesota. Too cold up there.

你 ：佛羅里達是個好玩的地方。你一直都住在這裡嗎？

酒保 ：不。我是從明尼蘇達搬來的。那裡太冷了。

---

📖 *Words and Phrases*

1. initiate [ɪ`nɪʃɪˌet] *v.* 開始；發起

2. Yankees [`jæŋkɪz] *n.* 【棒球】紐約洋基隊（前需加冠詞 the）

FYI 好用資訊

邁阿密餐廳今日菜單

# Today's Special

## Appetizers and Salads

QUESADILLA WITH LIME-GRILLED CHICKEN
monterey jack cheese and green tomatillo sauce

WARM SPINACH SALAD
with pistachio marinated goat cheese, tomatoes and red onions

PERUVIAN CEVICHE MIXTO
tilapia and shellfish in a spicy lime marinade, grilled corn, sweet potato

## Sandwiches

GRILLED CAJUN CHICKEN SANDWICH
on country bread with cajun mayonnaise, grilled onions and French fries

## Entrees

CRISPY SKIN YELLOWTAIL SNAPPER
sweet potato, wild mushroom risotto, organic arugula, kaffir lime butter

OAXACAN STYLE FRESH FLORIDA MAHI-MAHI FILET
Florida mahi-mahi roasted in banana leaves with oaxacan black fire-roasted salsa, with smoked onion, wild mushrooms and sweet corn tamale

## Desserts

CARAMELIZED MANGOES
with crisp pastry

Travel Tips 旅遊撇步一起走

　　在旅途中碰上很多人有一個壞處：你可能會因此而生病。在世界上的某些地區有像肝炎這類屬地區性的傳染病。前往這些地方旅遊之前應先接種適當的疫苗。事實上，假如你沒有提出文件證明自己接種過適當的疫苗的話，有些國家根本不讓你入境。在出遊之前，一定要事先計畫，因為有些預防針必須連續施打好幾個月。

Notes

# Notes

# CHAPTER 7

# SHOPPING

購物

# David

## 大衛

 Dialogue 對話

CD 1-56

**David is at the Chatuchak Market with a Thai girl.**

*David* : If you're going to keep me from getting [1]ripped off, you should at least tell me your name.

*Gayle* : My English name is Gayle. My Thai name is very long and difficult to [2]pronounce.

*David* : Well, Gayle, I'm David. Let's shop!

*Gayle* : OK, what do you need to get?

*David* : Stuff for my girlfriend. She'll kill me if I don't get her some Thai silk and also some [3]designer [4]knockoffs.

*Gayle* : Knockoffs?

*David* : You know, [5]fake [6]brand name goods. Clothing, bags, that kind of stuff.

*Gayle* : No problem. How about here? Gucci bags, Nike [7]trainers...?

*David* : Let's try and get a deal on a bag. That brown leather one.

*Gayle* : How much is this?

*Shopkeeper* : 1,000 baht.

*Gayle* : [8]No way, too much. I only have 200 baht.

*Shopkeeper* : 700 baht. My [9]final offer.

*Gayle* : Let's go.

*Shopkeeper* : Ah, OK, OK. 500 baht. You [10]drive a hard bargain.

*Gayle* : 400.

*Shopkeeper* : Done.

*David* : Wow, you haggle like a [11]master.

*Gayle* : Years of practice and, of course, that man is my uncle!

大衛和一位泰國女孩在乍都節市場。

大衛：假如你要幫忙我不被敲竹槓，起碼應該告訴我妳的名字吧。

蓋兒：我的英文名字叫蓋兒。我的泰國名字很長，而且很難念。

大衛：嗯，蓋兒，我叫大衛。咱們去買東西吧！

蓋兒：好，你需要買什麼？

大衛：給我女朋友的東西。假如我沒有買一些泰國絲以及一些名牌的仿製品給她的話，她會殺了我。

蓋兒：仿製品？

大衛：妳知道的，就是假的名牌商品。衣服呀、袋子之類的東西。

蓋兒：沒問題。這裡怎麼樣？古馳的包包、耐吉的慢跑鞋……？

大衛：咱們試著在包包上討個好價錢。就那個咖啡色的包包。

蓋兒：這個多少錢？

店員：一千銖。

蓋兒：沒這回事，太貴了。我只有兩百銖。

店員：七百銖。最低就這個價錢了。

蓋兒：我們走吧。

店員：啊，好啦，好啦。五百銖。妳真是會殺價。

蓋兒：四百。

店員：成交。

大衛：哇，妳殺起價來真像個大行家。

蓋兒：練了好幾年了。當然還有一點，那個男的是我叔叔！

## 🚌 *Words and Phrases*

1. rip off 敲詐；敲竹槓

2. pronounce [prə`naʊns] v. 發音

3. designer [dɪ`zaɪnɚ] n. 名設計師

4. knockoff [`nɑk`ɔf] n. 未經授權的仿冒品

5. fake [fek] adj. 贗

6. brand name 名牌

7. trainers [`trenɚ] n. 運動鞋（由training shoes 演變而來）

8. No way. 不可能；沒有這回事。

9. final [`faɪnl] adj. 最終的

10. drive a hard bargain 狠狠殺價

11. master [`mæstɚ] n. 能手；行家

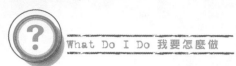 What Do I Do 我要怎麼做

CD 1-57

# The Counteroffer 還價

**(1)** Shopkeeper : I'll let you have it for 600 baht.

You : Is that your final offer? If it is, it's still ²way too high.

店員 ：我六百銖賣給你。

你 ：那是你的最低價錢嗎？假如是的話，那還是太太太貴了。

---

**(2)** Shopkeeper : I can't go any lower than 500.

You : Then thank you for your time, but I'll have to shop ³elsewhere.

店員 ：我不能比五百再低了。

你 ：那謝謝你的時間，我只好去別的地方買了。

---

**(3)** Shopkeeper : OK, how about 400?

You : ⁴Now you're talking. Make it 350 and you have a ⁵deal.

店員 ：好，四百怎麼樣？

你 ：總算有點像話了。三百五就成交。

📖 *Words and Phrases*

1. counteroffer [ˋkaʊntɚˏɔfɚ] *n.* 還價；反提案

2. way [we] *adv.* 遠遠地；大大地

3. elsewhere [ˋɛlsˏhwɛr] *adv.* 在別的地方

4. Now you're talking. 這才像話。

5. deal [dil] *n.* 成交

Getting What You Want 解決你的需求 CD 1-58

# Starting Negotiations 展開談判

**(1)** You : Is the price on this jacket negotiable?

Shopkeeper : Everything is negotiable.

你 ：這件外套的價格可以商量嗎？

店員 ：每樣東西都可以商量。

---

**(2)** You : I like this ¹handicraft, but the price listed seems too high.

Shopkeeper : How much seems right to you?

你 ：我喜歡這件手工藝品，可是標示的價格似乎太高了。

店員 ：你覺得應該要多少錢？

---

**(3)** You : How much would you let me have this for?

Shopkeeper : Oh, I'll give you a deal. Very good deal.

你 ：這個你願意賣我多少錢？

店員 ：喔，我會給你優惠，非常好的優惠。

*Words and Phrases*

1. handicraft [`hændɪ͵kræft] *n.* 手工製品；手工藝品

117

FYI 好用資訊

**key chain**

鑰匙圈

**doll**

娃娃

**trainers**

運動鞋

**hair braiding**

編髮

Travel Tips 旅遊撇步一起走

　　準備好試試自己殺價的本事了嗎？這裡有幾個祕訣可以讓你媲美專家。首先，花一點時間決定自己願意花多少錢買這樣東西。準備好以後，用眼神向店員示意，他們就會過來，並知道你已經準備交易。當他們第一次出價時，睜大眼睛、張大嘴巴表示你的驚訝。假如你願意付一百元，但他們要一百五十元，那麼你的第一次還價的價格應該是五十元左右。不要怕出低價，也不要怕冒犯賣方。他／她一定會裝出委屈或震驚的樣子，但那只是在演戲而已。賣方會逐漸降價，而且假如你堅持到底，最後你們就會取得折衷，你所付的價錢也會跟你所希望的價錢差不多。

Notes

# Marie & Celeste

瑪莉 & 賽麗絲特

Dialogue 對話

CD 1-59

**Marie and Celeste are shopping in a department store on the Champs Elysées.**

*Salesgirl*: May I help you?

*Marie*  : We're just looking, thanks.

*Celeste*  : Actually, do you have this dress in [2]a size 4? I can't see one.

*Salesgirl* : Just let me check.

*Marie*  : Celeste! That's not really [3]your kind of dress.

*Celeste*  : What do you mean?

*Marie*  : Well, it's short and [4]tight and...well...[5]sexy.

*Celeste*  : So? Can't I wear [6]nice clothes if I want?

*Marie*  : No need to [7]get hot under the collar. I'm just surprised.

*Celeste*  : Just [8]mind your own business. You're not my mother!

*Marie*  : Ahh! I know. You're thinking about dinner with Raymond tonight!

*Salesgirl* : Excuse me. We have one left [9]in stock. I'll just [10]fetch it for you to [11]try on.

(*A few minutes later*)

*Celeste*  : So what do you think?

*Salesgirl* : It looks perfect.

*Marie*  : I'm [12]keeping my nose out of your business!

*Celeste*  : I'll take it. Do you accept traveler's checks?

*Salesgirl* : Of course. I'll need to see some ID though.

*Celeste*  : [13]Here you are, my passport.

*Marie*  : I've changed my mind about dinner. I'm going back to the pension.

*Celeste*  : [14]Suit yourself!

瑪莉與賽麗絲特在香榭里舍大道上的一家百貨公司買東西。

銷售小姐：我可以為兩位效勞嗎？

瑪莉　　：我們只是看看而已，謝謝。

賽麗絲特：事實上，這件衣服你們有沒有四號的？我沒有看到。

銷售小姐：讓我看看。

瑪莉　　：賽麗絲特！那種衣服不太合你的型。

賽麗絲特：怎麼說？

瑪莉　　：妳看，它又短又緊，而且……嗯……很性感。

賽麗絲特：那又如何？難道我就不能在高興的時候穿點好衣服嗎？

瑪莉　　：不須要那麼激動，我只是驚訝罷了。

賽麗絲特：不要多管閒事，妳又不是我媽！

瑪莉　　：啊！我知道了。妳腦子想的是今晚跟雷蒙吃晚餐的那檔事。

銷售小姐：對不起。我們還有一件，我幫妳拿來試穿。

（幾分鐘後）

賽麗絲特：妳覺得怎麼樣呢？

銷售小姐：看起來好極了。

瑪莉　　：我不管妳了！

賽麗絲特：我要帶這件。你們接受旅行支票嗎？

銷售小姐：當然，可是我得看一下證件。

賽麗絲特：在這裡，我的護照。

瑪莉　　：晚餐的事我改變心意了。我要回去旅舍。

賽麗絲特：隨便妳！

## Words and Phrases

1. salesgirl [`selz͵gɝl] *n.* 銷售小姐

2. a size 4 四號尺寸的（衣物）

3. your kind of... 妳這種類型的……

4. tight [taɪt] *adj.* 緊身的

5. sexy [`sɛksɪ] *adj.* 性感的

6. nice [naɪs] *adj.* 像樣的；美好的

7. get hot under the collar 激動；惱怒

8. Mind your own business. 別多管閒事。

9. in stock 有貨的；有庫存的

10. fetch [fɛtʃ] *v.* 拿來；取來

11. try on 試穿

12. keep sb.'s nose out of sth. 不干涉；不過問

13. Here you are. 在這裡。（把東西給別人看時引起注意力的用詞）

14. Suit yourself. 隨便你。

121

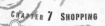

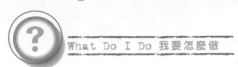

What Do I Do 我要怎麼做

CD 1-60

# Fun with Shopkeepers 和店員同樂

**(1)** Shopkeeper : May I have you?

You : I'm just ¹browsing. I'll let you know if I have any questions.

店員 ：我可以為您效勞嗎？

你 ：我只是看看而已。假如我有問題的話，會讓你知道的。

---

**(2)** Shopkeeper : That hat looks wonderful on you.

You : Oh, I like it, too. Let me just try a few others before I decide.

店員 ：那頂帽子你戴起來真適合。

你 ：噢，我也喜歡。讓我先多試幾頂再來決定。

---

**(3)** Shopkeeper : We'll have more colors in stock tomorrow.

You : Would you ²set aside a red one for me? I'd appreciate it.

店員 ：我們明天將會進更多的顏色。

你 ：能不能請你幫我預留一件紅色的？我會非常感激。

## Words and Phrases

1. browse [brauz] *v.* 瀏覽

2. set aside 留下；預留

Getting What You Want 解決你的需求

CD 1-61

# [1]Returning an Item 退貨

**(1) You** : I'd like to return this dress. It doesn't [2]fit right.

**Shopkeeper** : Do you have the receipt?

你 ：我想退這件衣服。不合穿。

店員 ：您有收據嗎？

---

**(2) You** : This CD player doesn't work. Can I [3]exchange it?

**Shopkeeper** : Sure. I'll get you another one.

你 ：這台CD播放機不靈光。我能換一台嗎？

店員 ：當然。我幫您拿另外一台。

---

**(3) You** : You charged me too much for this. I want my money back.

**Shopkeeper** : Sorry! [4]All sales are final.

你 ：你們這個賣我太貴了，我要退錢。

店員 ：抱歉！貨物既出，概不退還。

---

## Words and Phrases

1. return [rɪ`tɝn] v. 退貨；退還

2. fit [fɪt] v. 合身

3. exchange [ɪks`tʃendʒ] v. 換貨；用其他物品替代

4. All sales are final. 貨既售出，概不退換。

FYI 好用資訊

東方女性的身材和西方女性相比，一般而言要嬌小許多。若店內尺碼有提供
**petite size**（以 **P** 表示）以供選擇，相信對於東方女性來說會合身得多。
以下收錄各部位尺碼的測量法。

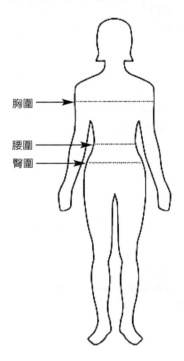

胸圍（**Bust**）
測量胸部最飽滿的部位

腰圍（**Waist**）
測量自然腰線，皮尺鬆鬆地繞腰部一圈

臀圍（**Hip**）
測量上臀部最飽滿的部位

（褲子的）管內縫（**Inseam**）
測量從跨下部位到腳底板的長度

### 嬌小尺碼（**160 cm** 以下身高女性）對照表

| | P/XS | P/S（P的小號） | | P/M（P的中號） | | P/L（P的大號） | |
|---|---|---|---|---|---|---|---|
| Size | 2P | 4P | 6P | 8P | 10P | 12P | 14P |
| Bust | 32 | 33 | 34 | 35 | 36 | 37$\frac{1}{2}$ | 39 |
| Waist | 23$\frac{1}{2}$ | 24$\frac{1}{2}$ | 25$\frac{1}{2}$ | 26$\frac{1}{2}$ | 27$\frac{1}{2}$ | 29 | 30$\frac{1}{2}$ |
| Hip | 34 | 35 | 36 | 37 | 38 | 39$\frac{1}{2}$ | 41 |

百貨公司賣的東西很多，但假如你想撿便宜，那就得去別的地方看了。在美國的很多城市以及歐洲的某些地方，像「精品重現（Elite Repeat）」或「二次機會（Second Chance）」這種專賣二手貨的商店頗為盛行。有些人對二手衣的觀念嗤之以鼻，但卻因此少撿了一些很划算的便宜。這些店裡有很多東西的品質都很高檔，就跟新的一樣，而且價錢只要百貨公司的幾分之一。如果要找稀有、高檔且具地方色彩的衣物，這些是很不錯的地方，而且重點是東西都很便宜。

Notes

# Kevin & Sarah

## 凱文 & 莎拉

 Dialogue 對話

CD 1-62

**Sarah and Kevin are buying souvenirs from the gift store at the Alligator ¹Ranch.**

*Kevin* : ²Oh man, that was great. That last alligator was a ³monster, almost 20 feet long!

*Sarah* : I've read about people like you in the newspapers—stupid tourists who get their leg bitten off because they get too close to wild animals!

*Kevin* : Take it easy, Sarah. I got some great ⁴shots of it ⁵chasing me up that tree!

*Sarah* : Didn't you hear the tour guide ⁶screaming his head off at you?

*Kevin* : I ⁷was caught up in the ⁸thrill of the chase! Let's go get some souvenirs. Bring the plastic.

*Sarah* : I can't believe I married an ⁹adrenaline ¹⁰junkie.

(*In the gift shop*)

*Kevin* : "I survived the alligator ranch." Excellent T-shirt. Let's get six.

*Clerk* : ¹¹Cash or card?

*Kevin* : ¹²Put it on my Visa card, please.

*Clerk* : That's 95 dollars and 94 cents. Can you sign the ¹³slip? Thanks for shopping at the Alligator Ranch.

*Kevin* : My pleasure. Have a nice day! We'll see you again soon.

*Sarah* : ¹⁴Over my dead body!

莎拉與凱文在鱷魚農場的禮品店裡買紀念品。

凱文：哇塞，真是太棒了。最後那一隻鱷魚簡直是隻怪物，幾乎有二十呎長。

莎拉：我在報上讀到過像你這種人的新聞——愚蠢的遊客因為太靠近野生動物而被咬斷腿。

凱文：放輕鬆，莎拉。我拍到一些它追趕我到樹上去時的精采鏡頭！

莎拉：你沒聽到導遊對你聲嘶力竭的吼叫嗎？

凱文：我在那場緊張刺激的追逐之中渾然忘我！咱們去買些紀念品吧。把信用卡帶著。

莎拉：我真不敢相信自己嫁了一個只要刺激不要命的傢伙。

（在禮品店裡）

凱文：「我從鱷魚農場活了下來。」這T恤太棒了，我們買個六件吧。

店員：付現還是刷卡？

凱文：麻煩刷我的威士卡。

店員：總共是九十五元九十四分。可以在簽單上簽個名嗎？感謝您來鱷魚農場消費。

凱文：是我的榮幸。祝你有個愉快的一天。我們不久還會再見的。

莎拉：我絕對不允許！

## Words and Phrases

1. ranch [ræntʃ] *n.* （專門飼養某種動物的）飼養場

2. Oh man. 老天。（表達一時的強烈情感的語氣詞）

3. monster [`mɑnstɚ] *n.* 異常巨大之物

4. shot [ʃɑt] *n.* （拍攝的）鏡頭、畫面

5. chase [tʃes] *v.* 追逐；追趕

6. scream sb.'s head off 聲嘶力竭地喊叫

7. get caught up 變得忘我

8. thrill [θrɪl] *n.* 緊張的快感；刺激的興奮

9. adrenaline [æd`rɛnlɪn] *n.* 腎上腺素

10. junkie [`dʒʌŋkɪ] *n.* 癮君子；對某事上癮的人

11. Cash or card? 付現還是刷卡？

12. put on sb.'s card 刷某人的信用卡

13. slip [slɪp] *n.* 紙條

14. Over my dead body. 除非我死了。

What Do I Do 我要怎麼做

CD 1-63

# Problems at the ¹Cash Register 收銀台前的問題

**①** Clerk : I'm sorry, sir, but the charges were ²declined.

You : Really? It should work. Would you try it again?

店員 ：抱歉，先生，您的金額被拒絕了。

你 ：真的嗎？應該可以才對。請再試一次好嗎？

---

**②** Clerk : Your total comes to $45.65.

You : Oops. Um, I'm afraid I don't have quite enough. I'll have to put these ³chocolate-covered strawberries back.

店員 ：您的消費總額為四十五‧六五元。

你 ：哎呀。嗯，恐怕我帶的錢不夠。我得把這些塗了巧克力的草莓放回去。

---

**③** Clerk : I'm sorry, sir, but we don't accept British currency here.

You : Oh! Then I'll use my Visa card. Can I?

店員 ：抱歉，先生，我們這裡不接受英國貨幣。

你 ：噢，那我用威士卡好了。可以嗎？

*Words and Phrases*

1. cash register [ˈkæʃˈrɛdʒɪstɚ] 收銀機

2. decline [dɪˈklaɪn] *v.* 拒絕

3. chocolate-covered [ˈtʃɔklɪtˈkʌvɚd] *adj.* 以巧克力覆蓋的

CD 1-64

# Special Request at the Shop 在店裡的特殊要求

**①** You : I'd like to send this home. Could you take care of that for me?

Clerk : No problem. Let me check on the ¹shipping and han-dling fee.

你 ：我想把這個寄回家。你們可以幫我處理嗎？

店員 ：沒問題。讓我查一下運費和手續費。

---

**②** You : Would it be possible for me to have this ²gift-wrapped?

Clerk : Sure, I'll be happy to do that for you.

你 ：這個可以幫我包裝起來嗎？

店員 ：當然，我很樂意為您服務。

---

**③** You : How is this going to appear on my credit card?

Clerk : Don't worry. The ³reference on your ⁴statement will be ⁵discreet.

你 ：這在我的信用卡明細上會怎麼顯示？

店員 ：不用擔心。您的明細會看不出這項消費的性質。

## Words and Phrases

1. shipping and handling fee  運送費和手續費

2. gift-wrapped [`gɪft‚ræpt] *adj.* （以精美禮品包裝紙、緞帶等）包裝的

3. reference [`rɛfrəns] *n.* 參照項目

4. statement [`stetmənt] *n.* 明細；結算表

5. discreet [dɪs`krit] *adj.* 謹慎的；不會洩露秘密的

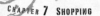

FYI 好用資訊

**cash register**
收銀機

**alligator**
鱷魚

**snow globe**
雪景球

**souvenir**
紀念品

Travel Tips 旅遊撇步一起走

　　大部分的遊客都會記得在觀光地點買禮物回家。假如你打算出遊，在出發前也別忘了買一點東西，這樣你就會有一些家鄉的紀念品當作禮物送給在路上交到的朋友。帶一些比較容易包裝與攜帶的家鄉特產，像T恤、零食等，這樣你的新朋友會覺得很高興。

# CHAPTER 8

# EATING OUT

在外用餐

# David
## 大衛

**David and Rick from the hostel are eating a** [1]**traditional Thai break-fast at a small food** [2]**stall.**

*David* : This is delicious soup. What are the [3]ingredients?

[4]*Vender* : [5]Jasmine rice, [6]garlic, Thai [7]pepper and shrimp. It's too [8]spicy for most foreigners.

*David* : Not for us Taiwanese! [9]The hotter the better is what I say.

*Vender* : This is called Khao Tom Koong. I can make it hotter if you wish.

*David* : Sure. [10]Suits me. Can I also have some of that fish and rice, please?

*Rick* : [11]Bad move, man. That stuff is super-[12]salty. Are you sure you're [13]up to it?

*David* : I'll [14]give it a go.

*Rick* : Eat a small piece of fish with a big [15]mouthful of rice and keep a [16]bucket of water [17]handy!

*David* : Mmm...you're right. It's kind of over-salty. Tea, please! Quick!

*Rick* : Told you! How about a banana [18]pancake and a cup of coffee?

*David* : Yeah. Just let me finish the soup. I think I'll [19]pass on the rest of the fish.

*Rick* : Um... You can't do that. The boss will be [20]offended.

*David* : Aargh!

大衛和在旅舍認識的瑞克在一個小吃攤上吃傳統的泰式早餐。

大衛：這湯真好喝。材料是什麼？

攤販：香米、大蒜、泰國辣椒和蝦子。對大部分的外國人來說都太辣了。

大衛：對我們台灣人來說不會！我說啊，愈辣愈好。

攤販：這叫做蝦飯湯。假如你要的話，我可以再弄辣一點。

大衛：好啊，正合我意。我能不能再來些那種魚配飯？

瑞克：不好不好，大哥。那玩意兒超鹽的，你確定你想吃嗎？

大衛：我想試試看。

瑞克：吃一小塊魚配一大口飯，並且準備好一桶水！

大衛：嗯……你說得沒錯，是有一點太鹹。麻煩給我茶，快！

瑞克：就跟你說吧。來份香蕉餅和一杯咖啡怎麼樣？

大衛：好，就讓我喝完這碗湯。我想剩下的魚我就不吃了。

瑞克：嗯……你不能這樣做，老闆會不高興的。

大衛：啊！

## Words and Phrases

1. traditional [trə`dɪʃən] *adj.* 傳統的

2. stall [stɔl] *n.* 攤位

3. ingredient [ɪn`gridɪənt] *n.* 材料；食材

4. vender [`vɛndə] *n.* 攤販

5. jasmine rice [`dʒæsmɪn͵raɪs] 泰國香米

6. garlic [`gɑrlɪk] *n.* 大蒜

7. pepper [`pɛpə] *n.* 辣椒；胡椒

8. spicy [`spaɪsɪ] *adj.* 辛辣的

9. The hotter the better. 愈辣愈好。

10. suit sb. 適合某人；合某人的胃口

11. bad move 不妥當的行動

12. salty [`sɔltɪ] *adj.* 鹹的

13. up to sth. 對某事有興趣；對某事準備好了

14. give sth. a go 試試看某事

15. mouthful [`maυθ͵fυl] *n.* 一嘴的；滿滿一口的

16. bucket [`bʌkɪt] *n.* 水桶；一桶之量

17. handy [`hændɪ] *adj.* 近便的；就在手搆得到之處的

18. pancake [`pæn͵kek] *n.* 薄餅

19. pass [pæs] *v.* 放棄；放過

20. offended [ə`fɛndɪd] *adj.* 感情被傷害的；被冒犯的

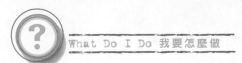

CD 2-02

# Before and After Mealtimes 用餐時間前後

**(1)** Friend: I don't feel like Chinese food again tonight.

You   : What do you feel like? I'll eat whatever.

朋友   :今天晚上我不想再吃中餐了。

你     :那你想吃什麼？任何東西我都吃。

---

**(2)** Friend: Let me get this one.

You   : No. You paid last time. This one's mine. I insist.

朋友   :這攤讓我請。

你     :不行。上次是你請的，這次換我請。我堅持。

---

**(3)** Friend: It'll be twenty minutes before a table 'opens.

You   : That's not bad. Let's have a drink at the bar while we wait.

朋友   :還要等二十分鐘的時間才會有桌子空出來。

你     :還不算太糟。讓我們去吧檯叫杯飲料，然後一邊等著。

*Words and Phrases*

1. open [ˋopən] *v.* 變得可以利用；有空缺

CD 2-03

# There's a Bug in My Soup 我的湯裡有隻蟲

**(1)** You : I ordered ¹trout, not ²tuna.

**Waitress** : I'm sorry. I'll take it back.

你 ：我點的是鱒魚，不是鮪魚。

服務生 ：對不起，我拿回去。

---

**(2)** You : This soup is cold. Would you warm it up for me?

**Waitress** : Sure. I'll be right back.

你 ：這湯冷掉了。可以幫我把它加熱嗎？

服務生 ：當然可以，我馬上回來。

---

**(3)** You : Excuse me, but I just found a hair in my ³pasta.

**Waitress** : I'm very sorry. I'll bring a fresh plate out for you.

你 ：對不起，我在我的通心麵裡發現一根頭髮。

服務生 ：非常抱歉，我幫您換新的一盤。

## Words and Phrases

1. trout [traʊt] *n.* 鱒魚

2. tuna [ˋtunə] *n.* 鮪魚；金槍魚

3. pasta [ˋpɑstɑ] *n.* （通心麵等）麵食

FYI 好用資訊

## 胃藥瓶上之部分標示文字

**Stomach Aid**

**Relieves**
* heartburn
* acid indigestion
* sour stomach
* upset stomach
* overindulgence in food and drink

**Warnings**
* Ask a doctor before use if you have kidney disease.
* Ask a doctor or pharmacist if you are taking prescription drugs. Antacids may interact with certain prescription drugs.
* Stop use and ask a doctor if symptoms persist for more than 2 weeks.
* Keep out of reach of children.

**Directions**
* Shake well before use.
* Take 2-4 teaspoonfuls between meals, at bedtime, or as directed by a doctor.
* Do not take more than 24 teaspoonfuls in a 24-hour period, or use the maximum dosage for more than 2 weeks.

Travel Tips 旅遊撇步一起走

　　假如你在旅行，尤其是到了開發中國家時，路邊攤吃多了，腸胃大概遲早都會吃出毛病。但只要採取下列的預防措施，就可以降低生重病的風險。不吃沒有煮過的魚和菜，水果要削皮，未經殺菌的乳製品也應避免。如果要安心喝水，一定要煮沸五分鐘（高緯度則需更久），或是使用殺菌錠。另外，別忘了，冰塊大概都沒有經過殺菌。對吃的東西是要小心，但也不需要太過疑神疑鬼。因為不管怎麼樣，你大概都還是會水土不服。

# Notes

# Marie & Celeste

瑪莉 & 賽麗絲特

Dialogue 對話

CD 2-04

**Celeste is meeting Raymond for dinner. Marie has stayed in the hotel.**

*Raymond* : Hello, Celeste. I'm glad that you could ¹make it. But where is Marie?

*Celeste* : We had a bit of a ²disagreement, so she stayed in the hotel.

*Raymond* : That is a ³pity.

*Celeste* : Yes. ⁴By the way, I forgot to ⁵mention that I'm a vegetarian. Will that be a problem?

*Raymond* : I don't think so. You can eat frog legs and ⁶snails?

*Celeste* : Are you kidding? I even ⁷feel bad about drinking milk!

*(One hour later)*

*Celeste* : Your brother is so charming. And the food is so ⁸rich and delicious.

*Raymond* : Yes, he used to be a ⁹chef in one of the big hotels.

*Celeste* : I never really liked red wine before, but this is fantastic.

*Raymond* : Yes, 1994 was an ¹⁰exceptional ¹¹vintage for that ¹²Burgundy.

*Celeste* : Oh, excuse me, that's my phone.

*Raymond* : Who was it?

*Celeste* : Marie. She can't find her ¹³inhaler and she's having an ¹⁴asthma ¹⁵attack. Our ¹⁶landlady isn't home so she wants me to go with her to the doctor. Sorry.

*Raymond* : No problem. I will ¹⁷give you a lift.

賽麗絲特和雷蒙見面共進晚餐，瑪莉則待在旅館。

雷蒙　　：哈囉，賽麗絲特，很高興妳能夠赴約。但是瑪莉呢？

賽麗絲特：我們起了點爭執，所以她待在旅館裡。

雷蒙　　：好可惜。

賽麗絲特：是啊。對了，我忘了提我吃素。這會是個問題嗎？

雷蒙　　：我不這麼認為。你能吃田雞腿和蝸牛嗎？

賽麗絲特：開什麼玩笑？我連喝牛奶都覺得良心不安。

（一小時後）

賽麗絲特：你哥哥真迷人，而食物相當濃郁、好吃。

雷蒙　　：是啊，他過去在一家大旅館當過主廚。

賽麗絲特：我從來沒真正喜歡過紅酒，但是這瓶棒透了。

雷蒙　　：是的，一九九四這個年份是那種勃艮第的高檔葡萄酒。

賽麗絲特：噢，抱歉，我的電話。

雷蒙　　：是誰？

賽麗絲特：瑪莉。她的氣喘發作了，卻找不到吸入器。我們的女房東不在家，所以她要我陪她去看醫生。抱歉。

雷蒙　　：沒問題。我載你一程。

## 🚌 *Words and Phrases*

1. make it 【口語】趕上、達成

2. disagreement [ˌdɪsəˈgrimənt] *n.* 意見不合；爭執

3. pity [ˈpɪtɪ] *n.* 憾事

4. by the way, ... 對了，……

5. mention [ˈmɛnʃən] *v.* 說到；提及

6. snail [snel] *n.* 蝸牛；螺

7. feel bad 覺得良心不安；感到內疚

8. rich [rɪtʃ] *adj.* 味道濃厚的；富含油脂的

9. chef [ʃɛf] *n.* 主廚；大廚

10. exceptional [ɪkˈsɛpʃənəl] *adj.* 優越的；傑出的

11. vintage [ˈvɪntɪdʒ] *n.* （葡萄酒的）佳釀（在特定的地方、豐收的年份與釀造工藝之優良葡萄酒）

12. Burgundy [ˈbɝgəndɪ] *n.* （產於法國勃艮第地區的）葡萄酒；（泛指產於其他地區的同種）紅葡萄酒

13. inhaler [ɪnˈhelɚ] *n.* 吸入輔助器

14. asthma [ˈæzmə] *n.* 氣喘；哮喘

15. attack [əˈtæk] *n.* 症狀發作

16. landlady [ˈlændˌledɪ] *n.* （旅館、寄住宿舍等的）女主人、老闆娘

17. give sb. a lift 送某人一程；讓某人搭便車

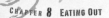

**What Do I Do** 我要怎麼做

 CD 2-05

# Restaurant ¹Situations 餐廳狀況

**(1)** ²Maître d': Do you have a ³reservation?

You : Yes. Lin. ⁴Party of four.

餐廳領班 ：您有訂位嗎？

你 ：有。姓林，四位。

---

**(2)** Waiter : Would you like a table, or a booth?

You : I'd prefer a ⁵booth.

服務生 ：您要桌子還是雅座？

你 ：我比較喜歡雅座。

---

**(3)** Waiter : Are you ready to order?

You : I think I need another minute.

服務生 ：您準備好要點菜了嗎？

你 ：我還需要一點時間。

---

📖 *Words and Phrases*

1. situation [ˌsɪtʃʊˋeʃən] *n.* 狀況；處境；局面

2. maître d' [ˋmetəˋdi] *n.* 【法】餐廳之中的領班（又作maître d'hôtel）

3. reservation [ˌrɛzəˋveʃən] *n.* 訂位

4. party [ˋpɑrtɪ] *n.* 一行人；一夥人

5. booth [buθ] *n.* 隔開的座位；雅座

Getting What You Want 解決你的需求

CD 2-06

# Special Requests in the Restaurant
## 在餐廳的特殊要求

**(1)** You　　: Are you positive this is not made with peanut oil? I'm
　　　　　　　¹allergic to peanuts.

**Waiter** : I better ²double-check with the chef.

你　　　：你確定這個沒用花生油嗎？我對花生過敏。

服務生 ：我最好再去跟廚師確認一下。

---

**(2)** You　　: I'd like the cream sauce ³on the side, please. Not on
　　　　　　　the pasta.

**Waiter** : Sure.

你　　　：我奶油醬要放邊邊，不要擺在麵上，麻煩你。

服務生 ：好的。

---

**(3)** You　　: We're going to ⁴split the lasagña. Would you please
　　　　　　　bring an extra plate?

**Waiter** : No problem.

你　　　：我們要分吃這盤千層麵。可以麻煩你多給一個盤子嗎？

服務生 ：沒問題。

## Words and Phrases

1. allergic [ə`lɝdʒɪk] *adj.* 對……過敏的

2. double-check [`dʌbl`tʃɛk] *v.* 覆核；再確認

3. on the side 作為配菜；放在一旁不要淋上去

4. split [splɪt] *v.* 【口語】分享

FYI 好用資訊

**spicy**

辣的

**booth**

雅座

**reservation**

訂位

**business hours**

營業時間

Travel Tips 旅遊撇步一起走

　　有人認為「小費」，根本是「保證快捷」（To Insure Promptness）的縮寫。其實給小費是表示你很滿意服務生、司機或門房對你所做的服務。每個地方給小費的習慣都不同。在美國的餐廳，通常他們會期待一五％到二十％的小費，但這項明細卻不會在帳單上被列出來。在法國，帳單上的總價通常已包含了小費，大約是一二～一五％。給小費在香港是慣例，但在日本則沒有那麼普遍。無論你去哪裡，給小費其實並沒有硬性的嚴格規定，它多半算是一種常識。當你得到特別棒的服務時，給多一點的小費；當服務很糟糕時，小費就給少一點，或者是完全不給。

# Notes

# Kevin & Sarah

## 凱文&莎拉

Dialogue 對話

CD 2-07

**After their exciting time at the alligator park Sarah and Kevin are enjoying their lunch at an** [1]all-you-can-eat [2]buffet **restaurant.**

*Sarah* : I thought the buffets in Taiwan were big, but this is [3]something else.

*Kevin* : [4]Unbelievable. The [5]variety of stuff and the size of the plates!

*Sarah* : Look at this. Beef, pork, chicken, [6]lobster, shrimp, lamb. All that's missing is alligator!

*Kevin* : High [7]protein stuff.

*Sarah* : Maybe it's part of the [8]Atkins Diet [9]fad.

*Kevin* : Could be. I'm not complaining though. I am pretty hungry. I could [10]handle a lobster or two.

*Sarah* : Even the salads have meat in them!

*Kevin* : Well, you're not a vegetarian, so what's the problem?

*Sarah* : It's just a bit [11]overwhelming. Look at the size of some of these people!

*Kevin* : [12]Don't sweat it. When we get back to the hotel we can [13]hit the gym for a couple of hours.

*Sarah* : Yes, you're right. We're on vacation. We should enjoy ourselves. Where's the ice cream counter with the 45 different [14]flavors?

經過鱷魚公園的刺激時刻後，莎拉與凱文在一家隨你吃到飽的自助餐廳享用午餐。

莎拉：我以為台灣的自助餐已經夠瞧的了，但和這個比真是小巫見大巫。

凱文：真不敢相信。種類之多，盤子之大！

莎拉：你看看這。牛肉、豬肉、雞肉、龍蝦、蝦子、羊肉，唯獨就缺了鱷魚肉！

凱文：高蛋白食物。

莎拉：說不定這是阿金飲食熱的一部分。

凱文：可能吧，但我可不是在嫌。我好餓，我可以吃它一、兩隻龍蝦。

莎拉：連沙拉裡面都有肉！

凱文：反正妳又不吃素，有什麼問題嗎？

莎拉：只是有點受不了。看看這裡某些人的體型！

凱文：別緊張。等我們回到旅館後，再在健身房中待他幾個小時就好了。

莎拉：沒錯，你說得對。我們在度假，應該好好享受。有四十五種不同口味冰淇淋的檯子在哪裡？

## Words and Phrases

1. all-you-can-eat *adj.* 隨你吃到飽的

2. buffet [bə`fe] *n.* 自助餐；自助餐檯（可以隨意選取菜色的餐廳）

3. something else 完全不同的另一回事

4. unbelievable [ˌʌnbə`livəb]] *adj.* 難以置信的

5. variety [və`raɪətɪ] *n.* 種類；變化

6. lobster [`lɑbstɚ] *n.* 龍蝦；大螯蝦

7. protein [`protiɪn] *n.* 蛋白質

8. Atkins Diet [`ætkɪnz`daɪət] 阿金飲食

9. fad [fæd] *n.* 一時的流行或是狂熱

10. handle [`hænd]] *v.* 有辦法解決（在此指吃得下）

11. overwhelming [ˌovɚ`hwɛlmɪŋ] *adj.* 壓倒性的；無法抵抗的

12. Don't sweat it. 別擔心。

13. hit [hɪt] *v.* 前往；上路

14. flavor [`flevɚ] *n.* 口味

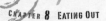
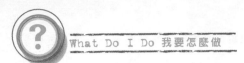 What Do I Do 我要怎麼做

 CD 2-08

# Time to Order 點餐了

**1** Waiter : Do you need another minute?

You : No, I'm ready to order. I'd like the ¹roast chicken.

服務生 ：您需要再等一下嗎？

你　　：不用，我可以點餐了。我要烤雞。

---

**2** Waiter : Do you have any question?

You : I'm feeling a bit ²indecisive. I wouldn't mind a ³recommendation.

服務生 ：您有任何疑問嗎？

你　　：我覺得有點舉棋不定。不妨給點建議吧。

---

**3** Waiter : Will that be all?

You : Actually, I'd also like an ⁴order of ⁵crab cakes ⁶to go—for later.

服務生 ：這樣就好了嗎？

你　　：事實上，我還要一份蟹肉餅——等下帶走。

## Words and Phrases

1. roast [rost] *adj.* 烤過的

2. indecisive [ˌɪndɪˋsaɪsɪv] *adj.* 無法決定的

3. recommendation [ˌrɛkəmɛnˋdeʃən] *n.* 推舉；建議

4. order [ˋɔrdə] *n.* 一份（餐）

5. crab cake [ˋkræbˌkek] 蟹肉餅

6. to go 外帶

CD 2-09

# When You Don't [1] <u>Feel Like</u> It 當你並不想的時候

**(1)** You　　: I don't feel like [2]<u>eating out</u> tonight. Go on without me.

Friend : OK. I'll see you later then.

你　　：我今晚不想在外面吃。你自己去吧。

朋友　：好吧，那晚一點再見了。

---

**(2)** You　　: I think I'll [3]<u>pass on</u> dessert. I'm [4]<u>full</u>.

Waiter : Just coffee then.

你　　：我想甜點我不用了。我已經吃飽了。

服務生：那光咖啡就好了。

---

**(3)** You　　: To be honest, I'm sick of [5]<u>fast food</u>. Let's eat something different.

Friend : [6]<u>I couldn't agree more.</u>

你　　：老實說，我討厭吃速食。咱們吃點不一樣的吧。

朋友　：我舉雙手贊成。

## 🚌 Words and Phrases

1. feel like　想要

2. eat out　外食；在外用餐

3. pass on sth.　【口語】拒絕；放棄

4. full [fʊl] *adj.* 吃飽了的

5. fast food　快餐；（麥當勞、肯德基、漢堡王之類的）簡便食物；速食

6. I couldn't agree more. 我完全贊成。

147

FYI 好用資訊

自助餐菜單

Billy Bob's BIG BUFFET
"Be all you can be-Eat all you can eat!"
Today's Specials
Lunch Special Standard Buffet $5.95
All-You-Can-Eat SEAFOOD $8.95
coffee and soft drinks Included
Try our famous homemade peach cobbler

Travel Tips 旅遊撇步一起走

　　要是你一家接一家到餐廳吃大餐，非變胖不可。假如你希望回家時的體型和出門前一樣，你就得注意自己所吃的東西。把乾果之類的健康零食帶在身上，這樣你就不會在餓著肚子的狀態之下進入餐館。當你點餐時，只要點夠吃的就好。假如點四盎司的牛排就已經夠填飽肚子，那就不要點十二盎司的。假如餐廳所給的份量都很大，那就和朋友共用一道主菜。不要不好意思問餐廳人員菜是怎麼料理的，或是請他們稍微改變一下料理方式。而且你一定要像在家的時候一樣，確實地作足夠的運動。假如你時常選擇走路而不是坐計程車，那你就不必太過擔心你所多吃的那一片雙層巧克力蛋糕了。

# CHAPTER 9
# TROUBLE

## 突發狀況

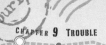

# David
## 大衛

CD 2-10

**An [1]overenthusiastic breakfast has left David with stomach problems.**

*Rick* : Don't say I didn't warn you.

*David* : Can a person die from [2]diarrhea?

*Rick* : Only by being [3]murdered if they don't clean up the bathroom when they're [4]through.

*David* : I need medicine, something to [5]settle my stomach.

*Rick* : Can you [6]make it to the drug store?

*David* : Only if we can get there and back in twenty minutes.

*(Five minutes later)*

*Rick* : This is the best drug store in the area. You can get everything here—even stuff that you would need a [7]prescription for back in the U.S.

*David* : I just need [8]Imodium and some [9]oral rehydration [10]solution.

*Rick* : OK. Hello, my friend has an [11]upset stomach. Do you have any Imodium?

[12]*Pharmacist* : Sure. I'll give you sixteen [13]tablets. Take two four times a day, for two days. If you don't feel better, go see a doctor.

*Rick* : How about oral rehydration [14]treatment?

*Pharmacist* : I think it is unnecessary. Just don't drink soda, or eat any [15]dairy products. Also, nothing fried or anything spicy.

*David* : So, bread and water, then?

*Pharmacist* : Or rice.

*Rick* : And next time [16]go easy on the breakfast soup!

*David* : Do you have a bathroom?

一頓太豐盛的早餐使大衛的腸胃出了問題。

瑞克：別說我沒有警告過你。

大衛：拉肚子會不會死人啊？

瑞克：只有在拉完之後沒有把廁所清乾淨才會被謀殺掉。

大衛：我需要一些藥來緩和胃痛。

瑞克：你撐得到藥局嗎？

大衛：要是我們能在二十分鐘之內來回的話。

（五分鐘之後）

瑞克：這是這附近最好的藥局。你要什麼有什麼，甚至連在美國必須有處方籤才能
　　　拿得到的藥都有。

大衛：我只需要止瀉藥和一些口服補水劑。

瑞克：好。你好，我朋友肚子不舒服。你們有賣止瀉藥嗎？

藥師：當然。我給你十六片藥片，一天四次，一次吃兩片，連續吃兩天。假如沒有
　　　好轉，那就去看醫生。

瑞克：需不需要吃口服補水劑呢？

藥師：我想不需要。只要別喝汽水或吃任何乳製品就行了。還有，不要吃炸的或辣
　　　的東西。

大衛：那就只有麵包和水囉？

藥師：或是米飯。

瑞克：而且下次早餐湯不要喝太猛！

大衛：請問這裡有廁所嗎？

## Words and Phrases

1. overenthusiastic [ˌovɚənˈθjuzɪˌæstɪk]
   *adj.* 過份熱情的（在此指太過豐盛的）

2. diarrhea [ˌdaɪəˈriə] *n.* 腹瀉；拉肚子

3. murder [ˈmɝdɚ] *v.* 謀殺

4. through [θru] *adj.* 完成；終了

5. settle [ˈsɛtl] *v.* 使穩定；使鎮靜

6. make it to... 撐到……

7. prescription [prɪˈskrɪpʃən] *n.* 處方；藥方

8. Imodium [ɪˈmodɪəm] *n.* 止瀉藥；痢達膠囊

9. oral rehydration [ˈorəl ˌrɪhaɪˈdreʃən] 口服補水沖劑；電解質口服液（於脫水時補充體內水分用）

10. solution [səˈluʃən] *n.* 溶劑；液劑

11. upset stomach [ʌpˈsɛtɪˈstʌmək] 腸胃不適（包括各種跟消化有關的不適，如胃酸過多、噁心等）

12. pharmacist [ˈfɑrməsɪst] *n.* 藥劑師

13. tablet [ˈtæblɪt] *n.* 藥片

14. treatment [ˈtritmənt] *n.* 治療；療法

15. dairy product [ˈdɛrɪ ˈprɑdʌkt] 乳製品

16. go easy on sth. 減低某事物的量；客氣地使用（吃、喝）某事物

What Do I Do 我要怎麼做

CD 2-11

# Not Feeling Well 覺得不舒服

(1) Friend : You don't look so good.

　　You : I don't feel well. I think it was something I ate.

　　朋友 : 你看起來不太對勁。

　　你 : 我覺得不舒服。我想是我吃壞東西了。

---

(2) Stranger : Are you okay?

　　You : I'm feeling ¹sick. I need a doctor.

　　陌生人 : 你還好吧？

　　你 : 我覺得想吐。我得看醫生。

---

(3) Friend : Should I call a doctor?

　　You : No. I'll be okay. I just need to rest.

　　朋友 : 需要我叫醫生嗎？

　　你 : 不用，我很快會沒事。我只是需要休息。

Words and Phrases

1. sick [sɪk] *adj.* 噁心的；想吐的；生病的；身體不舒服的

Getting What You Want 解決你的需求

 CD 2-12

## [1]Urgent Requests 緊急要求

**(1)** You : We need to get to a hospital as quickly as possible. Please hurry.

Taxi Driver : We'll be there in less than five minutes.

你 ：我們得盡快趕到醫院。麻煩快一點。

計程車司機：不到五分鐘我們就會到了。

---

**(2)** You : My friend is very sick. He needs to see a doctor right now.

Nurse : OK. Wait right here.

你 ：我朋友病得很重,他現在就得看醫生。

護士 ：好,在這裡等。

---

**(3)** You : You better stop the car. I'm going to be sick.

Driver : OK. I'm [2]pulling over.

你 ：你最好把車停下來,我要吐了。

司機 ：好,我現在就靠邊停。

📖 *Words and Phrases*

1. urgent [ˋɝdʒənt] *adj.* 事態緊急的

2. pull over 把車開到路邊

## 海氏催吐法

當身旁有人食物哽噎、溺水或是氣喘發作之時都可利用此種技巧救人一命。

欲參閱更詳盡的內容請上：
http://www.heimlichinstitute.org/howtodo.html

 Travel Tips 旅遊撇步一起走

  每個旅遊的人都應該隨身攜帶一個基本的急救箱。裡面應該準備消毒手套、包紮用品、抗菌濕紙巾和抗菌藥膏。自黏繃帶會很方便，也別忘了溫度計。當然剪刀和鑷子亦不可少。少量的非處方籤藥品應該足以應付大部分的小病痛。另外，阿斯匹靈或布洛芬（ibuprofen：鎮熱解痛劑）、止瀉藥以及治療胃部不適的治酸劑。假如你要去環境惡劣的地方旅行，再視需要加入其他東西（像是抗瘧疾藥和驅蟲藥）。

# Notes

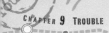

# Marie & Celeste

瑪莉 & 賽麗絲特

 Dialogue 對話

 CD 2-13

**Celeste and Raymond take Marie to the doctor.**

*Marie* : I can't [1]breathe. I can't find my inhaler anywhere.

*Raymond* : Do you have any idea what [2]brought on this attack?

*Marie* : No. Maybe it was the smoke at the place I went for dinner.

*Celeste* : (*To herself*) Maybe it was the place I went for dinner!

*Raymond* : OK, we are here now. You go inside, I will wait in the car.

(*In the doctor's office*)

*Doctor* : What is the problem, Madame?

*Marie* : Asthma. I don't have my inhaler.

*Doctor* : Here, breathe this [3]oxygen and I will write you a prescription for a new inhaler and some [4]steroids.

*Celeste* : Steroids?

*Doctor* : Yes, it is [5]common practice. Steroids [6]expand the [7]veins and [8]arteries.

*Marie* : We will be here for another ten days; can you give me [9]that many steroids?

*Doctor* : No. Five days only. If you still feel bad you will need to return.

*Celeste* : Excuse me, where is the [10]pharmacy?

*Doctor* : There is a [11]24-hour one on the next street, [12]parallel to this street.

*Marie* : Thanks.

賽麗絲特和雷蒙帶瑪莉去看醫生。

瑪莉　　　：我喘不過氣來了，又到處都找不到吸入器。

雷蒙　　　：你知不知道這次發作是什麼東西引起的？

瑪莉　　　：不知道。也許是我去吃晚餐的那個地方有煙的關係。

賽麗絲特：（自言自語）也許是我去吃晚餐的地方的關係！

雷蒙　　　：好了，現在我們到了。你們進去吧，我在車裡等。

（在醫生的診療室裡）

醫生　　　：小姐，妳有什麼問題？

瑪莉　　　：氣喘。我找不到我的吸入器。

醫生　　　：來，吸吸氧氣。我會開給你新的吸入器和一些類固醇。

賽麗絲特：類固醇？

醫生　　　：是啊，這是普遍的醫療方式。類固醇可以擴張靜脈和動脈。

瑪莉　　　：我們還要在這裡待十天，你能多給我那麼多的類固醇嗎？

醫生　　　：不行，只能給五天份。假如你還是不舒服的話，那就回來複診。

賽麗絲特：對不起，請問藥局在哪裡？

醫生　　　：在下一條街有一家二十四小時營業的藥局，跟這條街平行。

瑪莉　　　：謝謝。

## Words and Phrases

1. breath [briθ] *v.* 呼吸

2. bring on 帶來；引起；造成

3. oxygen [ˋɑksədʒən] *n.* 氧氣

4. steroid [ˋstɛrɔɪd] *n.* 類固醇

5. common practice [ˋkɑmənˋpræktɪs] 慣用療法

6. expand [ɪkˋspænd] *v.* 擴張

7. vein [ven] *n.* 靜脈

8. artery [ˋɑrtərɪ] *n.* 動脈

9. that many 那麼多的

10. pharmacy [ˋfɑrməsɪ] *n.* 藥局

11. 24-hour *adj.* 二十四小時的

12. parallel to... 與……平行

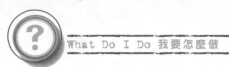

What Do I Do 我要怎麼做

CD 2-14

# Answering the Nurse's Questions
## 回答護士的問題

**(1)** Nurse : Are you currently taking any ¹medication?

You　　: No. Just ²aspirin ³every now and then.

護士　　：你目前有沒有服用任何藥物？

你　　　：沒有。只有偶爾會服用阿斯匹靈。

**(2)** Nurse : Do you have any ⁴allergies?

You　　: Not that I know of.

護士　　：你有任何的過敏嗎？

你　　　：就我所知沒有。

**(3)** Nurse : When did the ⁵symptoms start?

You　　: Yesterday.

護士　　：症狀是什麼時候開始的？

你　　　：昨天。

## Words and Phrases

1. medication [ˌmɛdɪˋkeʃən] *n.* 藥物

2. aspirin [ˋæspərɪn] *n.* 阿斯匹靈

3. every now and then  偶爾

4. allergy [ˋælədʒɪ] *n.* 過敏症

5. symptom [ˋsɪmptəm] *n.* 症狀

CD 2-15

## ¹Medical Questions 醫療問題

**1** You : Do these ²pills have any ³side effects?
Pharmacist : They'll probably make you a little ⁴drowsy.
你 ：這些藥丸會有任何的副作用嗎？
藥師 ：大概會使你有些昏昏欲睡。

---

**2** You : When will I start to feel better?
Doctor : Take it easy for a week ⁵or so and you'll start feel-ing better.
你 ：我什麼時候才會開始覺得好一點？
醫生 ：休息個一星期左右，你就會開始覺得好一點了。

---

**3** You : Am I OK to travel? I have a flight to catch tomor-row.
Doctor : Flying shouldn't be a problem. Just don't ⁶overexert yourself.
你 ：我能夠旅行嗎？我明天需要搭一班飛機。
醫生 ：坐飛機應該不是問題，只要不要使自己過度勞累即可。

## Words and Phrases

1. medical [ˋmɛdɪk!] *adj.* 醫藥上的；醫學上的

2. pill [pɪl] *n.* 藥丸

3. side effect [ˋsaɪdə͵fɛkt] 副作用

4. drowsy [ˋdraʊzɪ] *adj.* （令人）昏昏欲睡的

5. ... or so 接近……

6. overexert [͵ovɚɪgˋzɝt] *v.* （使）過分操勞

159

FYI 好用資訊

**dizzy**

頭暈

**vomit**

嘔吐

**drowsy**

昏昏欲睡

**expand**

擴張

Travel Tips 旅遊撇步一起走

　　在世界很多地方，愛滋病仍在蔓延。隨便、缺乏保護措施的性行為及靜脈注射藥物一直是主要的高傳染性活動。在醫院裡，要是受感染的病患用過的針頭沒有經過消毒，也可能傳染愛滋病毒（或其他重病，像是B型肝炎）。這種風險不高，但假如你在旅遊時真的要打針，最好檢查一下，以確定所用的針頭是拋棄式的或是已經過適當地消毒的。

# Notes

# Kevin & Sarah

## 凱文 & 莎拉

 Dialogue 對話

CD 2-16

**Sarah has had her bag ¹stolen at the restaurant. She is ²blaming Kevin.**

*Sarah* : I told you to watch the bag carefully.

*Kevin* : God, I just went to grab a couple of shrimps. It took one minute, ³tops. Who would've ⁴expected any of these people to be able to move so quickly?

*Sarah* : You ⁵dumbass. My credit card was in that bag, ⁶along with all our cash!

*Kevin* : At least the traveler's checks are in the hotel ⁷safe and I've got the camera.

*Sarah* : But we still need to call the police to report the ⁸theft.

*Kevin* : We should call the bank first and ⁹cancel the plastic.

*Sarah* : The number is in your ¹⁰money belt.

(*Later*)

*Kevin* : OK, the card's canceled. They can get a new one to us within five days.

*Sarah* : Now can we call the ¹¹cops?

*Waitress* : Is there a problem folks?

*Sarah* : Somebody stole my bag. We need to report it to the police.

*Waitress* : Honey, I'm so sorry. Use our phone to call 911.

*Sarah* : I don't think that they'll find the bag but we need a ¹²police report for the ¹³insurance company.

*Waitress* : I know. I'm terribly sorry. Don't' worry about the bill; it's ¹⁴on the house.

*Kevin* : Is it OK if I get another lobster ¹⁵claw?

莎拉的包包在餐廳被偷了,她怪罪於凱文。

莎拉　：我叫你要好好看著包包的。

凱文　：拜託,我只是去拿幾隻蝦,頂多花了一分鐘。誰會曉得這裡有人動作這麼快?

莎拉　：你這個白癡。我的信用卡在那個包包裡面,我們全部的現金也是!

凱文　：起碼旅行支票還好好地擺在旅館的保險箱裡,而且我也拿了相機。

莎拉　：可是我們還是得聯絡警方,報告這起竊盜案。

凱文　：我們應該先打電話給銀行把卡停掉。

莎拉　：電話號碼在你的腰帶式錢包裡。

（一會兒之後）

凱文　：好了,卡停掉了。他們可以在五天內發新卡給我們。

莎拉　：現在我們可以報警了嗎?

服務生：兩位,有問題嗎?

莎拉　：有人偷了我的包包,我們需要報警。

服務生：親愛的,真是抱歉。用我們的電話打九一一吧。

莎拉　：我不認為他們能找得到包包,可是我們保險公司需要一份報案記錄。

服務生：我知道,真的很抱歉。不用擔心帳單,這頓店裡請客。

凱文　：那我可以再吃一個龍蝦螯嗎?

## 🚌 Words and Phrases

1. stolen [`stolən] *adj.* 被偷了的

2. blame [blem] *v.* 責怪

3. ...tops. ……最多了。

4. expect [ɪk`spɛkt] *v.* 想到;預料到

5. dumbass [`dʌm,æs] *n.* 笨蛋

6. along with... 跟……一起

7. safe [sef] *n.* 保險箱

8. theft [θɛft] *n.* 竊盜（案）

9. cancel [`kænsl] *v.* 取消

10. money belt [`mʌnɪ,bɛlt] （腰帶式）錢包袋;裡面可以藏錢的腰帶

11. cop [kɑp] *n.* 【口語】警察

12. police report [pə`lisrɪ`pɔrt] 警方報案記錄

13. insurance company [ɪn`ʃurəns; `ɪnʃurəns `kʌmpənɪ] 保險公司

14. on the house 店家請客

15. claw [klɔ] *n.* 1.（蟹、蝦等的）螯; 2. 長而利的爪子（如貓爪）

163

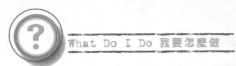

What Do I Do 我要怎麼做

CD 2-17

# Troubled Times 受難時刻

**(1)** Stranger : Are you OK? I saw you ¹<u>crash</u> your bike.

You : I think I'm OK. I'm just feeling a little ²<u>silly</u>.

陌生人 ：你還好嗎？我看到你撞壞了你的腳踏車。

你 ：我想我沒事。我只是覺得有點蠢。

**(2)** Police : Did you see the person who took your camera?

You : I sure did. I asked him to take my picture, and then he just ³<u>ran off</u>.

警察 ：你有看到拿走你相機的人嗎？

你 ：我當然看到了。我請他幫我拍照，結果他就這麼跑了。

**(3)** Police : We'll do our best, but it isn't too likely that we'll find your bag.

You : I know. But I'd like to fill out a report anyway, for insurance reasons.

警察 ：我們會盡力，可是我們幫你找到包包的機會不太大。

你 ：我知道。但是我還是要填報案記錄一保險上的需要。

Words and Phrases

1. crash [kræʃ] *v.* 猛撞；撞壞

2. silly [ˋsɪlɪ] *adj.* 傻的；愚蠢的

3. run off 逃走；跑掉

Getting What You Want 解決你的需求

CD 2-18

# ¹Confronting a Bad Guy 面對壞人

**①** You : I saw you take something from that woman's ²purse.
³Thief : No, you didn't—not if you know what's good for you.
你 ：我看見你從那位女士的錢包裡拿走東西。
小偷 ：不，你並沒有看到──你如果聰明的話，最好少管。

---

**②** You : Give my watch back. I won't leave until you return it.
Thief : ⁴Finder's keepers. I guess I could sell it to you, if you like.
你 ：把手錶還給我，你不還我我就不走。
小偷 ：誰撿到就是誰的。假如你要的話，我想我可以賣給你。

---

**③** You : Look, I don't want any trouble. This is all the money I have. Take it and go.
Thief : Thank you very much. And have a nice night.
你 ：聽好，我不想惹任何麻煩。這是我全部的家當，拿了就離開吧。
小偷 ：多謝，祝你有個愉快的夜晚。

## Words and Phrases

1. confront [kən`frʌnt] *n.* 面對

2. purse [pɝs] *n.* 錢包；手提包

3. thief [θif] *n.* 竊盜犯

4. Finder's keepers. 誰撿到就是誰的。

FYI 好用資訊

以下的報案記錄表是以加州大學爾灣分校的犯罪報告表為範本，可上網取得。網址是 http://www.police.uci.edu/reportform.html。

## Crime Report Form – Theft

1. Personal Information

    Name: (first) _____ (mi) _____ (last) _____

    Street Address:

    City:

    State:

    Zip Code:

    E-mail address:

    Home Phone:

    Cell Phone:

    Date of Birth:

    Social Security Number:

    Gender:

    Driver's License #: _____       State: _____

2. Crime Information

    Type of Crime:

    When was the property last seen:

    When was the property noticed stolen:

    Location where the crime occurred:

    Information about the suspect (if known):

    Description of crime/incident:

    Be very thorough. Describe everything you remember (Be sure to include Who, What, When, How, Why and Where):

在某些國家，扒手和小偷十分猖獗。小心警覺是防堵他們的第一步，但適當的準備也不可或缺。千萬不要讓當地的扒手有機可乘。假如你把錢擺在外面的口袋裡，他們就容易得手。大筆的現款和重要的文件要擺在腰帶式的錢包裡。把小錢包的繩帶纏繞在肩膀或腰部附近，然後把小錢包塞進褲子裡或是至於前方的褲頭裡。假如你有帶背包，在擁擠的地方要把它轉到身體前面。小偷最喜歡看當他們用刀子割開了遊客的包包之後，會掉出什麼東西來。假使你必須把包包放下來，千萬不要讓它離開你的視線，就算只是一下下都不要。綁一條帶子在你的大腿上，如此一來，假如有人想要搶了就跑，你就會知道。要提防小偷們的聯手，也就是說，由一個人設法分散你的注意力，再由另一個人偷走你的行李。祝你好運。

Notes

## Notes

# CHAPTER 10

# KEEPING IN TOUCH

## 與家人保持聯絡

# David

## 大衛

Dialogue 對話

CD 2-19

**David is looking for an** [1]**Internet café so that he can email his family.**

| | |
|---|---|
| *Rick* | : Are you feeling better? |
| *David* | : I'm [2]not quite 100%, but I'm getting there. I need another favor. |
| *Rick* | : [3]Shoot. |
| *David* | : I want to email my folks and check my [4]inbox. I'm [5]expecting some forms from my college. |
| *Rick* | : There is a computer here, with an ADSL [6]connection. Let's go talk to Prinachorn at the front desk. |
| *David* | : Do we have to? |
| *(Later)* | |
| *Prinachorn* | : Good morning! |
| *Rick* | : What's up, Prin? David wants to use the computer. |
| *Prinachorn* | : Cost is 1 baht per minute up to thirty minutes. After that it's 0.5 baht per minute up to one hour... |
| *David* | : ...ten minutes would be... |
| *Prinachorn* | : ...over one hour is 0.4 baht per minute and 10% off for two hours or more. No [7]downloading music, no [8]pornography. |
| *David* | : OK. |
| *Prinachorn* | : Please don't [9]install any programs because of [10]viruses and [11]sign out of your [12]account when you are finished. |
| *David* | : Thanks. Can I use it now? |
| *Prinachorn* | : No, sorry. The computer is [13]out of order. Please come back later. |

大衛正在找網咖，以便寄電子郵件給家人。

瑞克　　：你覺得好點了嗎？

大衛　　：還沒有完全恢復，但在逐步恢復當中。我需要你幫我另一個忙。

瑞克　　：說吧。

大衛　　：我想要寄電子郵件給家人並查看郵件。我在等我的學校寄一些表格來。

瑞克　　：這裡有一台電腦，接了ADSL。我們找櫃台的普林納瓊問問看。

大衛　　：我們一定得這樣做嗎？

（一會兒之後）

普林納瓊：早安！

瑞克　　：你好嗎，普林？大衛想要用電腦。

普林納瓊：費用是前三十分鐘每分鐘一銖，超過三十分鐘到一小時是每分鐘○‧五
　　　　　銖⋯⋯

大衛　　：⋯⋯十分鐘會是⋯⋯

普林納瓊：超過一小時是每分鐘○‧四銖，兩個小時以上再打九折。不能下載音
　　　　　樂，也不能瀏覽色情內容。

大衛　　：好。

普林納瓊：請不要安裝任何程式，以免中毒。當你用完時，請登出你的帳戶。

大衛　　：謝謝。我現在可以用嗎？

普林納瓊：抱歉，不行。電腦故障了，請稍後再來。

## Words and Phrases

1. Internet café [ˈɪntəˌnɛtkæˈfe] 網咖

2. not quite 100% 不是在最佳狀態

3. shoot [ʃut] v. 直說吧

4. inbox [ˈɪnbɑks] n. 收信匣

5. expect [ɪkˈspɛkt] v. 盼望；等待

6. connection [kəˈnɛkʃən] n. （網路）連線

7. download [ˈdaʊnˌlod] v. 下載

8. pornography [pɔrˈnɑgrəfɪ] n. 色情（包括一切任何形式，文字敘述、照片、電影等）

9. install [ɪnˈstɔl] v. （程式）安裝

10. virus [ˈvaɪrəs] n. 病毒

11. sign out 登出

12. account [əˈkaʊnt] n. 帳號

13. out of order 故障的

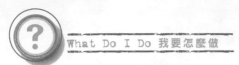

What Do I Do 我要怎麼做

CD 2-20

## ¹**Cyber Café** 網咖

**①** Clerk : Would you please ²turn down the ³volume on your computer?

You : No problem. Was I making a lot of noise?

店員 ：可以麻煩你把電腦的聲音調小一點嗎？

你 ：沒問題。我剛才很吵嗎？

---

**②** Clerk : Let's see, you were ⁴logged on for ten minutes. That'll be $4.

You : I have to pay for the ⁵full 1/2 hour?

店員 ：我看看，你登入了十分鐘，一共是四塊錢。

你 ：我要付整整半小時的錢？

---

**③** Clerk : Sir, we'd like to ask you not to download any new ⁶software.

You : That wasn't me. The guy before me did that.

店員 ：先生，請不要下載任何新的軟體。

你 ：那不關我的事，是我前面那個傢伙幹的。

## 🚌 *Words and Phrases*

1. cyber café [ˋsaɪbəˍkæˋfe] 網咖（同 Internet café）

2. turn down 降低

3. volume [ˋvɑljəm] *n.* 音量

4. log on 登入

5. full [fʊl] *adj.* 完整的

6. software [ˋsɔftˍwɛr] *n.* 軟體

Getting What You Want 解決你的需求

CD 2-21

# Cyber Café 網咖

**(1)** You : Can I use a ¹<u>floppy disk</u> here?

**Clerk:** No.

你　　：這裡可以用軟碟嗎？

店員　：不行。

---

**(2)** You : The connection seems really slow.

**Clerk:** I'm afraid it's like that sometimes.

你　　：連線速度似乎真的很慢。

店員　：恐怕有時候就是這個樣子。

---

**(3)** You : I've been ²<u>disconnected</u> three times. Do I still have to pay full price?

**Clerk:** No. We won't charge you for the time.

你　　：我斷線了三次。我還是得付全額嗎？

店員　：不用，這次不算你的時間。

📖 *Words and Phrases*

1. floppy disk [ˋflɑpɪˋdɪsk] 軟式磁碟（也直接稱為 floppy）

2. disconnect [͵dɪskəˋnɛkt] v. 離線；斷線

173

FYI 好用資訊

## 公共圖書館網路使用規範

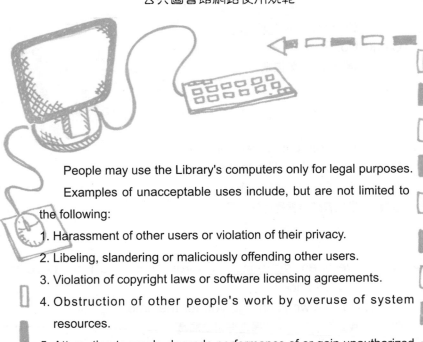

People may use the Library's computers only for legal purposes. Examples of unacceptable uses include, but are not limited to the following:

1. Harassment of other users or violation of their privacy.
2. Libeling, slandering or maliciously offending other users.
3. Violation of copyright laws or software licensing agreements.
4. Obstruction of other people's work by overuse of system resources.
5. Attempting to crash, degrade performance of or gain unauthorized access to the Library's or other computer systems and networks.
6. Damaging equipment, software or data belonging to the Library or other users.
7. Exposing children to harmful materials.
8. Violations may result in restrictions on library use. Illegal uses of computers may also be subject to prosecution by local, state or federal authorities.

Travel Tips 旅遊撇步一起走

　　假如你在旅行時打算上網，就需要有網路電子郵件帳號（像是 hotmail 或 yahoo）。如此一來，不需要特殊的軟體就可以收發電子郵件。你可以事先做點調查，看看在哪些地方可以登入。如果要查世界各地的網咖據點一覽表，請上 cybercaptive.com。

Notes

# Marie & Celeste
## 瑪莉＆賽麗絲特

Dialogue 對話

CD 2-22

**Marie wants to call her family to tell them that everything is OK.**

*Marie* : I wish I'd brought my ¹mobile phone and then we wouldn't have had to search for a ²pay phone.

*Celeste* : But your phone ³charger wouldn't have worked here, so after three days it would have been useless.

*Marie* : Pay phones are just so ⁴uncool.

*Celeste* : Oh, stop ⁵whining. We'll just go to the post office and use the phones there. We need to mail stuff ⁶anyway.

*(In the post office)*

*Marie* : I don't have any change.

*Celeste* : Just go buy a ⁷phone card then. Look, can't you read; "Counter 12—phone cards."

*Marie* : All right, take it easy. I told you I was sorry for ⁸spoiling your dinner with Raymond!

*Celeste* : Just buy the card.

*Marie* : Hi, I need to call Taiwan, but only for a few minutes. What ⁹value card should I get?

*Clerk* : Well, it's almost a euro a minute, so you should probably get at least a 10-euro card.

*Marie* : OK, that's fine.

*Celeste* : I'm going to buy some more postcards; I'll be back in a minute.

*Marie* : OK, I'll ask my mom to call yours.

瑪莉想要打電話給家人，告訴他們一切平安。

瑪莉　　：真希望我帶了行動電話，這樣我們就不必找公用電話了。

賽麗絲特：可是妳的電話充電器在這裡又不能用，所以三天後就無用武之地了。

瑪莉　　：公用電話簡直太遜了。

賽麗絲特：喂，別再抱怨了。我們就到郵局去用那裡的電話，反正我們也要寄東西。

（在郵局裡）

瑪莉　　：我一個零錢都沒有。

賽麗絲特：那就去買電話卡。瞧，妳沒有看到嗎，「十二號櫃台──電話卡」。

瑪莉　　：好嘛，放輕鬆點。我跟妳說過了，我很抱歉破壞了妳和雷蒙的晚餐！

賽麗絲特：買妳的卡就是了。

瑪莉　　：嗨，我必須打電話到台灣，可是只要打幾分鐘。我應該買哪種價值的卡？

櫃台人員：嗯，一分鐘幾乎要一歐元，所以你大概至少應該買十歐元的卡。

瑪莉　　：好，就買十歐元的。

賽麗絲特：我要多買幾張明信片，等下就回來。

瑪莉　　：好，我會叫我媽打電話給你媽。

## 🚌 *Words and Phrases*

1. mobile phone [`mobaɪl`fon]　行動電話；手機（＝cell phone）

2. pay phone [`pe͵fon] *n.* 公用電話

3. charger [`tʃɑrdʒɚ] *n.* 充電器

4. uncool [ʌn`kul] *adj.* 不酷的

5. whine [hwaɪn] *v.* 抱怨；訴苦

6. anyway [`ɛnɪ͵we] *adv.* 反正

7. phone card　電話卡

8. spoil [spɔɪl] *v.* 破壞；搞砸

9. value [`væljʊ] *n.* 價值；額度

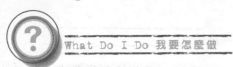

# ¹On the Phone 講電話

**①** Phone ²<u>Voice</u> : One minute remaining.

    You      : Mom, my card is about to ³<u>expire</u>. I love you and I'll call you again soon.

    電話語音 ：還有一分鐘。

    你     ：媽，我的卡快要用完了。我愛妳，我很快會再打給妳。

---

**②** Operator : How would you like to ⁴<u>place the call</u>?

    You      : I'd like to use a ⁵<u>calling card</u>.

    接線生 ：您的電話要怎麼付費？

    你     ：我要用電話卡。

---

**③** Friend    : Can I call you back?

    You      : I'm at a pay phone that does not receive ⁶<u>incoming calls</u>.

    朋友   ：我可以打回去給你嗎？

    你     ：我打的是公用電話，無法接聽來電。

## *Words and Phrases*

1. on the phone 講電話當中

2. voice [`vɔɪs] *n.* （電話中的）語音

3. expire [ɪk`spaɪr] *v.* 到期；期滿失效

4. place a call （透過接線生）打電話

5. calling card 電話卡（=phone card）

6. incoming call [`ɪn͵kʌmɪŋ`kɔl] 打進來的電話；來電

CD 2-24

Getting What You Want 解決你的需求

# Calling Card Question 電話卡的問題

**1** You : Which card has the best rate for calling Taiwan?

　　Clerk : This one is the best.

　　你 ：哪張卡的費率打回台灣最划算？

　　櫃台人員：這張最划算了。

---

**2** You : Does this card have a ¹connection fee?

　　Clerk : Yes. Fifty cents per call.

　　你 ：這張卡需要接線費嗎？

　　櫃台人員：是的，每通五毛錢。

---

**3** You : When will this card expire?

　　Clerk : It's ²good for two months.

　　你 ：這張卡什麼時候會過期？

　　櫃台人員：它有兩個月的期限。

🚌 *Words and Phrases*

1. connection fee 接線服務費

2. good for... 能用（一段時間）的

FYI 好用資訊

電話卡的使用說明

INTERNATIONAL
CALLING CARD

## PHONE CARD INSTRUCTIONS

To place a call:

1. Dial Your ACCESS NUMBER.
   - 1-800-xxx-xxx (English)
   - 1-800-xxx-xxx (Chinese)
2. Enter your PIN number.
3. Dial your DESTINATION NUMBER.
   - For International Calls
   - Dial 011 + Country Code + City Code + Number
   - For Domestic Calls
   - Dial 1 + Area Code + Number
4. Listen for your account balance and time available for this call.
5. Customer Service: service@phonetech.com

Travel Tips 旅遊撇步一起走

　　當你在國外時，用國際電話卡保持聯絡是個不錯的方法。最近幾年來，打國際電話的費用便宜了許多，但你在選購電話卡的時候還是得小心，有些還是會坑人的。它們在廣告上可能會宣稱每分鐘的費率很低，但卻會要求你付其他方面的費用。比方說，每通電話都會要收接線費，或者是月費很高，還有的是每通電話的最後都是以兩分鐘為單位來計費（比如，如你只打了十秒鐘，還是會以打了兩分鐘的價錢來計費）。最好貨比三家來找出最划算的方案，而且一定要注意收費細節。

Notes

# Kevin & Sarah
## 凱文＆莎拉

Dialogue 對話

CD 2-25

Sarah wants to call the bank in Taiwan to [1]confirm the loss of her credit card and tell them not to send another one.

*Sarah* : I think that we can [2]do without a credit card for the next ten days. We have plenty of traveler's checks. We [3]might as well use those.

*Kevin* : It's [4]up to you. You'll need to call the bank and ask them not to send another one though, because I told them to send it to the hotel.

*Sarah* : OK. You think my cell phone will work for an [5]international call?

*Kevin* : It should. But [6]keep it brief or it'll be expensive.

*Sarah* : What's the [7]code for Taiwan?

*Kevin* : 886.

*Sarah* : Hello, hello?

*Voice* : Changhwa Bank, International [8]Helpline. How can I help you?

*Sarah* : Hi. My name is Sarah Lin. My account number is...hang on... 3465271453. I'm in the U.S., and my credit card was stolen.

*Voice* : Yes, it was reported stolen at 5:53 today Taiwan time. We can get a new one to you in five days.

*Sarah* : Well, I'm calling to say that's not necessary. Please don't send the new card here. Just send it to my home address.

*Voice* : OK. We'll do that.

*Sarah* : (*Hanging up*) Well, that was [9]a piece of cake. Let's go spend those traveler's checks.

莎拉要打電話給台灣的銀行，以確定告知自己的信用卡遺失，並叫他們不要寄新卡。

莎拉：我想我們沒有信用卡也可以撐過接下來的十天。反正我們有很多旅行支票，我們用這些支票就好了。

凱文：看妳囉。可是妳得打電話給銀行，叫他們不要寄新卡來，因為我叫他們寄來旅館。

莎拉：好。你想我的手機可以打國際電話嗎？

凱文：應該可以。但要長話短說，否則會很貴。

莎拉：台灣的國際代碼是多少？

凱文：八八六。

莎拉：喂，喂？

對方：彰化銀行國際服務專線，需要什麼服務嗎？

莎拉：你好，我的名字是莎拉‧林。我的帳號是……等等……三四六五二七一四五三。我人在美國，我的信用卡被偷了。

對方：是的，它在台灣時間今天的五點五十三分時掛失。我們可以在五天內寄新卡給您。

莎拉：嗯，我打來是要跟妳說不用了。請不要把新卡寄來這裡，直接寄到我的住家地址就好了。

對方：好的，我們會這麼處理。

莎拉：（掛掉電話）嗯，真容易。走吧，咱們去花掉那些旅行支票吧。

## 🚌 *Words and Phrases*

1. confirm [kənˋfɝm] *v.* 確認

2. do without... 在沒有……的情況下

3. might as well... 不如就……

4. up to you 由你決定

5. international call 國際電話

6. keep it brief 盡量使它簡短；長話短說

7. code [kod] *n.* 碼（在此指一國的國碼）

8. helpline [ˋhɛlpˌlaɪn] *n.* 求助熱線

9. a piece of cake 太容易的事

What Do I Do 我要怎麼做

 CD 2-26

# Credit Card ¹Transactions 信用卡交易

① Clerk : I'm sorry. I've tried twice, but your card still won't work.

　　You　: I guess I'll have to pay cash.

　　店員　：抱歉，我試過兩次，可是您的卡還是不能用。

　　你　　：我想我只好付現了。

---

② Clerk : Please sign here.

　　You　: I need a receipt. Can I keep this ²copy?

　　店員　：請在這裡簽名。

　　你　　：我需要收據。我可以把這份留下來嗎？

---

③ Clerk : Could I please see some ID?

　　You　: How about a passport?

　　店員　：可以讓我看一下證件嗎？

　　你　　：護照可以嗎？

📦 *Words and Phrases*

1. transaction [træns`ækʃən] *n.* （業務的）交辦、處理

2. copy [`kɑpɪ] *n.* （文件）份

CD 2-27

# Credit Card Trouble 信用卡問題

**(1) You** : My Visa card was stolen. Has anyone used it?

[1]Customer Service : Let me check.

你 ：我的威士卡被偷了。有被人盜用嗎？

客服人員 ：我查一下。

---

**(2) You** : You [2]billed me for [3]purchases made after my card was stolen.

Customer Service : Your account number, please.

你 ：你們把我的卡被偷以後的消費金額都算進我的帳上了。

客服人員 ：麻煩您，給我您的帳號。

---

**(3) You** : Does my card provide insurance for a rental car?

Customer Service : Just a moment. I'm going to [4]transfer you.

你 ：我的卡有沒有提供租車的保險？

客服人員 ：稍等一下，我幫您轉接。

## Words and Phrases

1. customer service [`kʌstəmɚ͵sɝvɪs] 客服

2. bill [bɪl] v. 記為某人的帳

3. purchase [`pɝtʃəs] n. 購買

4. transfer [`trænsfɚ] v. 轉接

FYI 好用資訊

## 失竊信用卡遭盜刷之消費明細

| VISA Card Account Summary | | | |
|---|---|---|---|
| ACCOUNT NUMBER | XXXX-XXXX-XXXX-XXXX | | |
| PAYMENT DUE DATE | September 18, 2005 | | |
| CREDIT LIMIT | $5,000.00 | | |
| CREDIT AVAILABLE | $2,872.00 | | |
| | | | |
| **Transactions** | | | |
| Merchandise/Retail | August 23 | Vivaldi Café | $32.50 |
| | August 25 | Alligator Ranch Gift Shop | $75.00 |
| | August 25 | Four Seasons Buffet | $35.50 |
| | August 25 | Universal TV | $1200.00 |
| | August 25 | Jordan's Gems and Jewelry | $785.00 |

Travel Tips 旅遊撇步一起走

　　假如你要在旅途中帶著信用卡，一定要了解持卡人能享有哪些額外優惠？很多卡都提供免費或折扣的租車保險，另外可能還提供旅行險和醫療險。不妨好好利用信用卡所提供的一切優惠。

# CHAPTER 11

# GETTING THINGS DONE

## 事務辦理

# David

## 大衛

Dialogue 對話

CD 2-28

**David has gone to the bank. He is expecting his mother to ¹wire him some money.**

*David* : Good afternoon, I'm expecting a ²wire transfer.

*Clerk* : You name, please?

*David* : David Wang. The transfer is from the Chinatrust Commercial Bank in Taiwan. I'm not exactly sure of the amount.

*Clerk* : Here we are—from Wang Shu Chuan in Taipei. ³Payee David Wang. Can I see some ID please?

*David* : My passport.

*Clerk* : You'll need to fill out this form. Take a pen and sit down at the table over there.

*(A few minutes later)*

*Clerk* : ⁴All done?

*David* : I think so. It seems like a complicated form to just ⁵collect some money. I couldn't fill in the amount because you didn't tell me how much it was.

*Clerk* : Sorry. It's for 10,000 ⁶New Taiwan Dollars, which would be 11,539 baht at today's rate. Minus our 200 baht commission... that gives you 11,339 baht. Sign here and here and here.

*David* : Is that all? I shouldn't have told my mom that Thailand was so cheap, should I?

大衛到了銀行，他正等待他媽媽匯錢給他。

大衛：午安，我在等一筆電匯轉帳的錢。

行員：請問貴姓大名？

大衛：王大衛。是從台灣的中國信託商業銀行轉出的，我不確定確切的金額。

行員：查到了——轉帳人是台北的王淑娟，受款人是王大衛。能讓我看您的證件嗎？

大衛：我的護照。

行員：您需要把這張表格填好。您可以拿枝筆到那邊的桌子坐下來寫。

（幾分鐘後）

行員：都寫好了嗎？

大衛：我想是吧。為了領一點錢，這張表格似乎有點太複雜了。你沒有告訴我是多少錢，所以金額我沒辦法填。

行員：抱歉。是一萬塊新台幣，以今天的匯率換算是一萬一千五百三十九銖。扣掉兩百銖的手續費後……您可實領的金額是一萬一十三百三十九銖。請在這裡、這裡和這裡簽名。

大衛：這樣就可以了嗎？我真不該告訴我媽泰國的東西很便宜，對不對？

## 🚌Words and Phrases

1. wire [waɪr] *v.* 電匯

2. wire transfer [`waɪr͵trænsfɚ] 電匯轉帳

3. payee [pe`i] *n.* 受款人

4. all done 全部完成了

5. collect [kə`lɛkt] *v.* 領取

6. New Taiwan Dollar 新台幣

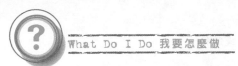

What Do I Do 我要怎麼做

CD 2-29

# Personal Information 個人資料

**(1)** Clerk : Is this your ²permanent address?

You : No. That's where I'm staying here in town.

店員 ：這是你的永久住址嗎？

你 ：不是，那是我目前在本城所待的地方。

---

**(2)** Clerk : Do you have a Visa card? I'll need that number.

You : Really? Why would you need that? I'm not buying anything.

店員 ：你有威士卡嗎？我需要那個卡號。

你 ：真的嗎？你為什麼會需要？我又沒有要買東西。

---

**(3)** Clerk : I'll need a phone number where you can be reached this week.

You : Sure. I'll give you the number of the hotel where I'm staying.

店員 ：我需要可以在本週中聯絡到你的電話號碼。

你 ：當然。我給你我目前所住旅館的號碼。

## Words and Phrases

1. personal information [ˈpɝsn̩l͵ɪnfɚˈmeʃən] 個人資料

2. permanent address [ˈpɝmənənt ˈædrɛs] 永久住址

CD 2-30

# Exchanging Money 換錢

**(1) You** : How much does the exchange rate ¹<u>vary</u> from day to day?

**²<u>Trader</u>** : Quite a bit sometimes. Today it's good.

你 ：匯率每天會變動多少？

交易商 ：有時候還不少。今天的匯率還不錯。

---

**(2) You** : How does the price you're offering compare to the bank's?

**Trader** : My price is better. Not ³<u>by a lot</u>, but it's a little better.

你 ：你給的價錢和銀行給的比起來怎麼樣？

交易商 ：我給的價錢比較好。不是好很多，可是還是好一些。

---

**(3) You** : I'd like to exchange NT$1,000 for local currency.

**⁴<u>Bank teller</u>** : Sure. Let me check on the exchange rate.

你 ：我想把一千元新台幣換成本地的貨幣。

銀行行員 ：好，讓我查看一下匯率。

## 🚌 *Words and Phrases*

1. vary [`vɛrɪ] *v.* 變更；變動

2. trader [`tredɚ] *n.* 商人

3. by a lot 大幅地

4. bank teller [`bæŋk͵tɛlɚ] 銀行出納員

FYI 好用資訊

國際匯率快算心法：

臺幣（**TWD**）／泰銖（**THB**）＝ 1:0.8
臺幣（**TWD**）／歐元（**EUR**）＝ 1:43
臺幣（**TWD**）／美元（**USD**）＝ 1:32

參考網站：**http://www.xe.com/ucc/**

Travel Tips 旅遊撇步一起走

　　旅途中若遇上錢不夠用，急需家人匯款，卻沒有在當地銀行開有戶頭的話，可以利用西聯匯款公司（Western Union）來匯款。匯款人不需要有銀行戶頭、不需要是當地公民、也不需要成為會員，只要填表完成匯款手續，受款人即可憑有效身分證明文件（如護照），在任何西聯匯款的據點領取款項。西聯匯款是此類服務中規模最大、觸角最廣的，全世界幾乎每個國家都設有據點提供匯款即取款，台灣目前在國泰世華銀行設有據點。此項服務酌收的手續費不低，卻是緊急情況下一條快速方便的途徑。請參考網站 http://www.westernunion.com。

# Notes

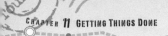

# Marie & Celeste

瑪莉 & 賽麗絲特

 Dialogue 對話

CD 2-31

**Marie and Celeste are in the post office sending postcards to their friends and family.**

*Marie* : There's something ¹<u>pointless</u> about postcards. They always seem to arrive just after you've arrived back from vacation with hundreds of photographs.

*Celeste* : Pointless or not, we have twenty of them to send and we need to do it now because we have to meet Raymond later to buy tickets for Le Moulin Rouge.

*Marie* : I'm not sure that I want to go see a ²<u>strip show</u>!

*Celeste* : First, it's a ³<u>cabaret</u>, not a strip show. Second, Raymond will be ⁴<u>upset</u> if you don't ⁵<u>show up</u>.

*Marie* : OK. Let's do the postcards.

*Celeste* : I'll take them.

*Clerk* : Yes?

*Celeste* : Twenty ⁶<u>stamps</u> for Taiwan, please.

*Clerk* : For postcards or letters?

*Celeste* : Postcards.

*Clerk* : 80 cents ⁷<u>apiece</u>. 16 euros total. You can put them in the green mailbox next to the door when you're finished.

*Celeste* : Thanks. Come on, Marie. I'm done. We'll have to ride fast to get to Le Moulin Rouge before five.

*Marie* : Take it easy, Celeste. We've got ⁸<u>plenty</u> of time.

瑪莉與賽麗絲特在郵局寄明信片給朋友及家人。

瑪莉　　：寄明信片好像沒有多大意義。它們似乎總是在妳已經度完假並帶著好幾
　　　　　百張照片回去以後才會寄到。

賽麗絲特：不管有沒有意義，我們有二十張要寄，而且現在就要寄，因為我們待會
　　　　　要跟雷蒙碰面，去買紅磨坊的票。

瑪莉　　：我可不確定我想去看脫衣舞表演！

賽麗絲特：第一，那是歌舞表演，不是脫衣舞。第二，假如妳不出現，雷蒙會不高
　　　　　興的。

瑪莉　　：好吧，我們把明信片的事辦好吧。

賽麗絲特：給我吧，我來。

櫃台人員：是的？

賽麗絲特：麻煩給我二十張寄去台灣的郵票。

櫃台人員：貼明信片還是信件？

賽麗絲特：明信片。

櫃台人員：每張八毛，總共十六歐元。等妳貼好以後，可以把它們投入大門旁邊的
　　　　　綠色郵筒。

賽麗絲特：謝謝。來吧，瑪莉。我弄好了。我們得騎快一點才能在五點以前趕到紅
　　　　　磨坊。

瑪莉　　：慢慢來，賽麗絲特。我們還有很多時間。

## 📖 Words and Phrases

1. pointless [`pɔɪntlɪs] *adj.* 無意義的

2. strip show [`strɪp ˏʃo] 脫衣表演

3. cabaret [ˏkæbə`re] *n.* 卡巴來歌舞表演

4. upset [ʌp`sɛt] *adj.* 不高興的

5. show up 出現；到、來

6. stamp [stæmp] *n.* 郵票

7. apiece [ə`pis] *adj.* 每個；各

8. plenty [`plɛntɪ] *n.* 充足；豐富

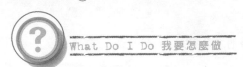

CD 2-32

## Mail 寄信

**1** Clerk : How would you like to send this letter?

You : How much will ¹air mail cost?

櫃台人員：你想要以哪種方式寄這封信？

你　　　：航空郵件要多少錢？

---

**2** Clerk : You haven't written a ²return address on the enve-lope.

You : I don't have one. I'm traveling.

櫃台人員：你的信封上沒有寫回函地址。

你　　　：我沒有回函地址，因為我在旅行。

---

**3** Clerk : Shall I put the ³postage on, or would you like to buy stamps?

You : I'd like to use stamps. Do you have any interesting ones?

櫃台人員：你要我貼上郵資，還是你想買郵票來貼？

你　　　：我要用郵票。你們有有趣的郵票嗎？

Words and Phrases

1. air mail [`ɛr‚mel] 航空郵件

2. return address 寄件人地址

3. postage [`postɪdʒ] *n.* 郵資

Getting What You Want 解決你的需求

CD 2-33

# Mail 寄信

① You　　： I need to send this in a hurry. Do you have ¹overnight mail?

Clerk　 ： Yes, we do. Let me weigh your package and I'll give you a price.

你　　　：我急著要寄這樣東西。你們有隔夜寄送嗎？

櫃台人員：是的，我們有。讓我先幫您的包裹秤一下，再告訴您價錢。

② You　　： How much longer will it take if I send this 2nd class rather than 1st?

Clerk　 ： Hard to say. First class is faster.

你　　　：假如我用第二類而不是第一類來寄這樣東西，速度會慢多少？

櫃台人員：很難說。第一類比較快。

③ You　　： If I mail this today, will it arrive by next Friday?

Clerk　 ： Yes, it should. But there are no ²guarantees.

你　　　：假如我今天把它寄出去，下星期五以前會到嗎？

櫃台人員：是的，應該會，可是我們不保證。

📖 *Words and Phrases*

1. overnight mail [ˌovəˈnaɪt ˈmel] 隔天送達的郵件

2. guarantee [ˌgærənˈti] *n.* 擔保；保證

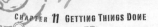

FYI 好用資訊

### 國際「隔日送達」郵件服務介紹

For your most urgent international shipments.

- Available 365 days a year for last-minute emergency shipments.
- Your deliveries to most major cities within hours (subject to flight availability).
- Call 1-800-974-7333 for a delivery quote and to arrange for pickup.
- The courier will bring an air waybill for you to complete.
- We track the status of your shipment and let you know when it arrives.
- Ship packages up to 2,200 lbs each (more with approval), and up to 48"x48"x70".

Travel Tips 旅遊撇步一起走

　　如果要讓寄給家鄉友人的明信片顯得有趣，記住一個最重要的原則，那就是要具體明確。不要寫說「我們昨天晚上在一家法國餐廳吃了一頓很棒的晚餐」，而應該寫寫主廚的拿手菜有多值得誇讚，譬如：「Veau et Coquilles St Jacques é la Francaise 是用大蒜及夏敦埃奶油醬嫩煎小牛肉片及海扇貝，我吃完後覺得它真是盤中極品。」小細節才能讓旅遊顯得不虛此行，而且這樣也最能向家鄉的友人表達出你所體驗到的感受。

```
Notes
```

# Kevin & Sarah
## 凱文＆莎拉

Dialogue 對話

CD 2-34

**Sarah and Kevin are deciding the best way to ¹deal with the stuff they've bought.**

*Sarah* : A ²solid week of shopping. Excellent!

*Kevin* : ³How the hell do you expect to carry all this stuff? We need a donkey.

*Sarah* : We're not going to carry it all. I have a plan. We're going to mail it. Call a taxi.

*(In the taxi)*

*Taxi Driver* : I'll have to charge you extra I'm afraid. Eight boxes is a lot.

*Sarah* : Sure. Here's twenty ⁴bucks. ⁵Keep the change.

*(In the post office)*

*Sarah* : I want to mail these boxes to Taiwan, please.

*Clerk* : Umm, I guess you want to send them ⁶surface rather than ⁷air?

*Sarah* : Surface would be fine. There's no ⁸rush. Air would be too expensive, I guess.

*Clerk* : At least you packed them well. Can you put them on the ⁹scales?

*Kevin* : What's the total?

*Clerk* : 97 ¹⁰kilos. Total amount ¹¹payable is US$314. I've insured them. Allow 3-6 weeks for delivery.

*Sarah* : What do I do if they don't show up after six weeks?

*Clerk* : Go to our ¹²website and enter your ¹³tracking numbers to find out where they are.

*Kevin* : Thanks.

莎拉與凱文在討論他們所買的東西要怎麼處理最好。

莎拉 ：整整血拼了一個禮拜。太棒了！

凱文 ：妳到底打算怎麼帶這些東西？我們需要一頭驢子。

莎拉 ：我們不會全部隨身帶著。我已經想好了，我們用寄的。叫計程車。

(在計程車上)

計程車司機：我恐怕得向你們收取額外的費用。八箱還挺多的。

莎拉 ：當然。這裡是二十塊，不用找。

(在郵局裡)

莎拉 ：麻煩你，我要把這些箱子寄到台灣。

櫃台人員 ：嗯，我想你要寄海陸而不是航空吧？

莎拉 ：海陸就可以了，不趕。我想航空會太貴。

櫃台人員 ：起碼妳打包得很好。能不能把它們放在磅秤上？

凱文 ：總共多重？

櫃台人員 ：九十七公斤，總須付金額是三百一十四美元。我已經幫它們加了保。
三到六週後可以寄到。

莎拉 ：假如六週後沒有送到，我該怎麼辦？

櫃台人員 ：上我們的網站輸入追蹤號碼，找看看它們在哪裡。

凱文 ：謝謝。

## Words and Phrases

1. deal with 處理

2. solid [`sɑlɪd] *adj.* 整整的

3. how the hell 到底

4. buck [bʌk] *n.* 【口語】一美元

5. Keep the change. 不用找了。

6. surface [`sɝfɪs] *adv.* 以水運（或陸運）
方式郵遞

7. air [ɛr] *adv.* 以航空方式郵遞

8. rush [rʌʃ] *n.* 急切；匆忙

9. scale [skel] *n.* 磅秤

10. kilo [`kɪlo] *n.* 公斤（kilogram 的簡稱）

11. payable [`peəbl] *adj.* 應支付的

12. website [`wɛb,saɪt] *n.* 網站

13. tracking number [`trækɪŋ ,nʌmbɚ] 追
蹤號碼

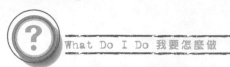

What Do I Do 我要怎麼做

CD 2-35

# Shipping 運費

**1** Clerk : You could add another 2 kilos and still ship this for the same price.

You : That's OK. I've already put everything in.

櫃台人員：你可以再加兩公斤，運費還是會一樣。

你 ：不用了。我已經把所有東西都裝進去了。

---

**2** Clerk : For a little bit extra, you could send this ²express mail.

You : How much extra? And how much faster is express mail?

櫃台人員：再加一點點錢，你就可以用快捷郵件來寄。

你 ：要加多少？快捷郵件會快多少？

---

**3** Clerk : Do you need POD — ³Proof of Delivery — for this?

You : No, that won't be necessary.

櫃台人員：你這樣東西需要 POD（投遞證明）嗎？

你 ：不用，沒這個必要。

*Words and Phrases*

1. shipping [ˋʃɪpɪŋ] *n.* 運費

2. express mail [ɪkˋsprɛs͵mel] 快遞；快捷

3. proof of delivery 投遞證明

Getting What You Want 解決你的需求

 CD 2-36

# Shipping 運費

**1** You : I'd like to insure this package.

**Clerk** : What is it?

你 ：我要幫這個包裹加保。

櫃台人員：包裹裡是什麼東西？

---

**2** You : I sent a package 6 weeks ago and it still hasn't arrived.

**Clerk** : I'm sorry. Let me have your tracking number and I'll ¹see about it.

你 ：我六個星期前寄了一個包裹，到現在還沒到。

櫃台人員：抱歉。把你的追蹤號碼給我，我來看看怎麼回事。

---

**3**

You : That seems very expensive. Is there a cheaper way?

**Clerk** : ²Not that I know of.

你 ：這樣似乎很貴。有沒有比較便宜的方法？

櫃台人員：我所知道的並沒有。

---

📖 *Words and Phrases*

1. see about... 處理……

2. Not that I know of. 我所知道的並沒有。

FYI 好用資訊

**packing peanuts**
填充泡綿

**scale**
磅秤

**stamp**
郵票

**postage**
郵資

Travel Tips 旅遊撇步一起走

　　每個國家的郵局服務品質有很大的差異。假如你在旅行途中想把貴重的東西寄回家，先打聽打聽，確定當地的郵務沒有腐敗及怠職的情況。萬一有，還是多付一點錢請私人貨運公司寄送比較好。

# CHAPTER '12

# OUT ON THE TOWN

# 市區遊玩

# David

## 大衛

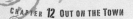

Dialogue 對話

CD 2-37

**David is meeting the Thai girl Gayle in a local bar.**

David : Sorry I'm late. I couldn't find the place.

Gayle : I thought you were going to [1]stand me up.

David : No. I'm just [2]hopeless with directions. I just got back from Chiangmai. You wouldn't believe how many times I got lost there. Can I get you a drink?

Gayle : Singha [3]beer, please.

David : A Singha and a [4]Johnnie Walker for me please, [5]on the rocks.

Barman : Coming right up. Do you want anything to eat?

David : Gayle?

Gayle : No, I'm fine.

David : Just a [6]bowl of [7]nuts then, please.

Barman : Here you go. Beer, whisky and nuts.

Gayle : So, David, have you enjoyed your stay?

David : Yeah. It's been nice; very different from Taiwan. Everyone is very [8]relaxed and friendly. Trekking in Chiangmai was great and I enjoyed Bangkok, although the traffic is a [9]joke.

Gayle : Will you come again?

David : I'd love to. Anyway, I'll give you my address and phone number. If you're ever in Taiwan, [10]look me up. I'll show you around.

Gayle : I will. Cheers!

David : Cheers!

大衛和泰國女孩蓋兒在當地的酒吧見面。

大衛：抱歉，我來晚了，我找不到這個地方。

蓋兒：我以為你會放我鴿子。

大衛：沒的事，我只是對方向沒有概念。我剛從清邁回來，你不會相信我在那裡迷了多少次路。我可以請妳喝杯飲料嗎？

蓋兒：獅牌啤酒，麻煩你。

大衛：麻煩給我一杯獅牌啤酒和一杯約翰走路，加冰塊。

酒保：馬上來。你們要吃什麼嗎？

大衛：蓋兒？

蓋兒：不用了，我不餓。

大衛：那就來一碗堅果，麻煩你。

酒保：兩位請用。啤酒、威士忌和堅果。

蓋兒：那，大衛，你在這段時間還玩得愉快嗎？

大衛：愉快，一直都挺不錯的，跟台灣很不一樣。這裡每個人都很悠閒跟友善。在清邁徒步旅行很棒。我很喜歡曼谷，只不過交通令人不敢恭維。

蓋兒：你還會再來嗎？

大衛：我很願意。這樣吧，我把我的地址和電話號碼給你。假如你有機會來台灣的話，一定要來找我，我帶你去逛逛。

蓋兒：我會的。乾杯！

大衛：乾杯！

## 🚌 Words and Phrases

1. stand sb. up 放某人鴿子

2. hopeless with... 對於……沒輒

3. beer [bɪr] *n.* 啤酒

4. Johnnie Walker [ˋdʒɑnɪˋwɔkɚ] 【酒】約翰走路（蘇格蘭的威士忌品牌）

5. on the rocks 加冰塊的

6. bowl [bol] *n.* 碗

7. nut [nʌt] *n.* 堅果、核仁之類的點心

8. relaxed [rɪˋlækst] *adj.* 輕鬆自在的

9. joke [dʒok] *n.* 可笑之事

10. look sb. up 拜訪某人；看望某人

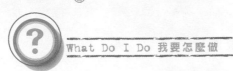

What Do I Do 我要怎麼做

CD 2-38

## Bar Time 酒吧時刻

**(1)** Bartender : ¹<u>What'll it be?</u>
You      : I'll have a beer.
酒保      ：要什麼？
你       ：我要啤酒。

---

**(2)** Bartender : That'll be two dollars.
You      : I'm going to be here for a while. Can I ²<u>run a tab</u>?
酒保      ：總共兩塊錢。
你       ：我要在這裡待一陣子。可以掛帳嗎？

---

**(3)** Bartender : I'll be with you in just a second.
You      : Thanks. There's no rush.
酒保      ：我馬上就會來招呼您。
你       ：謝謝，不急。

*Words and Phrases*

1. What'll it be? 要什麼？

2. run a tab 掛帳

Getting What You Want 解決你的需求

CD 2-39

# At the Bar 在酒吧裡

**(1) You** : I'm sorry, but this ¹margarita is too strong. I asked you to take it easy on the ²tequila.

**Bartender** : Yeah? Would you rather have a glass of milk?

你 ：對不起，這杯瑪格麗特太烈了。我告訴過你龍舌蘭加少一點。

酒保 ：是嗎？你要不要來杯牛奶算了？

**(2) You** : Do you serve food here?

**Bartender** : Nothing ³fancy. But I can fry you up a tasty cheese-burger if you want.

你 ：你這裡有吃的嗎？

酒保 ：沒有什麼太精緻的，不過假如你要的話，我可以幫你煎一份可口的起司漢堡。

**(3) You** : I'm ready to ⁴settle up.

**Bartender** : ⁵Alrighty. Your total comes to $10.75.

你 ：我準備好要結帳了。

酒保 ：好的。總共是十．七五元。

## Words and Phrases

1. margarita [ˌmɑrgəˈritə] 【酒】瑪格麗特（以龍舌蘭和檸檬汁調和而成的雞尾酒）

2. tequila [təˈkilə] *n.* 【酒】龍舌蘭（墨西哥蒸餾酒）

3. fancy [ˈfænsɪ] *adj.* 精心設計的

4. settle up　付清費用

5. alrighty [ɔlˈraɪtɪ] *adv.* 【俚】好、沒問題

209

bowl
碗

nuts
堅果

on the rocks
加冰塊的

shot glass
小玻璃酒杯

Travel Tips 旅遊撇步一起走

　　曼谷最熱門的夜生活據點之一就是帕彭路。這附近聚集了超過一百家的酒吧，還有無數的小販在混亂的夜市之中叫賣。那裡有各種食物能夠滿足各種人的口味，酒類飲料之多亦不在話下。它是西方人很喜歡去的地方，但要是你覺得不自在，那就不要去。帕彭路是曼谷的性交易中心，到處都是穿著清涼的阿哥哥舞者、吧女和人妖，而且他們都是明目張膽地做生意。

# Notes

# Marie & Celeste

### 瑪莉＆賽麗絲特

 Dialogue 對話

CD 2-40

**Marie and Celeste are with their French friend Raymond in Le Moulin Rouge.**

*Marie* : I hope this is going to be good—90 euros for a ticket!

*Celeste* : God, ¹you're such a ²whiner! Raymond paid. He's so ³sweet. He ⁴queued at the ⁵box office, he bought the best tickets in the ⁶balcony and you're still complaining.

*Marie* : I'm not complaining. I just hope it's good.

*Waiter* : Madams! Your champagne.

*Celeste* : Oh thank you. That's wonderful!

*Marie* : Thanks.

*Celeste* : I wonder where Raymond is?

*Marie* : He's down there near the ⁷orchestra, talking to a man in a red coat.

*Celeste* : Oh, what's happening? It looks like he's leaving! Give me the ⁸opera glasses!

*Marie* : No, they're mine. There's another man there now. They've ⁹grabbed Raymond and they're ¹⁰leading him away.

*Celeste* : No! What's going on?

*Strange Man* : Ladies, pardon me. You are Celeste Zhuang and Marie Chen?

*Celeste/Marie* : Yes.

*Strange Man* : I am ¹¹Inspector Delon. I'm afraid that your friend "Raymond" will be ¹²unable to join you for the ¹³show. I apologize. Enjoy your champagne!

*Celeste* : (¹⁴Shocked) Umm.

*Marie* : I always thought there was something ¹⁵fishy about that guy. He was just too nice!

瑪莉與賽麗絲特和她們的法國友人雷蒙在紅磨坊裡。

| | |
|---|---|
| 瑪莉 | ：我希望這場表演會很好看，一張票可要九十歐元呢！ |
| 賽麗絲特 | ：天哪，你還真是有夠愛抱怨！錢是雷蒙出的，他人真好。不但去售票處排隊，又買了最好的包廂座席，但妳還是在抱怨。 |
| 瑪莉 | ：我不是在抱怨，我只是希望這場表演會很好看。 |
| 服務生 | ：小姐！妳們的香檳。 |
| 賽麗絲特 | ：噢，謝謝你。真棒！ |
| 瑪莉 | ：謝謝。 |
| 賽麗絲特 | ：不知道雷蒙在哪裡？ |
| 瑪莉 | ：他就在樂隊席的旁邊，和一個穿紅外套的人講話。 |
| 賽麗絲特 | ：嗚，發生什麼事了？看起來他像是要走了！把觀劇望遠鏡給我！ |
| 瑪莉 | ：不要，望遠鏡是我的。現在那裡多了一個男的。他們抓住雷蒙，而且正在把他給帶走。 |
| 賽麗絲特 | ：不要！這是怎麼回事？ |
| 陌生男子 | ：小姐們，失禮了。你們是賽麗絲特‧莊和瑪莉‧陳嗎？ |
| 賽麗絲特 / 瑪莉 | ：是的。 |
| 陌生男子 | ：我是調查員德倫。恐怕你們的朋友「雷蒙」沒辦法和你們一起看秀了。我向你們致歉。好好享用妳們的香檳吧！ |
| 賽麗絲特 | ：（震驚狀）呃。 |
| 瑪莉 | ：我一直都覺得那傢伙有點可疑，因為他太客氣了！ |

## 🚌 Words and Phrases

1. You're such a... 你真是個……

2. whiner [`hwaɪnɚ] n. 抱怨者；懦弱者

3. sweet [swit] adj. 討人喜歡的

4. queue [kju] v. 排隊等候（由指當有繩段引導隊形的時候）

5. box office 售票亭

6. balcony [`bælkənɪ] n. （兩層劇院的）樓座；包廂

7. orchestra [`ɔrkɪstrə] n. 管弦樂團；管弦樂團之演奏席；正廳前排席

8. opera glasses 觀劇望遠鏡；劇院用的小望遠鏡

9. grab [græb] v. 抓住

10. lead sb. away 把某人帶走

11. inspector [ɪn`spɛktɚ] n. 探員

12. unable [ʌn`ebl] adj. 不能的；不會的

13. show [ʃo] n. 表演；演出

14. shocked [ʃakt] adj. 震驚的

15. fishy [`fɪʃɪ] n. 可疑的

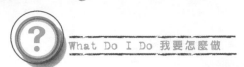

CD 2-41

# Meet the Police 與警察接觸

**(1)** Policeman : I'd like to ask you a few questions.

You　　　 : No problem, officer. Go ahead.

警察　　　：我想要問你幾個問題。

你：　　　：沒問題，警官，問吧。

---

**(2)** Policeman : You can't park here.

You　　　 : I'm sorry. I didn't see the sign. I see it now. I'm just leaving.

警察　　　：你不可以在這裡停車。

你　　　　：很抱歉，我剛剛沒看到標誌，現在才看到了。我這就走。

---

**(3)** Policeman : May I please see some 'identification?

You　　　 : I have my passport. Is that OK?

警察　　　：麻煩可以看一下你的證件嗎？

你　　　　：我有護照，可以嗎？

## Words and Phrases

1. identification [aɪˌdɛntəfəˋkeʃən] *n.* 身分證明

Getting What You Want 解決你的需求

CD 2-42

# ¹Notifying the ²Proper ³Authorities 知會有關當局

**①** You : My bag was stolen while I was on the Metro this morning.

Policeman : I'm sorry to hear that. Would you like to fill out a ⁴report?

你 ：我的袋子今早在地鐵上被偷了。

警察 ：很遺憾聽到這個消息。你要填報案單嗎？

---

**②** You : A ⁵suspicious⁶-looking man was ⁷hanging around my door last night.

Hotel Clerk : Did he have long red hair? That's just Ian, our Irish ⁸plumber.

你 ：昨晚有一個看起來很可疑的男子在我的門外徘徊。

旅館接待員 ：他是不是一頭紅色的長髮？那是伊恩，我們的愛爾蘭水電工。

---

**③** You : Where do I have to go to pay a ⁹parking ticket?

Policeman : You can just ¹⁰mail it in if you like.

你 ：違規停車罰單的錢要到哪裡去繳？

警察 ：假如你願意的話，可以就用寄的。

## 📖 Words and Phrases

1. notify [ˋnotəˏfaɪ] v. 通知；通報

2. proper [ˋprɑpɚ] adj. 正式的；合法的

3. authority [əˋθɔrətɪ] n. （常用複數）官方、當局

4. report [rɪˋport] n. 報告

5. suspicious [səˋspɪʃəs] adj. 可疑的；有蹊蹺的

6. -looking adj. 看起來……的（前頭可加任何合適的形容詞，如 nice-looking、funny-looking 等等）

7. hang around... 在……附近徘徊

8. plumber [ˋplʌmɚ] n. 鉛管工；水電工

9. parking ticket 停車罰單

10. mail sth. in 把某物郵寄到……

215

FYI 好用資訊

瑪莉從報紙上撕下的「騙子雷蒙」被逮捕的消息

## Counterfeiter Captured at Le Moulin Rouge

Paris

A man taken into custody yesterday at Le Moulin Rouge is alleged to be the ringleader of a counterfeiting operation based in Paris.

When he was captured yesterday evening the Albanian Arshi Bunjaku had in his possession passports from six different countries and more than 15,000 in counterfeit euros.

Inspector Franck Delon said that Bunjaku was using a French alias—Raymond Bellamont.

Travel Tips 旅遊撇步一起走

　　假如你在國外的時候需要警察幫忙，多數會獲得專業、殷勤的協助。但遺憾的是，有些地方的警察幾乎跟罪犯一樣麻煩。例如在墨西哥市，警察索賄的惡形惡狀可說是眾所皆知。有很多人被搶了以後都不會費事去找警察，因為他們不想再被「搶」一次。要隨時注意當地的情況，並做好適應的準備。

# Notes

# Kevin & Sarah

### 凱文＆莎拉

 Dialogue 對話

CD 2-43

**Sarah and Kevin are drinking in a typical** [1]**waterfront bar.**

*Kevin* : I love this Latin music.

*Sarah* : It's kind of dark though. It's [2]<u>hard to tell</u>, but can you see any other women in here?

*Kevin* : I hadn't really looked, but no. What do you want to drink?

*Sarah* : A margarita, please. Easy on the tequila.

*Bartender* : What can I get you?

*Kevin* : A [3]<u>Bud</u> for me and a margarita for my wife, please.

*Bartender* : You're tourists, huh?

*Kevin* : Yeah. We've been staying at the Four Seasons.

*Bartender* : We don't get many tourists in here. Excuse me a moment. "Ladies and Gentlemen, [4]<u>put your hands together</u> and give a warm welcome to Candy...Candeee!!"

*Customer* : All right! Yeah! Whooo!!

*Bartender* : Now, a Bud and a margarita, right?

*Kevin* : Uh, [5]<u>make it</u> two Buds and a margarita.

(*Two minutes later*)

*Kevin* : Here you are, one margarita!

*Sarah* : Kevin! This is a [6]<u>strip bar</u>! There is a nearly [7]<u>naked</u> woman dancing on the [8]<u>stage</u> over there!

*Kevin* : I really had no idea. Just let me finish my drink and we can go.

*Sarah* : Two beers?

*Kevin* : The bartender made a mistake. I didn't want to hurt his [9]<u>feel-ings</u>!

莎拉與凱文到了一家典型的濱水酒吧裡喝酒。

凱文：我愛死這種拉丁音樂了。

莎拉：但這裡有點暗。雖然看不清楚，不過你有沒有看到有其他的女生？

凱文：我沒認真看，但應該沒有。妳想喝什麼？

莎拉：麻煩給我一杯瑪格麗特，龍舌蘭加少一點。

酒保：兩位要喝什麼？

凱文：麻煩給我一杯百威，給我太太一杯瑪格麗特。

酒保：你們是觀光客吧？

凱文：是啊，我們住在四季大飯店。

酒保：到我們這裡來的觀光客不多。失陪一下。「各位女士先生，請以熱烈的掌聲
　　　歡迎康蒂……康蒂── ！

客人：好呀！耶！哇！

酒保：好了，一杯百威和一杯瑪格麗特，對嗎？

凱文：呃，改成兩杯百威和一杯瑪格麗特。

（兩分鐘後）

凱文：來，這是妳的，一杯瑪格麗特！

莎拉：凱文！這是個脫衣酒吧！那裡的舞台上有一個幾近全裸的女人在跳舞！

凱文：我真的不知道。讓我把酒給喝完，然後我們就可以走了。

莎拉：兩杯啤酒？

凱文：酒保弄錯了，但我不想傷他的心！

## 🚌 Words and Phrases

1. waterfront [`wɔtɚ͵frʌnt] *adj.* 靠碼頭
的；靠海岸的；濱水區的

2. hard to tell　很難講

3. Bud [bʌd] *n.* 百威（Budweiser 或是
Bud Light 的簡稱；美國的暢銷啤酒
品牌）

4. put your hands together　拍手

5. make it...　使（它）成為某種狀態

6. strip bar [`strɪp͵bɑr]　脫衣酒吧

7. naked [`nekɪd] *adj.* 赤裸的

8. stage [stedʒ] *n.* 舞台

9. feeling [`filɪŋ] *n.* 感情；感受

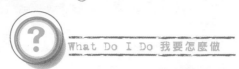

What Do I Do 我要怎麼做

 CD 2-44

# ¹<u>Awkward</u> ²<u>Red Light</u> Moments 棘手的危險時刻

**①** Bambi : Would you like a ³<u>private dance</u>? You won't be disappointed.

You : Not just now, thank you. I'm just having a drink.

班比 ：要不要來一段私舞？你不會失望的。

你 ：現在不用，謝謝。我只是來喝一杯。

**②** ⁴<u>Street Hustler</u> : Hey, honey, you feel like some ⁵<u>company</u> tonight?

You : No, no thank you. I've already got plans.

流鶯 ：嘿，甜心，今天晚上想找個人陪嗎？

你 ：不，不用了，謝謝，我有別的事。

**③** Dancer : Can I do something special for you?

You : You're already very special. Just ⁶<u>keep up</u> the good work.

舞者 ：我可以給你來段特別的嗎？

你 ：妳已經很特別了，只要繼續維持這種好的表現就可以了。

## Words and Phrases

1. awkward [`ɔkwɚd] *adj.* 尷尬的；棘手的

2. red light 紅燈（red-light district 爲紅燈區或風化區之意）

3. private dance 私舞（指脫衣舞孃不在台上，而是在你付錢之後到你面前爲你而跳的一段舞，但通常有規定只准欣賞而不准碰觸）

4. street hustler [`strit͵hʌsḷɚ] 流鶯；阻街女郎

5. company [`kʌmpənɪ] *n.* 伴；作伴

6. keep up *v.* 保持；維持

Getting What You Want 解決你的需求

CD 2-45

# Where Am I? 這是哪裡？

**(1)** You　　　: Wait a second, is this a [gay] bar?

Bartender : Yes, it is.

你　　　：等等，這是同志酒吧嗎？

酒保　　：是的，沒錯。

---

**(2)** You　　　: You said you were taking me to a nice place. This place looks dangerous.

Taxi Driver : [Looks] are [deceiving]! Go inside! You will be happy!

你　　　：你說過你要帶我去一個好地方的。這個地方看起來挺危險的。

計程車司機：外表會騙人！進去吧！你會很開心的！

---

**(3)** You　　　: Excuse me, I'm a little lost. Can you tell me where the exit is?

Guard　 : You're in B3. You need to take the elevator up to the [ground floor].

你　　　：對不起，我有點迷路了。你能告訴我出口在哪裡嗎？

警衛　　：這裡是 B3。你得搭電梯到大廳。

## Words and Phrases

1. gay [ge] *n.* 常指男同性戀者（lesbian 則為女同性戀）

2. look [lʊk] *n.* 外表（常用複數）

3. deceiving [dɪˋsivɪŋ] *adj.* 騙人的

4. ground floor 一樓（有接待處的樓層）

221

FYI 好用資訊

**opera glasses**
觀劇望眼鏡

**box office**
售票亭

**flier**
廣告傳單

**brochure**
小冊子

Travel Tips 旅遊撇步一起走

　　旅遊時冒冒險很有趣，但探險及找樂子的衝動也會使某些遊客渾然忘我而魯莽行事。在台北或馬德里，無論是白天或夜晚，你隨時都可以放心地到處走走。但要是在邁阿密或里約熱內盧，你就不能這麼做了。這些城市裡有些地區相當危險。當個精明的遊客，養成打聽這類事情的習慣，而不要冒不必要的險。

# CHAPTER '13

# GOING HOME

回程

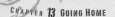

# David
## 大衛

**David arrives at the airport expecting to get on the 11:00 a.m. flight.**

*David* : Good morning, here's my return ticket.

*Check-In* : Good morning. Taipei, right?

*David* : Yes. Can you put me in No Smoking, please?

*Check-In* : Certainly. Er, I'm sorry sir, but we seem to have a bit of a problem.

*David* : Really? I confirmed my flight 3 days ago. There was no ¹mention of any problems then.

*Check-In* : I don't know how it happened, but we seem to have ²overbooked this flight. I'm terribly sorry, but I can't let you check in.

*David* : ³You're kidding me, right? Can you get me on the next flight?

*Check-In* : I'll see what I can do. Yes, yes, there is a flight tonight at 7:00. I've ⁴upgraded you to ⁵business class and I can give you US$50 in meal ⁶vouchers for your lunch and dinner in the airport. I'm really very sorry.

*David* : ⁷Never mind. These things happen. At least I'll get to fly business class. I'll come back later.

大衛到達機場，預計搭乘早上十一點的飛機。

大衛 ：早。這是我的回程票。

登機手續辦理處：早。台北，對嗎？

大衛 ：對。可不可以麻煩你幫我劃在禁菸區？

登機手續辦理處：當然可以。呃，先生，抱歉，似乎出了一點狀況。

大衛 ：真的嗎？我在三天前就已經確認班機了，當時沒說有任何問題呀。

登機手續辦理處：我不知道怎麼會這樣，可是這班飛機我們似乎接受了過多的訂位。
我深感抱歉，可是我沒辦法讓你辦理登機。

大衛 ：你在跟我開玩笑吧？能讓我搭下一班飛機嗎？

登機手續辦理處：我看看有沒有辦法。有，有，今晚七點有一班飛機。我已幫你升等
到商務艙，而且我可以給你五十美元的餐券，以便你在機場吃中餐
和晚餐。我真的很抱歉。

大衛 ：算了，這種事的確會發生。至少我有商務艙可以搭。我待會再回來。

## Words and Phrases

1. mention [`mɛnʃən] *n.* 說到；提及

2. overbook [ˌovɚ`buk] *v.* 接受過多的訂位

3. You're kidding me. 你在開我玩笑。

4. upgrade [`ʌpgred] *v.* 升級；升等

5. business class 商務艙

6. voucher [`vautʃɚ] *n.* 現金替用券；優待券

7. Never mind. 算了。

225

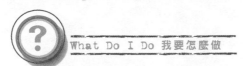

What Do I Do 我要怎麼做

CD 2-47

## Plane Pain 搭機的苦惱

**1** Flight Attendant : I'm sorry, but we've overbooked this flight. Would anybody be willing to ¹give up their seat in exchange for a free ²round-trip ticket?

You : Hey! I'll take that deal!

空服員 ：對不起，我們這班飛機超劃座位了。有沒有人願意以讓位來交換免費的來回機票？

你 ：嘿，這好康我要！

---

**2** Clerk : The flight has been ³delayed.

You : Do you have any idea when it will leave?

櫃台人員 ：飛機誤點了。

你 ：你們知道什麼時候可以起飛嗎？

---

**3** Clerk : I'm sorry, but that flight has been canceled ⁴due to ⁵weather conditions.

You : Is the airline providing hotel vouchers?

櫃台人員 ：抱歉，這班飛機因為天候狀況而被取消了。

你 ：航空公司有提供旅館住宿券嗎？

## Words and Phrases

1. give up 放棄

2. round-trip ticket *n.* 來回機票

3. delay [dɪ`le] *v.* 延遲；延誤

4. due to ... 由於

5. weather [`wɛðɚ] *n.* 天氣

Getting What You Want 解決你的需求

 CD 2-48

# This Seat ¹Stinks 這個位子爛透了

**(1) You** : If there are any extra seats in business class, I wouldn't mind sitting up there.

**Flight Attendant** : I'm sorry, sir. Your ticket is for ²cabin class.

你 ：假如商務艙有多出的位子的話，我不介意坐到那裡去。

服務員 ：抱歉，先生，您的票是經濟艙的。

---

**(2) You** : I ³noticed there is an empty seat up by the ⁴bulkhead. Could I move there?

**Flight Attendant** : Let me check to make sure the seat is not ⁵occupied.

你 ：我注意到隔板旁有一個空位。我能換到那裡去嗎？

服務員 ：讓我查一下以確認那個位子沒有人坐。

---

**(3) You** : I'm not ⁶comfortable sitting right next to the bathroom door. Is another seat available?

**Flight Attendant** : Just a moment. I'll check.

你 ：緊鄰廁所門的位子坐我覺得不舒服，還有別的空位嗎？

服務員 ：稍等一下，我查查看。

## Words and Phrases

1. stink [stɪŋk] *v.* 發臭；糟透

2. cabin class 經濟艙

3. notice [`notɪs] *v.* 注意到

4. bulkhead [`bʌlkˌhɛd] *n.* 隔離壁（經濟艙機門旁的首排座位，空間較大，常

預留給行動不便或是帶有嬰兒的旅客乘坐）

5. occupied [`ɑkjəˌpaɪd] *adj.* 佔用的

6. comfortable [`kʌmfɚtəbl] *adj.* 舒適的；愜意的

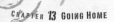

FYI 好用資訊

### 曼谷國際機場機場稅的說明

Bangkok Airport's Departure Tax—the Passenger Service Charge (PSC) is paid at counters and automatic vending machines. All passengers—international and domestic have to pay.

The Passenger Service Charge is 500 baht for international passengers, 50 baht for domestic departures.

The PSC can also be paid in US dollars (USD$11) at the PSC counter.

Travel Tips 旅遊撇步一起走

在搭飛機旅行時,不妨把隨時會用到的東西盡量塞在隨身提袋裡,以防萬一自己跟其他的行李被分隔兩地。如此一來,縱使你的袋子不見了或是錯過轉接班機,你還有必需品可以用,而且可以在比較輕鬆、沒有太大壓力的情況下,因應計畫的改變。

## Notes

# Marie & Celeste

瑪莉 & 賽麗絲特

 Dialogue 對話

CD 2-49

**Celeste is trying to change the date of her flight because she's upset about what happened with Raymond.**

Marie : Come on, Celeste. It's not like you were planning to marry the guy!

Celeste : I know, but that doesn't mean that I want to [1]find out he's a [2]con man who [3]makes his living [4]cheating and [5]robbing tourists!

Marie : I understand that you're upset, but do we really need to head for home early?

Celeste : You stay if you want to, but I don't [6]feel up to it.

Voice : Hello, China Airlines, may I help you?

Celeste : Hi, my name's Celeste Zhuang. I'm booked on the flight back to Taipei from Paris on the 22nd. I wonder if I could move my booking to tomorrow, the 20th.

Voice : Let me check the computer. No, I'm sorry, the 20th is fully booked, as is the 21st. If it's an [7]emergency I could put you on the [8]standby list.

Celeste : Standby? Oh, no thanks. That's too [9]risky. Can I just confirm my booking for the 22nd then?

Voice : Certainly. Are you traveling alone?

Celeste : No, I'd also like to confirm the booking of Marie Chen. Thanks.

Marie : So [10]now what? Are you going to stay in and [11]sulk?

Celeste : No. We're on vacation. Let's go and do some [12]comfort shopping.

賽麗絲特想更改搭機的日期，因為她對於雷蒙的事感到很煩亂。

瑪莉　　：別這樣嘛，賽麗絲特。妳又不是打算要嫁給那個傢伙！

賽麗絲特：我知道，可是那並不表示我就想知道他其實是個靠欺騙與搶劫觀光客維生的騙子！

瑪莉　　：我知道妳很氣，可是我們真的需要提早返家嗎？

賽麗絲特：假如你要留下就留下，我可不想。

人聲　　：哈囉，中華航空，可以為您服務嗎？

賽麗絲特：嗨，我的名字是賽麗絲特・莊，我預訂了二十二號從巴黎回台北的班機。不知道能不能把我的預訂改成明天，也就是二十號。

人聲　　：讓我查查電腦。抱歉，不行，二十號的預訂已經全都滿了，二十一號也一樣。假如是緊急情況的話，我可以幫您排在候補名單上。

賽麗絲特：候補？噢，不用了，謝謝，那樣太冒險了。這樣的話，我可以就確認一下我二十二號的預約嗎？

人聲　　：當然可以。您是一個人搭機嗎？

賽麗絲特：不是，我還要確認一下瑪莉・陳的訂位，謝謝。

瑪莉　　：那現在要怎麼辦？你要待在旅館裡生悶氣嗎？

賽麗絲特：不，我們可是在度假。我們出去血拚發洩一下。

## Words and Phrases

1. find out 發現；得知

2. con man [`kɑn͵mæn] 騙子；賺取不義之財的人

3. make sb.'s living 謀生

4. cheat [tʃit] v. 欺騙

5. rob [rɑb] v. 搶劫

6. feel up to sth. 想要（做）某事

7. emergency [ɪ`mɝdʒənsɪ] n. 緊急情況

8. standby list 候補名單

9. risky [`rɪskɪ] adj. 有風險的；沒把握的

10. Now what? 現在要怎樣？

11. sulk [sʌlk] v. 慍怒；悶悶不樂

12. comfort shopping 用以作為慰藉的購物

What Do I Do 我要怎麼做

CD 2-50

# Let's Get Out of Here 咱們離開這裡吧

**(1)** Clerk　：I'm sorry, Miss. Your ticket is for tomorrow.

　You　　：I know, but I really need to fly today. Isn't it possible to change the ticket?

　櫃台人員：抱歉，小姐，您的票是明天的。

　你　　　：我知道，可是我真的得在今天飛。難道沒有可能換票嗎？

---

**(2)** Clerk　：There are no seats on the four o'clock flight, but there is one available on flight 831, leaving in fifteen minutes.

　You　　：That's great! I'll take it. Do I have time to make it to the gate?

　櫃台人員：四點的飛機沒有位子了，不過八三一班次還有一個空位，它在十五分鐘之後起飛。

　你　　　：那太好了！我要坐。我還有時間趕到登機門嗎？

---

**(3)** Clerk　：I'm very sorry, Miss, but your flight has been canceled due to the ¹severe weather conditions. Weather ²permitting, it'll leave tomorrow.

　You　　：OK. Is the airline offering hotel vouchers?

　櫃台人員：我很抱歉，小姐，您的班機因為天候狀況惡劣而被取消了。只要天候允許，明天就會起飛。

　你　　　：好吧。航空公司有提供旅館住宿券嗎？

## Words and Phrases

1. severe [sə`vɪr] *adj.* 嚴重的；嚴峻的

2. permit [pə`mɪt] *v.* 允許；准許；許可

Getting What You Want 解決你的需求

CD 2-51

# Change of Plans 變更計畫

**1** You : I've decided to stay in Paris a while longer. Is there any chance I could get a ¹<u>refund</u> on my ticket?

Travel Agent : No, I'm sorry. But for another $100, I can change the ticket to another, later date.

你 ：我決定要在巴黎待久一點。有沒有可能退掉我的機票？

旅遊業者 ：不行，很抱歉。但是加上一百塊，我可以幫你改成另外一個比較晚的日期。

**2** You : I just noticed that my flight to Taipei has a long ²<u>layover</u> in Bangkok. Are there any ³<u>direct flights</u>?

Travel Agent : No, there aren't. But I might be able to book you on a flight that goes through Tokyo if you'd like.

你 ：我剛剛才注意到我那班飛往台北的班機在曼谷會作很久的停留。有直飛的班機嗎？

旅遊業者 ：沒有，並沒有。不過假如你願意的話，我倒是可以幫你改訂途經東京的班機。

**3** You : My flight was canceled and I'd like to stay another night. Will that be OK?

Hotel Clerk : Absolutely, Miss. We're happy to have you.

你 ：我的班機被取消了，我想多待一個晚上。這樣可以嗎？

旅館接待 ：當然可以，小姐。我們很高興您能留下。

📖 *Words and Phrases*

1. refund [`ri͵fʌnd] *n.* 償還金額

2. layover [`le͵ovɚ] *n.* 中途停留

3. direct flight 直飛；直航

FYI 好用資訊

**itinerary**
行程表

**travel agency**
旅行社

**airbus**
空中巴士（短程噴射機）

**flight information monitor**
班機時刻表

Travel Tips 旅遊撇步一起走

　　經驗老道的旅客都知道，延宕、天候以及其他種種可能會讓人不愉快的突發狀況在所難免。他們都知道該如何輕鬆面對，不要讓這些問題掃了自己的興。有時候，意料之外的改道或中途停下來反而會變成旅程中最值得回味與珍惜的部分。你可以把原訂計畫泡湯視為測試本身應變能力的機會，並欣然接受這段原本會令你不愉快的意外之旅。

# Notes

# Kevin & Sarah

### 凱文 & 莎拉

Dialogue 對話

CD 2-52

**Sarah and Kevin are checking out of their hotel.**

*Sarah* : Did you look around carefully? Don't forget your camera this time.

*Kevin* : I've got it right here, next to my [1]signed photo of Candy!

*Sarah* : Very [2]amusing. Pay the bill, funny guy!

*Kevin* : Hi, we're checking out. Can we [3]settle the bill? Room 1209.

*Clerk* : Yes, wait a second, room 1209. That's US$1217.

*Sarah* : How much?!

*Clerk* : US$1217, madam. If you wait a moment the computer will print out an [4]itemized bill for you.

*Kevin* : OK, thanks. Let me see. Eight nights at US$95 per night; three massages at US$45 each; four lunches and six dinners.; US$175 at the bar. OK, that seems right. Here you go.

*Clerk* : Thank you. US$1300 in traveler's checks. Here's your US$83 change. Would you like me to [5]call you a cab?

*Sarah* : Please. To the airport. Our flight doesn't leave until lunchtime, but we'd like to get there early and check in our stuff.

*Kevin* : Then we can wait forever for our luggage in Taipei!

編按：「US$」的發音可唸為「US dollars」或是「dollars US」，金額數字可放前面也可放後面，但不可放 US 與 dollars 之間。

莎拉與凱文在辦理退房。

莎拉　　：你到處都仔細地看過了嗎？這次可別把你的相機給忘了。

凱文　　：它就在這兒呢，放在康蒂的簽名照旁邊！

莎拉　　：很逗趣。付帳吧，愛耍寶的傢伙！

凱文　　：嗨，我們要退房。可以結帳了嗎？一二○九號房。

櫃台人員：可以，請稍等。一二○九號房一共是一千二百一十七美元。

莎拉　　：多少錢？！

櫃台人員：小姐，是一千二百一十七美元。若兩位稍等一下，電腦會幫你們把帳單明細列印出來。

凱文　　：好的，謝謝。我看看。八個晚上，每晚九十五美元；三次按摩，每次四十五美元；四頓中餐加六頓晚餐；在酒吧裡花了一百七十五美元。好，看來沒錯。錢在這兒。

櫃台人員：謝謝您。收您一千三百美元旅行支票，找您八十三美元。兩位需要我幫你們叫計程車嗎？

莎拉　　：麻煩你，到機場。我們的飛機要到午餐時間才會起飛，不過我們想早點到那裡登記托運我們的東西。

凱文　　：然後我們就可以在台北等行李等一輩子！

## 🚌 Words and Phrases

1. signed [saɪnd] *adj.* 簽過名的

2. amusing [ə`mjuzɪŋ] *adj.* 有趣的；逗趣的

3. settle [`sɛtl] *v.* 結帳

4. itemize [`aɪtəm͵aɪz] *v.* 列出條目

5. call sb. a cab 替某人叫計程車

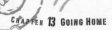

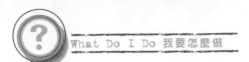

**What Do I Do** 我要怎麼做

CD 2-53

# Departure 出境

**① Clerk** : You're ¹<u>running</u> a little <u>late</u>, sir. ²<u>Passengers</u> are already ³<u>boarding</u>.

**You** : I know. I'll hurry. Don't let them leave without me!

**辦事員** : 你來晚了一點，先生。乘客都已經在登機了。

**你** : 我知道，我會儘快。別讓他們丟下我離開！

---

**② Travel Agent** : For international flights, we recommend that you arrive at the airport two hours early.

**You** : Okay. That seems like a lot of extra time, but I guess it's good to ⁴<u>play it safe</u>.

**旅遊業者** : 坐國際班機，我們建議您提早兩個小時到機場。

**你** : 好。看起來時間還很充裕，不過我想還是謹慎為妙。

---

**③ Clerk** : I'm sorry, sir. Boarding has ended for flight 7779. Would you like me to book you on another flight?

**You** : Yes, please. I'd appreciate that.

**櫃台人員** : 抱歉，先生，七七七九號班機已經截止登機。您要不要我幫您訂另一班飛機？

**你** : 好，麻煩你，謝謝。

*Words and Phrases*

1. running late 來遲了；來晚了

2. passenger [`pæsn̩dʒɚ] *n.* 乘客

3. board [bord] *v.* 登機

4. play it safe 小心行事；不冒險

Getting What You Want 解決你的需求

 CD 2-54

# Disputing a Bill 質疑帳單

**① You** : This is not right. I never ordered champagne from room service.

**Clerk** : Are you sure? Perhaps you had a little too much and forgot.

你 ：這不對。我根本沒叫過客房服務的香檳。

櫃台人員：你確定嗎？也許你稍微喝多了些，所以忘了。

---

**② You** : What's this? How can you charge so much for local phone calls?

**Clerk** : I'm sorry, sir. That's standard.

你 ：這是怎麼回事？你們的市內電話怎麼會這麼貴？

櫃台人員： 抱歉，先生，那是公定價。

---

**③ You** : Would you please add this up, please? It seems too expensive.

**Clerk** : Certainly. Perhaps there is some mistake.

你 ：可以麻煩你再把總數加一加嗎？似乎太貴了。

櫃台人員：沒問題，也許是哪裡算錯了。

## Words and Phrases

1. dispute [dɪsˋpjut] *v.* 爭論；對（結果等）懷疑

2. room service 客房服務

3. standard [ˋstændəd] *adj.* 標準的

4. add sth. up 計算某項帳目的總數

FYI 好用資訊

對於健康與運動愈來愈重視的美國人，就連在機場裡面也都設有健身中心提供等機的人消磨時間。這些健身中心多為旅館所提供，有時設置在機場外圍的附近，搭乘交通工具之後才能到達；有時則是在機場中的登機門附近就有設置。邁阿密國際機場的健身中心就是設置在機場當中，開放時間為上午六點到晚上十點，收費為八美元，得以使用一整天。

查詢全美與加拿大機場健身中心的網址為：

http://www.airportgyms.com/gyms/index.html

Travel Tips 旅遊撇步一起走

在許多地方，旅客可以在機場外的路邊，也就是說還沒進機場就先托運。假如可以的話，你一定要把握這樣的機會。如此一來，就不必在機場裡面的櫃台排隊排很久了。

# CHAPTER '14

# LOOKING BACK

和親友分享

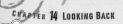

# David

## 大衛

 Dialogue 對話

CD 2-55

**David is out with his girlfriend talking about his trip.**

David : I bought you a couple of things while I was there — this bag and some of that ¹cotton ²print material you like.

Miss Liao : Wow, thanks. It looks like a Gucci bag.

David : It looks like one, but it's a knock-off. It wasn't expensive.

Miss Liao : It's still very good ³quality. I can't believe that you chose it your-self.

David : Actually, somebody did give me a few tips on bargaining.

Miss Liao : A girl?

David : Umm, yes. I ⁴ran into her in one of the markets while I was shop-ping.

Miss Liao : Not in a bar?

David : No. She was very nice. She wanted to practice her English and we went out for drinks on my last night. She helped me a lot.

Miss Liao : Really.

David : Yes, really. She was a nice person and I ⁵imagine I'll never see her again. Open the other package and look at the material.

Miss Liao : I'm sorry. I shouldn't have spoken like that. The gifts are lovely. Oh! Your phone?

David : Hi. Yes, this is David Wang. Who? Gayle! Hi! What? Next month? Yes, of course, no problem. Yes, bye. ⁶Uh oh!

大衛和他的女友出去，他們在討論他此次的旅遊。

大衛　：我在那裡的時候幫妳買了幾樣東西——這個包包，還有一些妳喜歡的棉質
　　　　印花布料。

廖小姐：哇，謝謝。它看起來像是古馳的包包。

大衛　：看起來像，但它其實是仿製品，並不貴。

廖小姐：但是質感還是很好。我真不敢相信是你自己選的。

大衛　：事實上的確有人教了我幾個討價還價的撇步。

廖小姐：女孩子？

大衛　：嗯，是的。我在買東西時，在其中一個市場碰到她。

廖小姐：不是在酒吧？

大衛　：不是。她人很好。她想練習英文，我們在我要走的前一天晚上出去喝了幾
　　　　杯。

廖小姐：是哦。

大衛　：是啊，真的。她人很好，我想我再也不會見到她了。打開其他的袋子，看
　　　　看布料吧。

廖小姐：對不起，我不應該那麼說的。這些禮物真可愛。喔！你的電話？

大衛　：嗨，我是王大衛。誰？蓋兒？嗨！什麼？下個月？好，當然，沒問題。
　　　　好，再見。完蛋了！

## 🚌 Words and Phrases

1. cotton [`katn̩] *n.* 棉質物

2. print [prɪnt] *n.* 印花

3. quality [`kwɑlətɪ] *n.* 品質；質感

4. run into sb. 碰上某人

5. imagine [ɪ`mædʒɪn] *v.* 想像

6. Uh oh! 完蛋了！

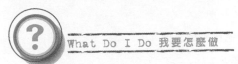

What Do I Do 我要怎麼做

CD 2-56

# Glad to Be Back 很高興回來

**①** Friend : Are you happy to be home?

You　: I guess so. I'm a little sad that my trip had to end. I had a great time.

朋友　：你回家了，高不高興？

你　　：我想是吧。我有點難過旅程非結束不可，不過我玩得很開心。

---

**②** Friend : Did you do a lot of ¹touristy stuff?

You　: Some. Mostly I just wandered about, meeting people, eating, looking, having a good time.

朋友　：你做了很多觀光客都喜歡做的事嗎？

你　　：做了一些。我大部分的時候只是在閒逛、認識人、吃東西、東看西看、開開心心的。

---

**③** Friend : Do you think you'll go back?

You　: As soon as possible. I loved it over there.

朋友　：你覺得你會再回去嗎？

你　　：愈快愈好。我喜歡那裡。

*Words and Phrases*

1. **touristy** [ˋturəstɪ] *adj.* 遊客喜歡的、常做的

CD 2-57

# Sharing Your Trip 分享你的旅遊經歷

**1** You : Do you want to hear a crazy story?

Friend : Sure. Is this something else that happened to you in Bangkok?

你 ：想不想聽個瘋狂的故事？

朋友 ：好啊。是你在曼谷發生的另外一件事嗎？

**2** You : I've got a lot of pictures of my trip if you'd like to see them sometime.

Friend : I'd love to.

你 ：假如你想看的話，我在旅途中拍了很多照片。

朋友 ：好啊。

**3** You : I brought some things home from my trip. Would you like to see them?

Friend : Sure. What did you bring?

你 ：我在途中帶了一些東西回來。要不要哪一天看一看？

朋友 ：當然要。你帶了什麼？

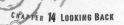

FYI 好用資訊

在外旅遊一定會遇上許多有趣,並令你大開眼界的人或事。在這個網站上有許多的同好在此發表自己的旅遊照片與遊記,邀請你一同分享他們的經驗與見聞:

**http://www.travelblog.org**

Travel Tips 旅遊撇步一起走

旅行似乎能把時間拉長。你可能只去了一個星期,感覺上卻像是經歷了一個月。有時候在一段愉快的旅行後,回到家反而會產生強烈的失落感。在經歷過許許多多的冒險後,家居生活自然顯得既緩慢又無聊。盡量和你在旅行時所交到的新朋友保持聯絡,也可以注意一下你去過的地方發生了什麼事。多做這類的事可以幫助你輕鬆回到原來的生活軌道。當然,你更可以隨時開始規劃下一次的旅遊。

# Notes

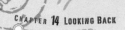

# Marie & Celeste

瑪莉 & 賽麗絲特

 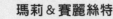

CD 2-58

**Marie and Celeste are discussing their trip with colleagues in the office.**

| | |
|---|---|
| *Marie* | : And this handsome guy is the ¹criminal ²mastermind that Celeste fell in love with! |
| *Celeste* | : God Marie, I thought we weren't going to mention that! |
| *Marie* | : It just ³slipped out, sorry. |
| *Colleague 1* | : Was he really a criminal or are you just ⁴leading us on? |
| *Marie* | : You see this photo — that's the Moulin Rouge by the way — well, if you look carefully at the ⁵bottom left, you can see Raymond being ⁶arrested by the police! |
| *Celeste* | : Oh, please, enough. It's not funny. Here, look everyone! We bought Body Shop stuff for all of you! |
| *Colleagues 1, 2 & 3* | : Thanks. That's perfect! |
| *Celeste* | : Check out these photos of Versailles. Fantastic, isn't it? |
| *Colleague 2* | : Who is this ⁷creepy old guy? |
| *Marie* | : Ah, that's Monsieur Roncart. We rented scooters from him. He thought he was rather ⁸charming. |
| *Celeste* | : We thought he was a ⁹dirty old man! But he did give us a discount. |
| *Marie* | : (*Imitating M Roncart*) "Ah, for such beautiful young girls I can always make it a little cheaper." |
| *Celeste* | : Yeah, looking back, except for the Raymond thing, it was a pretty good trip. |
| *Marie* | : ¹⁰Hear! Hear! |

瑪莉與賽麗絲特在辦公室和同事們討論她們的旅遊經歷。

| | |
|---|---|
| 瑪莉 | ：而這個帥哥就是賽麗絲特愛上的那個犯罪首腦！ |
| 賽麗絲特 | ：天哪，瑪莉，我以為不會再談那件事了！ |
| 瑪莉 | ：不小心就脫口而出，抱歉。 |
| 同事甲 | ：他真的是罪犯，還是妳們在唬弄我們？ |
| 瑪莉 | ：你看這張照片——順帶一提，那是紅磨坊——嗯，只要妳仔細看左下角，你們就可以看到雷蒙正被警方逮捕！ |
| 賽麗絲特 | ：哦，拜託，夠了，這並不有趣。嘿，大家看！我們買了美體小舖的東西給大家！ |
| 同事甲、乙、丙 | ：謝謝，太棒了。 |
| 賽麗絲特 | ：看看這些凡爾賽宮的照片，很棒，不是嗎？ |
| 同事乙 | ：這個令人起雞皮疙瘩的老傢伙是誰？ |
| 瑪莉 | ：啊，那是朗卡特先生，我們的機車就是跟他租的。他還覺得自己挺有魅力的。 |
| 賽麗絲特 | ：我們覺得他是個老不修！不過他的確有給我們打折。 |
| 瑪莉 | ：（模仿朗卡特先生）「啊，為了這麼漂亮的年輕女孩，我總是可以再算便宜一點的。」 |
| 賽麗絲特 | ：是啊，回想起來，除了雷蒙事件以外，這趟旅遊真是相當不錯。 |
| 瑪莉 | ：的確如此！ |

## Words and Phrases

1. criminal [`krɪmən!] adj. 罪犯的
2. mastermind [`mæstɚ,maɪnd] n. 主謀；幕後操縱者
3. slip out 脫口說出
4. lead sb. on 哄騙
5. bottom left 左下方
6. arrest [ə`rɛst] v. 逮捕
7. creepy [`kripɪ] adj. 令人毛骨悚然的
8. charming [`tʃɑrmɪŋ] adj. 迷人的
9. dirty old man 老不修
10 Hear! Hear! 說得好！

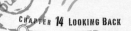

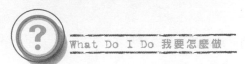
What Do I Do 我要怎麼做

CD 2-59

# How Was Your Trip? 你這趟旅行怎麼樣？

**(1)** Friend : How was the food?

You　 : I thought it was delicious.

朋友　：吃的東西怎麼樣？

你　　：我認為很好吃。

---

**(2)** Friend : Were the people you met friendly?

You　 : For the most part, yes. I ran into just a couple ¹unpleasant ²types.

朋友　：你遇到的人友善嗎？

你　　：大致上來說是的。我只碰到了幾個討厭的傢伙。

---

**(3)** Friend : Were you able to ³get by without speaking much French?

You　 : Actually, my French improved a lot while I was in Paris. But many people do understand English too.

朋友　：你不會說多少法文，有辦法應付嗎？

你　　：事實上，我在巴黎的時候，法文進步了不少。不過其實還是有很多人聽得懂英文。

## Words and Phrases

1. unpleasant [ʌnˋplɛzn̩t] *adj.* 令人不愉快的

2. type [taɪp] *n.* 類型；……類的人

3. get by　過得去；勉強對付過去

Getting What You Want 解決你的需求

CD 2-60

# **Getting Your Pictures** [1]**Developed** 沖洗照片

**(1)** You : I'd like a [2]double set of [3]three-by-five [4]prints.

Clerk: No problem. Come back in an hour.

你　　：我要洗兩份三乘五的照片。

店員　：沒問題。一個小時之後來拿。

---

**(2)** You : How much would an [5]eight-by-ten [6]enlargement of this one cost?

Clerk: That would be $12.95.

你　　：把這張放大成八乘十要多少錢？

店員　：要十二‧九五元。

---

**(3)** You : I had a lot of trouble with my [7]flash. If there's anything you can do to save these pictures, I'd really appreciate it.

Clerk: I'll see what I can do.

你　　：我的閃光燈老是出狀況。假如你能有辦法挽救這些照片的話，我會感激不盡。

店員　：我看看有什麼我能做的。

📖*Words and Phrases*

1. develop [dɪˋvɛləp] *v.* （底片）顯影；（照片）沖洗

2. double set 兩組

3. three-by-five 三×五吋

4. print [prɪnt] *n.* （由底片洗出的）照片

5. eight-by-ten 八×十吋

6. enlargement [ɪnˋlɑrdʒmənt] *n.* 放大

7. flash [flæʃ] *n.* 閃光燈

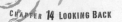

FYI 好用資訊

**photo frame**
相框

**negative**
負片

**film**
底片

**disposable camera**
即可拍相機

Travel Tips 旅遊撇步一起走

　　旅遊有一個奇特的現象，最糟的旅遊有時候反而是最棒的旅遊。困難與麻煩最容易被人們記住。旅遊者常發現自己會興致勃勃地一再講述「糟糕旅遊」的故事。公車陷入泥沼的時刻會成為珍貴的回憶，而躺在海灘上的浪漫時刻卻會逐漸淡去以致被人遺忘。

# Notes

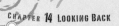

# Kevin & Sarah

## 凱文＆莎拉

Dialogue 對話

CD 2-61

**Sarah and Kevin are showing photos of their trip to Kevin's mother.**

*Kevin* : See! Look at the size of the teeth on that one! [1]<u>If it hadn't been for the</u> tree it would have bitten my leg off!

*Sarah* : Kevin was doing his Dr. Doolittle "talk to the animals" [2]<u>impression</u>. The tour guide [3]<u>went crazy</u>.

*Kevin's Mom* : Now that you're married, aren't you [4]<u>a little old for</u> stupid [5]<u>stunts</u> like that?

*Kevin* : Come on, Mom! I was [6]<u>running on</u> [7]<u>pure</u> adrenaline. You should have seen Sarah's face! It took about eleven flavors of ice cream just to calm her down.

*Sarah* : Very funny. At least I didn't [8]<u>run up</u> a US$175 bar bill!

*Kevin* : Mom, open the package.

*Kevin's Mom* : A T-shirt. "I survived the alligator ranch." Thanks. It's just what I wanted.

*Sarah* : It was Kevin's idea. I wanted to get you some perfume. Don't worry though, we've got about eight boxes of clothes and other stuff coming by surface mail.

*Kevin* : Come on, Mom, check out the rest of the photos.

*Kevin's Mom* : "The Naked Parrot [9]<u>Lounge</u>." What an interesting name for a bar!

*Sarah* : Yes, I [10]<u>practically</u> had to [11]<u>drag</u> Kevin out of there!

*Kevin* : Sarah!!

莎拉與凱文把他們的旅遊照片拿給凱文的母親看。

凱文　　：瞧！您看那隻的牙齒有多大！假如不是那棵樹的話，我的腿早就被咬斷了！

莎拉　　：當時凱文在模仿怪醫杜立德「和動物說話」的本事。導遊簡直要抓狂了。

凱文的媽：你都已經結婚了，你不覺得做這種沒大腦的特技表演有點幼稚嗎？

凱文　　：哎呀，媽！當時我是完全靠腎上腺素在支撐的。您應該看看當時莎拉的臉的！她大概吃了十一種口味的冰淇淋才冷靜下來。

莎拉　　：笑死人了。至少我沒有在酒吧喝掉一百七十五美元！

凱文　　：媽，打開袋子。

凱文的媽：一件 T 恤，「我從鱷魚農場活了下來。」謝謝。這正是我想要的。

莎拉　　：那是凱文的主意，我本來想買香水給您的。不過別擔心，我們用海運寄了約八箱左右的衣服和其他東西回來。

凱文　　：來吧，媽，看看其他的照片。

凱文的媽：「赤裸鸚鵡坊」。這家酒吧的名字真有趣！

莎拉　　：是啊，我幾乎得用拖的才把凱文給拉出那家酒吧！

凱文　　：莎拉！！

## Words and Phrases

1. If it hadn't been for the... 要不是……的話

2. impression [ɪm`prɛʃən] n. 滑稽模倣

3. go crazy 發瘋

4. a little old for... 對於做……來說年紀有點大

5. stunt [stʌnt] n. 特技

6. run on... 靠……維持

7. pure [pjʊr] adj. 純粹的（此為加重語氣）

8. run up 達到（一個數字）

9. lounge [laʊndʒ] n. 酒吧間；高級酒吧

10. practically [`præktɪk]ɪ] adv. 幾乎；差不多

11. drag [dræg] v. 硬拉；硬拖

CD 2-62

## What Do I Do 我要怎麼做

# Explaining That Strange Photo to a Foreign Friend 向外國朋友解釋那張怪異的照片

**(1)** Mom : Is this a picture of somebody's ¹butt?

You : Well, I'll be... you're right. I don't know how that got in there.

媽 ：這張是某人屁股的照片嗎？

你 ：嗯，我……你說對了。我不知道它怎麼會混在那裡面。

---

**(2)** Friend : Did you ²make friends with this guy? He looks like a ³gangster!

You : A gangster! Hardly! He was my dance ⁴instructor.

朋友 ：你跟這傢伙交了朋友嗎？他看起來像是個流氓！

你 ：流氓！才不是咧。他是我的舞蹈教練。

---

**(3)** Friend : Look at the color of the ocean. It's beautiful.

You : You should have been there. That picture ⁵doesn't do it justice.

朋友 ：看看海的顏色，真美。

你 ：你真應該親自到那裡的。那張照片顯現不出實際上有多美。

## 📖 Words and Phrases

1. butt [bʌt] *n.* 屁股

2. make friends 交朋友

3. gangster [ˋgæŋstɚ] *n.* 流氓；歹徒

4. instructor [ɪnˋstrʌktɚ] *n.* 指導教練

5. doesn't do sth. justice 不能公道地評價某物（在此指照片無法顯示出實際的景色有多美）

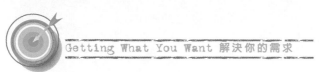

Getting What You Want 解決你的需求　　　　　　CD 2-63

# Going Again 再去一次

**(1)** You　　: I've already started planning my next trip.
　　Friend : You just got home yesterday.
　　你　　 : 我已經開始計畫我下一次的旅行了。
　　朋友　 : 你昨天才剛到家。

---

**(2)** You　　: Travel is ¹addictive. I can't wait to go somewhere new.
　　Friend : Can I go with you this time?
　　你　　 : 旅行會使人上癮。我等不及要去新的地方了。
　　朋友　 : 這次我可以跟你一起去嗎？

---

**(3)** You　　: I think I'm going to ²quit my job and wander the ³earth.
　　Friend : Umm... OK, that sounds like a real ⁴solid plan.
　　你　　 : 我想我把工作辭掉去環遊世界。
　　朋友　 : 嗯……好。聽起來還真像是個相當不錯的計畫。

## Words and Phrases

1. addictive [ə`dɪktɪv] *adj.* 使人上癮的

2. quit [kwɪt] *v.* 辭去（工作）

3. earth [ɝθ] *n.* 地球

4. solid [`sɑlɪd] *adj.* 實在的；穩健的；出色的

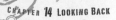

FYI 好用資訊

## 雙 D 康蒂的簽名照（凱文的收藏）

Travel Tips 旅遊撇步一起走

　　旅行是件很棒的事，它是生活中的一大樂趣。旅行可以開拓你的視野、增長你的見聞，並讓你充滿活力。所以，不要待在家裡，走出去。走吧，現在就出發！祝你一路順風！

# Notes

註：⑨代表此字彙出現在第九章

# *WORDS & PHRASES INDEX* 字詞檢索

⑨ artery *n.* 動脈

② as well as... 亦、也

⑥ ashamed *adj.* 覺得丟臉的；不好意思的

⑨ aspirin *n.* 阿斯匹靈

① assistance *n.* 幫忙；援助

⑧ asthma *n.* 氣喘；哮喘

③ at any time 任何時候

⑧ Atkins Diet 阿金飲食

⑧ attack *n.* 症狀發作

⑥ authentic *adj.* 道地的

⑫ authority *n.* (常用複數) 官方、當局

③ available *adj.* 可獲得的

⑫ awkward *adj.* 尷尬的；棘手的

# B

① backpacker *n.* 自助旅行者

③ backpacking *n.* 背著背包到處遠行 (通常是年輕人以有限的預算做自助旅遊)

⑧ bad move 不妥當的行動

③ baht *n.* 銖 (泰國貨幣單位)

⑫ balcony *n.* (兩層劇院的) 樓座；包廂

⑪ bank teller 銀行出納員

③ bar *n.* 酒吧

③ barely *adv.* 幾乎不能

① bargain *n.* 條件優惠的買賣

⑥ bargain *v.* 討價還價；就價格進行談判

⑥ barman *n.* 【英】酒保 (美國多用 bartender)

⑥ bartender *n.* 【美】酒保 (= barman)

③ bath towel 浴巾

④ be used to... 習慣了 (做)……

⑫ beer *n.* 啤酒

⑤ berth *n.* (船、火車的) 臥鋪、鋪位

③ beverage *n.* (通常指水以外的) 飲料

⑩ bill *v.* 記為某人的帳

③ bistro *n.* (特指法國非正式的) 小酒店、小餐館

⑨ blame *v.* 責怪

⑬ board *v.* 登機

① boarding pass 登機證

① book *v.* 訂 (票)

③ booking *n.* (席位等的) 預定

⑧ booth *n.* 隔開的座位；雅座

④ border *n.* 邊界

⑭ bottom left 左卜方

⑫ bowl *n.* 碗

⑫ box office 售票亭

⑦ brand name 名牌

② break *v.* 換開

⑨ breathe *v.* 呼吸

⑨ bring on *v.* 帶來；引起；造成

① brochure *n.* 【較英式的說法】宣傳品；小冊子

⑦ browse *v.* 瀏覽

⑧ bucket *n.* 水桶；一桶之量

⑫ Bud *n.* 百威 (Budweiser 或是 Bud Light 的簡稱；美國的暢銷啤酒品牌)

⑤ buddy *n.* 夥伴；老兄

③ budget *adj.* 省錢的

⑧ buffet *n.* 自助餐；自助餐檯（可以隨意選取菜色的餐廳）

⑬ bulkhead *n.* 隔離壁（經濟艙機門旁的首排座位，空間較大，常預留給行動不便或是帶有嬰兒的旅客乘坐）

⑧ Burgundy *n.* （產於法國勃艮第地區的）葡萄酒；（泛指其他地區同種）紅葡萄酒

③ business *n.* 事；事情

⑬ business class 商務艙

⑭ butt *n.* 屁股

⑪ by a lot 大幅地

⑧ by the way, ... 對了，……

# C

⑪ cabaret *n.* 卡巴來歌舞表演

⑬ cabin class 經濟艙

① cabin crew 機組人員

⑬ call sb. a cab 替某人叫計程車

⑩ calling card 電話卡

① can *n.* （可樂等的）罐

⑨ cancel *v.* 取消

⑥ card *n.* 名片

③ cardkey *n.* 鑰匙卡

② carousel *n.* （行李）旋轉式傳送帶；行李轉盤

⑤ carriage *n.* （鐵路）客車車廂

⑦ Cash or card? 付現還是刷卡？

⑦ cash register 收銀機

② cashier *n.* 出納；出納員

① catalog *n.* 目錄

⑥ catch *v.* 追上；趕上；搭上

① Certainly. 當然可以。

④ Champs Elysees 香榭麗舍大道

② change *n.* （找回的）零錢

② change *v.* 換（錢）

⑤ change *n.* 變更；更動

③ charge *n.* 索價；收費

⑩ charger *n.* 充電器

⑭ charming *adj.* 迷人的

⑦ chase *v.* 追逐；追趕

④ Chatuchak weekend market 乍都節週末市場（為曼谷最大的市場）

⑬ cheat *v.* 欺騙

② check-in *n.* 辦理登機手續

③ check on 檢查

① check out 看一看

③ check out 退房

④ check out 看看；得到證實

⑧ chef *n.* 主廚；大廚

① children's meal 兒童餐

⑦ chocolate-covered *adj.* 以巧克力覆蓋的

② cigar *n.* 雪茄

④ clarify *v.* 解釋清楚；澄清

⑤ class *n.* 等級

⑨ claw *n.* （蟹、蝦等的）螯；長而利的爪子

⑥ clean *adv.* 完全地

② clerk *n.* （旅館）接待員；售貨員；職

員；辦事人員

⑩ code *n.* 碼（在此指一國的國碼）

② coin *n.* 硬幣

① colleague *n.* 同事

② collect *v.* 領取

④ come down 降價

② come off 卸下

⑤ come to... 總計為⋯⋯

⑬ comfort shopping 用以作為慰藉的購物

⑬ comfortable *adj.* 舒適的；愜意的

② commission *n.* 手續費；佣金；回扣

⑨ common practice 慣用療法

⑫ company *n.* 伴；作伴

⑤ compartment *n.*（客車、船艙、臥車車廂等的）隔間、車室

③ complicated *adj.* 複雜的

⑬ con man 騙子；賺取不義之財的人

④ concern *n.* 擔心；利害關係

④ concierge *n.*（尤指歐洲各國旅館的）服務台職員

⑩ confirm *v.* 確認

⑨ confront *v.* 面對

⑥ congested *adj.* 壅塞的

③ connect to... 連接到⋯⋯

⑩ connection *n.*（網路）連線

⑩ connection fee 接線服務費

⑨ cop *n.*【口語】警察

① copy *n.*（書、雜誌等出版品的）一份；

一冊

③ corridor *n.* 走廊

⑭ cotton *n.* 棉質物

② counter *n.* 櫃台

⑦ counteroffer *n.* 還價；反提案

⑧ crab cake 蟹肉餅

⑨ crash *v.* 猛撞；撞壞

⑭ creepy *adj.* 令人毛骨悚然的

⑭ criminal *adj.* 罪犯的

⑥ cuisine *n.* 烹調；料理

④ culture center 文化中心

① currency *n.* 貨幣

④ current *adj.* 當下的；最新的

⑩ customer service 客服

② customs *n.* 海關

⑩ cyber café 網咖（同 Internet café）

# D

④ daily *adj.* 按日的

⑨ dairy product 乳製品

⑤ deal *v.* 打交道；對待；應付

⑤ deal *n.* 有利的交易

⑦ deal *n.* 成交

⑪ deal with 處理

⑫ deceiving *adj.* 騙人的

② declare *v.*（向海關）申報（納稅品等）

⑦ decline *v.* 拒絕

④ deco *n.* 裝飾（decoration 的略式）

⑬ delay *v.* 延遲；延誤

② denomination *n.*（貨幣）面額

⑤ departure *n.* 啟程；出發

⑤ deposit *n.* 訂金；保證金

② describe *v.* 描述

⑦ designer *n.* 名設計師

③ detail *v.* 詳細說明

⑭ develop *v.*（底片）顯影；（照片）沖洗

⑨ diarrhea *n.* 腹瀉；拉肚子

⑬ direct flight 直飛；直航

③ direction *n.* 行進路線；方向；指引

⑭ dirty old man 老不修

⑧ disagreement *n.* 意見不合；爭執

⑩ disconnect *v.* 離線；斷線

⑦ discreet *adj.* 謹慎的；不會洩露秘密的

② disembarkation *n.* 入境（disemba-rkation card 為入境卡）

⑤ dispose *v.* 丟棄（注意後接介係詞 of）

⑬ dispute *v.* 爭論；對（結果等）懷疑

④ district *n.* 泛指地方、區域

④ do *v.* 做；從事

⑩ do without... 在沒有……的情況下

⑭ doesn't do sth. justice 不能公道地評價某物（在此指照片無法顯示出實際的景色有多美）

③ don't hesitate to... 不必猶豫……

⑧ Don't sweat it. 別擔心。

③ dorm bed 宿舍床位

③ double *n.* 雙人房

⑧ double-check *v.* 覆核；再確認

⑭ double set 兩組

⑩ download *v.* 下載

② downtown *adv.* 往、在市中心（鬧區）

⑭ drag *v.* 硬拉；硬拖

⑦ drive a hard bargain 狠狠殺價

⑥ drop *n.* 滴

⑨ drowsy *adj.*（令人）昏昏欲睡的

⑤ drunk *adj.* 酒醉的

⑥ drunken *adj.* 醉酒的；喝醉了的

① dual *adj.* 雙重的；二元的

⑤ due *adj.* 預計到達

⑬ due to... 由於

② duffel bag 簡易行李袋（設計很簡單，手提和肩背皆可）

⑨ dumbass *n.* 笨蛋

① duty-free *adj.* 免稅的

# E

⑥ early start 早早動身

⑭ earth *n.* 地球

⑧ eat out 外食；在外用餐

⑤ economical *adj.* 節省的；省錢的

③ Eiffel Tower 艾菲爾鐵塔

⑭ eight-by-ten 八×十吋

⑦ elsewhere *adv.* 在別的地方

⑬ emergency *n.* 緊急情況

③ empty *adj.* 空的；無人居住的

② end *n.* 終端；盡頭

⑭ enlargement *n.* 放大

④ enter v. 入場;進入

⑥ espresso n. 濃縮咖啡

⑤ eternity n. 永恆(在此是強調等了非常久的一段時間)

② euro n. 歐元(符號為 €)

④ every adj. 每隔……的

⑨ every now and then 偶爾

⑧ exceptional adj. 優越的;傑出的

② exchange v. 兌換(貨幣)

⑦ exchange v. 換貨;用其他物品替代

② exchange rate 外匯兌換率

② exit n. 出口

⑨ expand v. 擴張

⑨ expect v. 想到;預料到

⑩ expect v. 盼望;等待

⑩ expire v. 到期;期滿失效

③ explore v. 勘查,探險

⑪ express mail 快遞;快捷

⑥ extend v. 延長;提供

④ extra adj. 額外的

# F

③ facilities n. 設備;設施

⑧ fad n. 一時的流行或是狂熱

⑦ fake adj. 贋品的;假造的

⑤ fan n. 風扇

⑫ fancy adj. 精心設計的

③ fantastic adj. 極好的;了不起的

⑧ fast food 快餐;(麥當勞、肯德基、漢堡王之類的)簡便食物;速食

① fasten v. 繫緊;扣緊

③ fee n. 費用

⑧ feel bad 覺得良心不安;感到內疚

⑧ feel like 想要

⑬ feel up to sth. 想要(做)某事

⑫ feeling n. 感情;感受

⑦ fetch v. 拿來;取來

④ figure n. 數字;金額

② fill out 填寫(書、報表等)

⑦ final adj. 最終的

⑬ find out 發現;得知

⑨ Finder's keepers. 誰撿到就是誰的。

⑫ fishy adj. 可疑的

① fit v. 正好吻合;放得下

⑦ fit v. 合身

⑤ flag sth. down 把……招下來

⑭ flash n. 閃光燈

⑧ flavor n. 口味

② flight n. 飛行

③ flight n. 樓梯(兩個休息平台之間的一段樓梯)

① flight attendant (客機上)空服人員(總稱為 cabin crew,另外,駕駛艙人員則為 cockpit crew)

② flight number 班機號碼

⑩ floppy disk 軟式磁碟(也直接稱為 floppy)

④ folks n. 各位

⑫ hang around... 在⋯⋯附近徘徊

⑫ hard to tell 很難講

⑥ have one's heart in... 對⋯⋯感濃厚興趣

④ head v. 朝⋯⋯前往

④ head out 出發

⑭ Hear! Hear! 說得好！

⑤ helmet n. 頭盔；安全帽

⑩ helpline n. 求助熱線

⑦ Here you are. 在這裡。（把東西給別人看時引起注意力的用詞）

④ highlight n. 壓軸；最有趣之處

④ historical adj. 歷史的；歷史上著名的

⑧ hit v. 前往；上路

④ hit the sack 就寢；上床睡覺

⑫ hopeless with... 對於⋯⋯沒轍

③ host n.（旅館等的）主人

③ hostel n. 招待所；小旅館（招待開著汽車、騎自行車或步行的青年旅遊者）

③ house band 駐唱樂團（house 可指旅館、飯店）

⑤ How can I be of assistance? 我能夠幫得上忙嗎？

② How do you want the money? 你的款項要以哪些面額呈現？

⑪ how the hell 到底

④ How was your sleep? 睡得怎麼樣？

⑧ I couldn't agree more. 我完全贊成。

④ I should know better. 我本該知道的。

③ I'll tell you what. 這樣好了。

⑥ I've got no idea. 我不知道。

⑫ identification n. 身分證明

⑭ If it hadn't been for the... 要不是⋯⋯的話

⑭ imagine v. 想像

② immigration n. 入境處

⑨ Imodium n. 止瀉藥；痢達膠囊

⑭ impression n. 滑稽模倣

⑤ in advance 事前地；預先地

⑦ in stock 有貨的；有庫存的

⑤ in the back 在後方的

⑩ inbox n. 收信匣

⑤ included adj. 有包含在內的

⑩ incoming call n. 打進來的電話；來電

⑧ indecisive adj. 無法決定的

③ inexpensive adj. 花費不多的

⑧ ingredient n. 材料；食材

⑧ inhaler n. 吸入輔助器

⑥ initiate v. 開始；發起

⑫ inspector n. 探員

⑩ install v.（程式）安裝

⑭ instructor n. 指導教練

⑤ insurance n. 保險

⑨ insurance company 保險公司

⑩ international call 國際電話

② international driver's license 國際

267

funny-looking 等等）

⑭ lounge *n.* 酒吧間；高級酒吧

⑥ Louvre *n.* 羅浮宮

② luggage *n.* 行李

# M

② madam *n.*【尊稱】小姐；女士

⑫ mail sth. in 把某物郵寄到……

⑧ maître d' 【法】餐廳之中的領班（又作 maître d'hôtel）

⑭ make friends 交朋友

⑧ make it 【口語】趕上、達成

⑫ make it... 使（它）成為某種狀態

⑨ make it to... 撐到……

⑬ make sb.'s living 謀生

④ mall *n.*（車子不得入內的）商店區、商業大街

⑤ mano a mano 單挑的；獨自面對面的

⑫ margarita *n.*【酒】瑪格麗特（以龍舌蘭和檸檬汁調和而成的雞尾酒）

⑦ master *n.* 能手；行家

⑭ mastermind *n.* 主謀；幕後操縱者

⑥ material *n.* 衣料；材料

① mealtime *n.* 用餐時間

⑨ medical *adj.* 醫藥上的；醫學上的

⑨ medication *n.* 藥物

⑧ mention *v.* 說到；提及

⑤ mess *n.* 髒亂；凌亂

③ metro *n.* 地下鐵、捷運等交通設施

③ mezzanine *n.* 閣樓；夾層（指上下樓層之間的一個局部樓層）

⑩ might as well... 不如就……

⑤ mileage *n.* 英里里程

⑦ Mind your own business. 別多管閒事。

② minus *prep.* 去除

④ miss *v.* 錯過

③ mistake *n.* 錯誤；過錯

⑥ mistake sb. for... 誤認某人為……

⑥ mistaken *adj.* 弄錯的

③ Mme *n.* 夫人；太太；女士（Madame 的縮寫，用於非英美地區、尤其是法國已婚婦女姓名前的尊稱，相當於美語中的 Mrs.，有時也用作對年長未婚女子的尊稱）

⑩ mobile phone 行動電話；手機（＝ cell phone）

⑨ money belt （腰帶式）錢包袋；裡面可以藏錢的腰帶

② monitor *n.*（電腦）螢幕

④ monsieur *n.*【法文】先生（相當於美語中的 Mr.或 Sir）

⑦ monster *n.* 異常巨大之物

⑧ mouthful *n.* 一嘴的；滿滿一口的

② multiple-entry visa 多次入境簽證

⑨ murder *v.* 謀殺

# N

⑫ naked *adj.* 赤裸的

④ national park 國家公園

⑨ oxygen *n.* 氧氣

# P

⑧ pancake *n.* 薄餅

② paperwork *n.* 文書工作

⑨ parallel to... 與……平行

⑫ parking ticket 停車罰單

⑧ party *n.* 一行人；一夥人

④ pass *n.* 免費入場證；通行證

⑧ pass *v.* 放棄；放過

⑧ pass on sth. 【口語】拒絕；放棄

⑬ passenger *n.* 乘客

② passport *n.* 護照

⑧ pasta *n.* (通心麵等) 麵食

⑩ pay phone 公用電話

⑪ payable *adj.* 應支付的

⑪ payee *n.* 受款人

③ pension *n.* (歐洲，尤其是法國、比利時等地的) 膳宿公寓；小旅社；民宿

⑧ pepper *n.* 辣椒；胡椒

① per person 每一人

① perfume *n.* (女用) 香水

⑪ permanent address 永久住址

⑬ permit *v.* 允許；准許；許可

⑪ personal information 個人資料

⑥ pest *n.* 討厭、難纏的人

④ pet *v.* 撫摸

⑨ pharmacist *n.* 藥劑師

⑨ pharmacy *n.* 藥局

② phase out 分階段逐步停止使用 (或生產、實行)；逐步結束、被淘汰

⑩ phone *n.* 電話卡

② photo ID 有照證件 (= picture ID)

① pick up 買；帶；弄到手

⑨ pill *n.* 藥丸

⑧ pity *n.* 憾事

⑩ place a call *v.* (透過接線生) 打電話

④ places of interest 名勝

② planned duration 準備停留的時間

① plastic *n.* 信用卡 (credit card 的口語講法)

⑤ platform *n.* 月台

⑬ play it safe 小心行事；不冒險

⑪ plenty *n.* 充足；豐富

⑫ plumber *n.* 鉛管工；水電工

③ plus *prep.* 加上

⑪ pointless *adj.* 無意義的

⑨ police report *n.* 警方報告

⑤ por favor【西班牙文】請 (相當於英文的 please)

⑩ pornography *n.* 色情 (包括一切任何形式，如文字敘述、照片、電影等)

⑤ positive *adj.* 確定的；確信的

⑪ postage *n.* 郵資

⑭ practically *adv.* 幾乎；差不多

⑨ prescription *n.* 處方；藥方

⑭ print *n.* 印花

⑭ print *n.* (由底片洗出的) 照片

③ private *adj.* 私人的；個人的

⑫ private dance　私舞（指脫衣舞孃不在台上，而是在你付錢之後到你面前為你而跳的一段舞，但通常有規定只准欣賞而不准碰觸）

⑦ pronounce *v.* 發音

⑪ proof of delivery　投遞證明

⑫ proper *adj.* 正式的；合法的

⑧ protein *n.* 蛋白質

⑤ public transportation　大眾運輸

⑨ pull over *v.* 把車開到路邊

⑩ purchase *n.* 購買

⑭ pure *adj.* 純粹的（此為加重語氣）

⑨ purse *n.* 錢包；手提包

⑦ put on sb.'s card　刷某人的信用卡

⑫ put your hands together　拍手

# Q

④ Q and A　問答

⑭ quality *n.* 品質；質感

⑫ queue *v.* 排隊等候（由指當有繩段引導隊形的時候）

⑭ quit *v.* 辭去（工作）

# R

⑦ ranch *n.* （專門飼養某種動物的）飼養場

③ range *n.* 範圍；一批、一組、一套

③ rat *n.* 老鼠（mouse 指的是體型較小、較可愛的鼠科）

③ rather than... 而不是⋯⋯

③ reach *v.* 與⋯⋯取得聯繫

① receipt *n.* 收據

④ recommend *v.* 建議；推薦

⑧ recommendation *n.* 推舉；建議

⑫ red light　紅燈（red-light district 為紅燈區、風化區之意）

① red wine *n.* 紅（葡萄）酒

⑦ reference *n.* 參照項目

① refill *v.* 續杯；再注入

⑬ refund *n.* 償還金額

⑤ refundable *adj.* 可退還的

⑤ regular *adj.* 普通的

⑫ relaxed *adj.* 輕鬆自在的

④ remind *v.* 提醒

⑤ rent *v.* 租用

② rental car　租車

⑫ report *n.* 報告

① request *v.* 懇請；請求

⑧ reservation *n.* 訂位

⑦ return *v.* 退貨；退還

⑪ return address　寄件人地址

⑤ return ticket　回程票

② reverse *v.* 背面的；翻過來另一面的

⑧ rich *adj.* 味道濃厚的；富含油脂的

① right away　馬上；即刻

② rip sb. off　敲竹槓

⑬ risky *adj.* 有風險的；沒把握的

⑧ roast *adj.* 烤過的

⑬ rob *v.* 搶劫

① roll *n.* 麵包捲

③ roof *n.* 屋頂

⑬ room service 客房服務

⑤ round trip 來回；全程

⑬ round-trip ticket 來回機票

④ roundup *n.*（新聞等的）綜述、概要、摘要

④ route *n.* 路線

⑤ rude *adj.* 無理的；粗暴的

① rudely *adv.* 無禮地

⑫ run a tab 掛帳

⑭ run into sb. 碰上某人

⑨ run off 逃走；跑掉

⑭ run on... 靠……維持

⑭ run up 達到（一個數字）

⑬ running late 來遲的

⑪ rush *n.* 急切；匆忙

# S

⑨ safe *n.* 保險箱

⑦ salesgirl *n.* 銷售小姐

⑧ salty *adj.* 鹹的

⑪ scale *n.* 磅秤

① scent *n.*【英】香水

④ scooter *n.* 小型摩托車

⑦ scream sb.'s head off 聲嘶力竭地喊叫

① seat *n.* 座位

① seat pocket 椅背上的置物袋

⑪ see about... 處理……

⑥ see the sights 瀏覽風光

⑦ set aside 留下；預留

⑨ settle *v.* 使穩定；使鎮靜

⑬ settle *v.* 結帳

⑫ settle up 付清費用

⑬ severe *adj.* 嚴重的；嚴峻的

⑦ sexy *adj.* 性感的

① shape *v.* 做成……的形狀

⑥ share *v.* 分享；共用

① ship *v.* 寄送

⑪ shipping *n.* 運費

⑦ shipping and handling fee 運送費和手續費

⑫ shocked *adj.* 震驚的

⑩ shoot *v.* 直說吧

⑥ shopkeeper *n.* 店主

⑦ shot *n.*（拍攝的）鏡頭、畫面

⑫ show *n.* 表演；演出

④ show sb. around 帶某人參觀

⑪ show up 出現；到、來

② shuttle bus 接駁公車

⑨ sick *adj.* 噁心的；想吐的；生病的；身體不舒服的

⑨ side effect 副作用

④ sightseeing *n.* 觀光；遊覽

① sign *v.* 簽字

② sign *n.* 標示

⑩ sign out 登出

⑬ signed *adj.* 簽過名的

273

遞

⑫ suspicious *adj.* 可疑的；有蹊蹺的

⑤ swear *v.* 發誓

⑫ sweet *adj.* 討人喜歡的

⑨ symptom *n.* 症狀

# T

⑨ tablet *n.* 藥片

① take a flight 飛行；搭機

⑥ take advantage 佔便宜

⑤ take care of sth. 處理某事

⑥ take in 觀看；盡收眼底

① take off 起飛

③ take out 扣除；去除

③ take sb. up on sth. 接受某人提出的提議、賭注、挑戰等

② task *n.* 任務

⑫ tequila *n.*【酒】龍舌蘭（墨西哥蒸餾酒）

② terminal *n.* 航空站

⑤ thank goodness 謝天謝地

⑨ that many 那麼多的

② That would explain it. 難怪。

⑧ The hotter the better. 愈辣愈好。

⑨ theft *n.* 竊盜（案）

⑨ thief *n.* 竊盜犯

⑭ three-by-five 三×五吋

⑦ thrill *n.* 緊張的快感；刺激的興奮

⑨ through *adj.* 完成；終了

④ ticket taker 收票員

⑦ tight *adj.* 緊身的

① time zone 時區

④ tip *n.* 提醒；建議；暗示

⑧ to go 外帶

① toiletries *n.* 梳妝用品（包括洗髮精、香水、牙刷、牙膏等）

⑨ ...tops. ……最多了。

⑤ total *n.* 全額；總數

③ tour *n.*（景點等的）遊歷；參觀

④ Tourist Information Bureau 旅遊局

⑭ touristy *adj.* 遊客喜歡的、常做的

⑪ tracking number 追蹤號碼

⑪ trader *n.* 商人

⑧ traditional *adj.* 傳統的

⑦ trainers *n.* 運動鞋（由 training shoes 演變而來）

⑩ transaction *n.*（業務的）交辦、處理

⑩ transfer *v.* 轉接

② transportation *n.* 交通工具

⑨ treatment *n.* 治療；療法

④ trekking *n.* 徒步旅行；長途跋涉

① trolley *n.* 手推車（除了餐車之外，也用以指機上賣免稅商品的推車或機場中放行李的推車）

⑧ trout *n.* 鱒魚

⑦ try on 試穿

⑧ tuna *n.* 鮪魚；金槍魚

⑩ turn down 降低

⑭ type *n.* 類型；……類的人

# U

⑭ Uh oh! 完蛋了！

⑫ unable *adj.* 不能的；不會的

⑧ unbelievable *adj.* 難以置信的

⑩ uncool *adj.* 不酷的

⑭ unpleasant *adj.* 令人不愉快的

⑤ until *prep.* 直到

⑧ up for sth. 對某事有興趣；對某事準備好了

④ up my alley 合我的胃口、能力

⑩ up to you 由你決定

⑬ upgrade *v.* 升級；升等

① upright *adj.* 垂直的；打直的

⑪ upset *adj.* 不高興的

⑨ upset stomach 腸胃不適（包括各種跟消化有關的不適，如胃酸過多、噁心等）

⑨ urgent *adj.* 事態緊急的

① utensil *n.* 餐具

# V

⑩ value *n.* 價值；額度

⑧ variety *n.* 種類；變化

⑪ vary *v.* 變更；變動

① vegetarian *adj.* 素食的

⑤ vehicle *n.* 車輛

⑨ vein *n.* 靜脈

⑧ vender *n.* 攤販

⑥ Versailles *n.* 凡爾賽宮

④ Vimanmek Palace 威瑪曼宮（又稱為雲天石宮）

⑧ vintage *n.* （葡萄酒的）佳釀（在特定的地方、豐收的年份與釀造工藝之優良葡萄酒）

⑩ virus *n.* 病毒

② visa *n.* 簽證

⑩ voice *n.* （電話中的）語音

⑩ volume *n.* 音量

⑬ voucher *n.* 現金替用卷；優待卷

# W

③ wake-up call 起床呼叫電話（＝ morning call）

④ wander *v.* 漫遊

④ Wat Arun 黎明寺（＝ The Temple of Dawn，又稱為鄭皇廟）

⑫ waterfront *adj.* 靠碼頭的；靠海岸的；濱水區的

⑦ way *adv.* 遠遠地；大大地

⑬ weather *n.* 天氣

⑪ website *n.* 網站

④ weekly *adj.* 按週的

④ well-known *adj.* 知名的

⑥ What do you have in mind? 你有什麼盤算？

⑫ What'll it be? 要什麼？

④ What's up? 近來如何？（非常口語的打招呼方式）

⑩ whine *v.* 抱怨；訴苦

⑫ whiner *n.* 抱怨者；懦弱者

⑤ whisky *n.* 威士忌

① white wine 白（葡萄）酒

① window *n.* 窗

① window shade 遮陽板

⑪ wire *v.* 電匯

⑪ wire transfer 電匯轉帳

⑤ working *adj.* 運作的；運轉的

⑤ would have been... 可能早就……

⑥ Would you like to do something?
你想做些什麼嗎？

⑥ wrestle *v.* 摔角；角力

⑥ Yankees *n.*【棒球】紐約洋基隊（前需
加冠詞 the）

① You won't get very far. 行不通。

⑬ You're kidding me. 你在開我玩笑。

⑫ You're such a... 你真是個……

⑦ your kind of... 你這種類型的……

國家圖書館出版品預行編目資料

會話震撼教育. 旅遊篇 = Conversation Boosters.
Travel / Jeffrey Gordon 作;戴至中譯.
－－初版. －－臺北市;貝塔語言,2005〔民 94〕
　　面;　　　公分

ISBN　957-729-467-7（平裝附光碟片）

1. 英國語言－會話

805.188　　　　　　　　　　　　　　93020402

# 會話震撼教育——旅遊篇
## Conversation Boosters — Travel

作　　　者 / Jeffrey Gordon
總 編 審 / 王復國
譯　　　者 / 戴至中
執行編輯 / 諸葛蓓芸、莊碧娟

出　　　版 / 貝塔語言出版有限公司
地　　　址 / 台北市 100 館前路 12 號 11 樓
電　　　話 / (02)2314-2525
傳　　　真 / (02)2312-3535
郵　　　撥 / 19493777 貝塔出版有限公司
客服專線 / (02)2314-3535
客服信箱 / btservice@betamedia.com.tw

總 經 銷 / 凌域國際股份有限公司
地　　　址 / 台北縣五股工業區五工五路 38 號 7 樓
電　　　話 / (02)2298-3838
傳　　　真 / (02)2298-1498

出版日期 / 2005 年 1 月初版一刷
定　　　價 / 350 元
ISBN： 957-729-467-7

Conversation Boosters — Travel
Copyright 2005 by Beta Multimedia Publishing

喚醒你的英文語感！

對折後釘好，直接寄回即可！

100 台北市中正區館前路12號11樓

 貝塔語言出版 收
Beta Multimedia Publishing

 寄件者住址

**貝塔語言出版**
Beta Multimedia Publishing

讀者服務專線（02）2314-3535　　讀者服務傳真（02）2312-353
客戶服務信箱　btservice@betamedia.com.tw
**www.betamedia.com.tw**

謝謝您購買本書！！

貝塔語言擁有最優良之英文學習書籍，為提供您最佳的英語學習資訊，您可填妥此表後寄回（免貼郵票）將可不定期收到本公司最新發行書訊及活動訊息！

姓名：＿＿＿＿＿＿＿＿＿＿　性別：□男 □女　生日：＿＿＿年＿＿＿月＿＿＿日

電話：(公)＿＿＿＿＿＿＿＿＿(宅)＿＿＿＿＿＿＿＿＿(手機)＿＿＿＿＿＿＿＿＿

電子信箱：＿＿＿＿＿＿＿＿＿＿＿＿＿＿＿＿＿＿＿＿＿＿＿＿

學歷：□高中職含以下　□專科　□大學　□研究所含以上

職業：□金融 □服務 □傳播 □製造 □資訊 □軍公教 □出版
　　　□自由 □教育 □學生 □其他

職級：□企業負責人 □高階主管 □中階主管 □職員 □專業人士

1. 您購買的書籍是？＿＿＿＿＿＿＿＿＿＿＿＿＿＿＿

2. 您從何處得知本產品？(可複選)
　　　□書店 □網路 □書展 □校園活動 □廣告信函 □他人推薦 □新聞報導 □其他

3. 您覺得本產品價格：
　　　□偏高 □合理 □偏低

4. 請問目前您每週花了多少時間學英語？
　　　□ 不到十分鐘 □ 十分鐘以上，但不到半小時 □ 半小時以上，但不到一小時
　　　□ 一小時以上，但不到兩小時 □ 兩個小時以上 □ 不一定

5. 通常在選擇語言學習書時，哪些因素是您會考慮的？
　　　□ 封面 □ 內容、實用性 □ 品牌 □ 媒體、朋友推薦 □ 價格□ 其他＿＿＿＿＿

6. 市面上您最需要的語言書種類為？
　　　□ 聽力 □ 閱讀 □ 文法 □ 口説 □ 寫作 □ 其他＿＿＿＿＿

7. 通常您會透過何種方式選購語言學習書籍？
　　　□ 書店門市 □ 網路書店 □ 郵購 □ 直接找出版社 □ 學校或公司團購
　　　□ 其他＿＿＿＿＿＿

8. 給我們的建議：＿＿＿＿＿＿＿＿＿＿＿＿＿＿＿＿＿＿＿＿
＿＿＿＿＿＿＿＿＿＿＿＿＿＿＿＿＿＿＿＿＿＿＿＿＿＿＿＿

喚醒你的英文語感！

Get a Feel for English !